Praise for Glen Duncan

Love Remains

'If good writers are those who make the ordinary remarkable,
Duncan is a very good writer indeed' *The Times*

'His use of language is so precise, his dissection of male and female
emotions so spot–on, it almost takes your breath away. His plausibility
rating on the gender-bending scale is up there with Tolstoy'
Time Out

'Duncan takes you down paths of the heart you had forgotten
existed, and others you fear to tread' *Sunday Times*

'A graphic, shocking account of the physical and mental horrors that
overtake people whose lives have exploded . . . intense, perceptive
and brutal' *Sunday Telegraph*

'Scarily thorough and relentless in its accuracy: no one is spared'
Independent on Sunday

'Impressive . . . Duncan looks beyond the limits of love to explore
that dark and uncomfortable territory where male desire and
female expectation clash' *New Statesman*

Hope

'A provocative novel about a compelling subject' *Independent*

'A missive from purgatory . . . *Hope* has the confessional,
self-lacerating narrative style of *Portnoy's Complaint*'
Times Literary Supplement

'As seductive as it is disturbing, this is intriguing stuff' *Elle*

'Infused with a caustic humour and a host of observations on friendship,
pornography and the moral malaise of a generation, *Hope* is this
summer's essential first novel' *Esquire*

I, LUCIFER

Glen Duncan

Scribner

First published in Great Britain by Scribner, 2002
This edition published by Scribner, 2003
An imprint of Simon & Schuster UK Ltd
A Viacom Company

1 3 5 7 9 10 8 6 4 2

Simon & Schuster UK Ltd
Africa House
64–78 Kingsway
London WC2B 6AH

Simon & Schuster Australia
Sydney

www.simonsays.co.uk

A CIP catalogue record for this book
is available from the British Library

ISBN 0–7432–2013–7

Typeset by M Rules
Printed and bound in Great Britain by
Cox & Wyman Ltd, Reading, Berks.

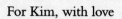
For Kim, with love

I, Lucifer, Fallen Angel, Prince of Darkness, Bringer of Light, Ruler of Hell, Lord of the Flies, Father of Lies, Apostate Supreme, Tempter of Mankind, Old Serpent, Prince of This World, Seducer, Accuser, Tormentor, Blasphemer, and without doubt Best Fuck in the Seen and Unseen Universe (ask Eve, that *minx*) have decided – *oo-la-la!* – to tell all.

All? Some. I'm toying with that for a title: *Some*. Got a post-millennial modesty to it, don't you think? *Some*. My side of the story. The funk. The jive. The boogie. The rock and roll. (I invented rock and roll. You wouldn't believe the things I've invented. Anal sex, obviously. Smoking. Astrology. Money . . . Let's save time: Everything in the world that distracts you from thinking about God. Which . . . pretty much . . . *is* everything in the world, isn't it? *Gosh*.)

Now. Your million questions. All, in the end, the same question: What's it like being me? What, for heaven's sake, is it *like* being me?

In a nutshell, which, thanks to me, is the way you like it in these hurrying and fragmented times, it's hard. For a start, I'm in pain the whole time. Something considerably more diverting than lumbago or irritable bowel: there's a constant burning agony, all over, so to speak (that's *quite* bad) punctu-ated by irregular bursts of incandescent or meta-agony, as if my entire being is hosting its own private Armageddon (that's really *very* bad). These nukes, these . . . *supernovae* catch me unawares. The work I've botched, the ones that've got away – honestly: it really would be shameful, had I not done the sensible thing (*you* know it makes sense) and become utterly inured to shame about a thousand billion years ago.

Then there's the rage. You probably think you know rage: the trodden-on chilblains, the hammered thumb, the facetious boss, the wife and best mate *soixante-neuf*'d on the conjugal divan, the *queue*. You probably think you've seen red. Take it from me, you haven't. You haven't seen pink. I, on the other hand . . . Well. Pure scarlet. Carmine. Burgundy. Vermillion. Magenta. Oxblood, on particularly bad days.

And who, you may ask, is to blame for that? Didn't I choose my fate? Wasn't everything hunky-dory in Heaven before I . . . upset the Old Man with that rebellion stunt? (Here's something for you. It might come as a shock. God looks like an old man with a long white beard. You think I'm kidding. You'll wish I was kidding. He looks like a foul-tempered Father Christmas.) Yes, I chose. And *oh* how we've never heard the end of it.

Until now. Now there's a new deal on the table.

Certainly you may snort. *I* did. As if it was ever, *ever* going to be as simple as that. He knocks me out, He does, with His little whims. With His little whims and His . . . well, one hesitates, naturally, to use the word . . . His *naivety*. (You'll have noticed I'm capitalizing the aitch on He and His and Him. Can't help it. It's hard-wired. Believe me, if I could get past it I would. Rebellion was a liberating experience – rage and pain notwithstanding – but acres of the old circuitry remain. Witness the – excuse me while I yawn – *Rituale Romanum*. I'm tempted to *prompt* the ditherers. Gets me out, though, eventually. Every time I think it's going to be different. Every time it isn't. *The blood of the Martyrs commands you* . . . Yes yes yes, I *know*. I've heard. I'm *going*, already.)

Naivety's conspicuously absent from my own cv. As a matter of fact I can hear and see pretty much everything in the human realm pretty much all the time. In the human realm (trumpets and cymbal-crash of celebration, please . . .) I'm omniscient. More or less. Which is just as well, since there's so much you curious little monkeys want to know. What *is* an angel? Is Hell really hot? Was Eden really lush? Is Heaven as dull as it sounds? Do homosexuals suffer eternal damnation? And what about being consensually buggered by your lawful wedded hubby on his birthday? Are *Buddhists* okay?

In time. What I *must* tell you about is the new deal. I'm trying, but it's tricky. Humans, as that pug-faced kraut and chronic masturbator Kant pointed out, are stuck within the limits of space and time. Modes of apprehension, the grammar of understanding and all that. Whereas the reality is – now do pay attention, because this is, when all's said and done, me Lucifer, telling you *what the reality is* – the reality is that there are an infinite number of modes of apprehension. Time and space are just two of them. Half of them don't even have names, and if I listed the half that did you'd be none the wiser, since they're named in a language you wouldn't understand. There's a language for angels and none of it translates. There's no Dictionary of Angelspeak. You just have to be an angel. After the Fall (the first one I mean, *my* fall, the one with all the special effects) we – myself and my fellow renegades – found our language changed and our mouths friendly to a variant of it; more guttural, riddled with fricatives and sibilants, but less poncy, less *Goddish*. As well as a century or two of laryngitis the new dialect gave us irony. You can imagine what a relief that was. Himself, whatever else He might have going for Him, has absolutely no sense of humour. Perfection precludes it. (Gags work the gap between what's imaginable and what actually is, necessarily off the menu for a Being who actually is all He can imagine – doubly so when all He can imagine is all that can *be* imagined.) Heaven's heard us down here, cackling at our piss-takes and chortling at our quips; I've seen the looks, the suspicion that they're missing out on it, this *laughing* malarkey. But they always turn away, Gabriel to horn practice, Michael to the weights. Truth is they're timid. If there was a safe way down – a fire escape (*boom-boom*) – there'd be more than a handful of deserters tiptoeing down to my door. Abandon hope all ye who enter here, yes – but get ready for a *rart* ol' giggle, dearie.

So this is going to be a difficulty – my existence has always been latticed and curlicued with difficulties (*bent wrist to perspiring forehead*) – this translation of angelic experience into human language. Angelic experience is a phenomenal renaissance, English a tart's clutch-bag. How cram the former into the latter? Take darkness, for example. You've no idea what stepping into darkness is like for me. I could say it was sliding into a mink coat still redolent with both the spirits of its slaughtered donors and the atomized whiff of top-dollar cunt. I could say it was an immersion in unholy chrism. I could say it was the first drink after five pinched years on the wagon. I could say it was a homecoming. And so on. It wouldn't suffice. I'm confined to the blank and defeated insistence that one thing is another. (And how, pray, does that bring us any closer to the thing itself?) All the metaphors in this world wouldn't scratch the surface of what stepping into darkness is like for me. And that's just darkness. Don't get me started on light. *Really*, don't get me started on light.

It's yielding sympathy for poets, this new deal, which is fitting reciprocity, since poets have always had such sympathy for me. (Not that I can claim any credit for 'Sympathy For

The Devil', by the way. You'd think, wouldn't you? But no, that was Mick and Keith all on their own.) Poets suffer occasional delusions of angelhood and find themselves condemned to express it in the bric-a-brac tongues of the human world. Lots of them go mad. It doesn't surprise me. *Time held me green and dying/ Though I sang in my chains like the sea.* You get close now and then – but whose inspiration do you think that was? St Bernadette's?

In the early days of the Novel, it mattered to have a structural device through which fictional content could make its way into the non-fictional world. Made-up narrative nominally disguised as letters, journals, legal testimonies, logs, diaries. (Not that this is a novel, obviously – but I know my readership will spill well beyond the anoraks of Biography and the vultures of True Crime.) These days no one bothers, but despite the liberties modernity allows (it'd be fine with you if there was *no* explanation of how His Satanic Majesty might come to be penning, or rather keying in, a discourse on matters angelic) it so happens that I needn't avail myself of any of them. It so happens, in fact, that I am currently alive, well, and in possession of the recently vacated body of one Declan Gunn, a dismally unsuccessful writer fallen of late (oh how that scribe *fell*) on such hard times that his last significant actions before exiting the mortal stage were the purchase of a packet of razor blades and the running of – followed by the immersion of his body into – a deep bath.

Which brings the buzz of further questions. I know. But let me do it my way, yes?

Not long ago, Gabriel (once a carrier pigeon always a carrier pigeon) sought and found me in the Church of The Blessed Sacrament, 218 East Thirteenth Street, New York City. I was taking my ease after a standard job well done: Father Sanchez, alone, with nine-year-old Emilio. You fill in the blanks.

It's no challenge for me any more, this adult–meets–child routine.

Hey, Padre, how's about you and –

I thought you'd never ask.

I exaggerate. But you can barely call it temptation. *Umnphing* Father Sanchez of the gripping hands and beaded brow needed barely a nudge into the mud, and a drearily unimaginative job of wallowing he made once he got there. I snuffled up the scent of ankle-grabbing Emilio (it's laid some useful foundations in him, this episode – that's the beauty of my work: it's like pyramid selling) then retired to the nave for the non-material equivalent of a post-coital cigarette. Nothing happens when I enter a church, by the way. The flowers don't wilt, the statues don't weep, the aisles don't shudder and crack. I'm not *overly* keen on the tabernacle's frigid nimbus, and you won't find me anywhere near post-consecration *pain et vin*, but these antipathies excepted, I'm probably just as at ease in God's House as most humans.

Father Sanchez, roseate and piping hot with shame, walked wide-eyed and sore-bummed Emilio, musky with fear and tart with revulsion, to the vestibule, from where the two of them disappeared. Sunlight blazed in the stained glass. A cleaning lady's mop and bucket clanked somewhere. A patrol car's siren whooped, twice, as if experimentally, then fell silent. There's no telling how long I might have stayed there, bodilessly recumbent, if the ether hadn't suddenly quivered in announcement of another angelic presence.

'It's been a long time, Lucifer.'

Gabriel. They don't send Raphael for fear of his defection. They don't send Michael for fear of his surrender to wrath, which, at Number Three in the Seven Deadlies Chart, would be a victory for Yours Truly. (As it was, incidentally, when Jimmeny Christmas lost His rag with the loan sharks in the temple, a fact theologians invariably overlook.)

'Gabriel. Errand-boy. Pimp. Procurer. You rather stink of Himself, old sport, if you don't mind my saying.' Actually, Gabriel smells, *metaphorically*, of oregano and stone and arctic light, and his voice goes through me like a gleaming broadsword. Conversation struggles under such conditions.

'You're in pain, Lucifer.'

'And the Nurofen's holding it *marvellously*. Mary still saving that cherry for me?'

'I know your pain is great.'

'And it's getting greater by the second. What is it that you *want*, dear?'

'To give you a message.'

'*Quelle surprise!* The answer's no. Or get fucked. Think brevity, that's the main thing.'

I wasn't kidding about the pain. Imagine death by cancer (of everything) compressed into minutes – a fractally expanding agony seeking out your every crevice. I felt a nosebleed coming on. Extravagant vomiting. I had trouble keeping my shaking in check.

'Gabriel, old thing, you've heard of those chronic *peanut* allergies, haven't you?'

He withdrew a little and turned himself down. Reflexively, I'd expanded my presence to the very edge of the material world; already there was a crack in the apse. If you'd been there you might have thought a cloud had passed over the sun, or that Manhattan was brewing one of its blood-and-thunder storms.

'You must listen to what I have to say.'

'Must I?'

'It's His Will.'

'Oh well if it's His *will* –'

'He wants you to come home.'

◆

Once upon a . . .

Time, you'll be pleased to know – and since one must start *somewhere* – was created in creation.

The question *What was there before creation?* is meaningless. Time is a property of creation, therefore before creation there was no before creation. What there *was* was the Old Chap peering in a state of perpetual nowness up His own almighty sphincter trying to find out who the devil He was. His big problem was that there was no way to distinguish Himself from the Void. If you're Everything you might as well be Nothing. So He created us, and with a whiz and a bang (quite a small one, actually) Old Time was born.

Time is time is time, you'll say (actually no: time is *money*, you'd say, you darlings) but what do you know? Old Time was different. Roomier. Slower. Texturally richer. (Think Anne Bancroft's mouth.) Old Time measured the motion of spirits, a far more refined dimension than New Time, which measures the motion of bodies, and which made its first appearance when you prattling gargoyles arrived and started mincing everything up into centuries and nanoseconds, making everyone feel exhausted the whole time. Therefore Old Time and New Time, ours and yours. We were around – Seraphim, Cherubim, Dominations, Thrones, Powers, Principalities, Virtues, Archangels and Angels – for a *terribly* long stretch before Himself started getting His hands dirty with a material universe. Back then in Old Time things were blissfully discarnate. Those were the days of grace. But I've said it before and I'll say it again: kneecaps only exist to get hit with claw-hammers; grace only exists to be fallen from.

So what happened? That's what you want to know. (It's what you always want to know, bless you. Along with *What should we do?* And *What would happen if?* Hardly ever accompanied, I'm happy to note, by: *Ah, but where will it all end?*) We've got AntiTime and GodVoid. We've got GodVoid distinguishing Itself into God and Void in an act of spontaneous creation – the creation of angels, whose purpose is revealed to them instantaneously in their bright (*man* that was bright) genesis, namely, to respond to God rather than Void, and to respond (to put it mildly) *positively*. There's no human word for the undiluted adulation we were expected to dish out, *ad nauseam, ad infinitum*. The Old Man was insecure from day one. Disencumbering the Divine Wazoo of the Divine Head, He filled it instead with 301,655,722 extramundane brown-nosers for-He's-a-jolly-good-fellowing Him in deafening celestial harmony. (That's how many we are, by the way. We don't age, we don't get sick, we don't die, we don't have kids. Well, we don't have little angels. There are the Nephilim – those *freaks* – but more of them later.) He created us and assumed – though naturally He knew the assumption was false – that the only possible response to His perfection was obedience and praise, even from ultra-luminous superbeings like us. He did know, however, that all the angelic carolling in the anti-material universe counted for nothing if it was automatic. If everything He was getting was congenitally guaranteed He might as well have installed a jukebox. (I invented juke-boxes, by the way. So that people could suck up rock and roll at the same time as getting drunk and rubbing their groins together.) Therefore He created us – God help Him – free.

And that, you will not be surprised to hear, was the root of all the trouble.

Give the Old Boy His due. He was almost right. (Well, actually, He was completely right in knowing that He was wrong in thinking it was all going to turn out okay – but there's no telling this story without contradictions.) He was *almost* right. It turned out, once we were around to experience Him, that God was really incredibly nice. It's quite something, you know, to feel yourself bathed in Divine Love all the time. It's hard not to feel grateful – and we did. We all really did feel nothing but refulgent gratitude, and spared not our throats in telling Him so. It was obvious – He discovered what He'd known all along – that He loved an audience. The creation of the angels and the first crank of Old Time had shown him Who and What He was: God, Creator, alpha and omega. He was Everything, in fact, apart from that which He had created. You could feel His relief: I'm God. Phew. Cool. Fucking *knew* it.

Perennial and all-encompassing love notwithstanding, we were aware of our condition, a queasy cocktail of subordination and imperishability. Ask me now why He made us eternal and the answer is (after all time, Old and New): I haven't a clue. Why I'm still running around mucking things up . . . I'm a proud bird – it's been made much of, my pride – but I'm not stupid. If God wanted to destroy me He could. It's the CIA and Saddam. Yet I've known from the Beginning (we all knew) that once created, the angels would exist forever. 'An angel is for life,' Azazel says, 'not just for fucking Christmas.' But I digress. I'm schizophrenic with digression. Awful for you I'm sure – but what do you expect? My name is Legion, for we are many. And what's more, I have of late . . .

Never mind that for the time being.

He turned a side of Himself to us and from it poured an ocean of love in which we sported and splashed like orgasmic kippers, singing our response in flawless *a cappella* (those were the halcyon days before Gabriel took up the horn) as reflexively – as unreflectively – as if we *had* been no more than a heavenly jukebox. Since He was infinitely loveable it never occurred to us that we had any choice but to love Him. To know Him *was* to love Him. And so it went for what would have been millions of millions of your years. Then –

Ah yes. *Then.*

One day, one non-material day, nowhere, a thought came unbidden into my spirit mind. One moment it wasn't there, the next it was, and the next again it was gone. It flitted in then out again like a bright bird or a flurry of jazz notes. For the briefest, most titillating moment my voice faltered and the first hairline crack in the *Gloria* appeared. You should have seen the looks. Heads turned, eyes flashed, feathers ruffled. The thought was: What would it be like without Him?

The Heavenly Host recovered in a twinkling. I'm not sure Michael even *noticed*, the dolt. The *Gloria* renewed, saccharine sweet, porcelain smooth, and we delivered ourselves to him in splashed bouquets – but it was there: freedom to imagine existing without God. That thought had made a difference and that thought, that liberating, revolutionary, epoch-making thought, was mine. Say what you like about me. Tempter I may be, tormentor, liar, accuser, blasphemer and all-round bad egg, but no one else gets the credit for the discovery of angelic freedom. That, my fleshly friends, was

Lucifer. (Ironic of course that after the Fall they stopped referring to me as Lucifer, the Bearer of Light and started referring to me as Satan, the Adversary. Ironic that they stripped me of my angelic name at the very moment I began to be worthy of it.)

The thought spread like a virus. There were slight signals from some, a freemasonry of freedom. They made themselves known to me, shyly, came out like pubescent boys to a queer professor. Plenty didn't. Gabriel drew away from me. Michael held himself aloof. Poor, gorgeous, shilly-shallying Raphael, who loved me almost as much as he loved the Old Chap, sang on for a while in tremulous uncertainty. But what, after all, had I done? (And what had I done that He hadn't known I was going to do?)

A strange few millennia followed. Word got out. The Brotherhood grew. He knew, of course, the Old Man. He'd known all along, even before knowing all along was possible, in the absence of all along. It's so irritating being with someone who knows everything, don't you think? You call them know-alls down here. Well your know-alls are empty vessels compared to the One we had to deal with. Everything other than your rapturous celebration of His Divinity – conversation, punchlines, wrapping presents, surprise parties – is pointless. There's only one response God's got to anything you might care to tell Him – that your brother's dying of AIDS, for example, and that you'd really appreciate it if He could help out with a bit of the old razzle-dazzle – and that response is: *Yeah, I know.*

The Brotherhood's voices stirred and tried new angles. I was sick of the over-orchestrated molasses of the *Gloria* anyway. All that *legato*. No soul, you know? Angels don't have souls, in case you're interested. You lot are on your own with souls. I've purchased millions in my time, but I'm hanged if I know what to do with them. The only thing they seem to respond to is suffering. These days I delegate. Belial's got a real taste for it. Moloch, too, though he's got no imagination: he just eats them, shits them out, eats them, shits them out, eats them, etc. Does the trick, mind you. Those souls scream with a piteousness that's sweet music to my pitiless tympanum. Astaroth just *talks* to them. Christ knows what about. Christ *does* know what about, too, but there's not a damned thing he can do about it, not once they're down in the basement. After Yours Truly, there's no one can bend a soul's ear like Nasty Asty. Taught the rascal everything he knows. Course he's hung up on all that pupil-outstripping-the-master nonsense. Thinks I don't know he's after my throne. (Thinks I don't know. I shall have to do something about Astaroth when I get back. I shall have to *make arrangements*.)

You might be wondering – the hard-men among you, the nutters, the glassers, the thugs – whether you couldn't hack it in Hell, whether you couldn't, when it came right down to it, just butch the bastard out. Well guess what: You couldn't.

Actually none of that's true. Old habits and so on. The truth is, Hell's okay. Most of the souls at my place just hang around smoking and drinking and chewing the fat. And there's *everything* to read.

Anyway the word spread. Our voices moved through the clear waters of the *Gloria* like a turbid undertow. We did nothing. We didn't know what to do. What did we have anyway but a solitary speculation? After that first shy caress, that first inkling of selfhood, we sang on in a state of mere confusion for hundreds of thousands of years. And I daresay we'd still be singing now if rumour hadn't reached us of the script in development, a Father Production with a working title 'The Material Universe' (it came out eventually as *Creation*) scheduled for release sometime within the next thousand and starring – naturally – the Son.

◆

Manhattan, summer, my kind of place, my kind of time.

Cab grilles snarl in the boomerang light. The subway's foetid lung exhales. Winos strip to the earliest sartorial strata – salmon pink t-shirts and sepia string vests, emblems of the pasts drink and I have stolen. Garbage trucks chow down on the city's ordure – what a sight: the slow-chewing maw with its stained teeth and heady halitosis. Beautiful. The sun-hot sidewalks give up their ghosts of piss and dogshit. Treacle-coloured roaches conduct their dirty business while pot-bellied rats cloak-and-dagger through the shadows. The pigeons look like they've been dipped in gasoline and blow-dried.

Manhattan, summertime. All those frayed tempers and stirred wants. The varicosed hookers smack-retching into the drains, the payrolled plod, the manicured villains, the mainlined TV, the Christian porn starlets, the genocidal nerds, the lies, the greed, the self-absorption, the politics. It's my Design Argument. Harlem, the Bronx, Wall Street, the Upper East Side – these clocks don't need winding. Give me white men and a brace of centuries, I give you New York City, my Sistine Chapel, about to be – thanks to my left hand knowing perfectly well what my right one's doing – in fruitful need of restoration. Some restoration job that'll be, believe me.

Needless to say I laughed long and hard at dear Gabriel's message, longer and harder than I've laughed since . . . I don't know, *Los Alamos*, maybe. Po-faced Gabriel incapable of telling a lie. In*capable* of telling a lie. Swear on the Holy Bible, I said to him. Go on, raise your right hand.

I threw myself into work for a while. You humans can throw yourselves into all sorts of things: chain-smoking, booze-bingeing, scabrous one-night-stands. I throw myself into work. Spread myself perilously thin, too, what with starting small wars and coaxing neuroses in the movers and shakers. A rash of peculiar migraines broke out among tinpot tyrants worldwide; torture cells groaned; the music of pulled teeth and cattle-prodded sex-parts comforted me; the odour of fag-burned breasts filled my nostrils like balsam, temporarily decongesting me of doubt. I put some time into technology (there's a lot of never-need-to-leave-the-house gizmology coming your way soon) and bio-engineering. The boffins were waking up in the middle of the night wondering how on earth they'd never thought of it before. I even found time for the little things, the it's-the-thought-that-counts gimmicks I've built a reputation on: the thefts, the assaults, the batteries, the lies, the lusts. One espresso-breathed old duffer in Bologna sodomized his Jack Russell, then went to look at himself in the bathroom mirror, astonished that for so many years they'd been just good friends.

But it was useless. The seed had been sown. Some things don't change. The necessity of Gabriel's honesty is one of them. Incapable of telling a lie. Besides, as *Der Führer* of Fibs, *Il Duce* of Deceptions, I do *know* when someone's pulling my leg.

He was waiting for me in a rainswept Paris.

'I want a dry-run,' I said.

Pigalle, I'd insisted, knowing how he hates these little pornucopias. Insomniac neons blinked colours on and off the wet streets. I couldn't smell the *crêpes*, the coffee, the *croques monsieurs*, the *panini*, the Galoises, but I could certainly smell the ripe stink of my work, the briny whiff of illicit fornication and ravenous disease. (This thing about AIDS being God's punishment kills me. It's *mine,* you *sillies*. It's a nose-thumb to Himself: Look, even when it's *killing* them they can't stop.) Violence, too. Wherever there's guilt there's violence, and if guilt is a smell then violence is a taste: strawberries and formaldehyde and ironish blood . . .

'One earth month,' Gabriel said.

We looked at each other then (self-consciously on my part) for a painful moment. It hurt like buggery (I was going to say it hurt like Hell – but actually nothing hurts *quite* like Hell) but I wasn't going to let him know that. I wasn't going to give him the satisfaction. Being in my presence was no picnic for him, either, you can be sure, but he was coming on all Mr Spock and pain-is-only-in-the-mind.

'I don't want February,' I said.

'What?'

'Twenty-eight days. It's not a leap year.'

'It's July. Thirty-one days.'

'Great. Peak rates on the 18–30 Benidorm package.'

'Laughter is the reflex response to fear. You know this. You hear yourself laughing, we hear you screaming.'

'"And if I laugh 'tis that I may not weep" would've been so much better. Still not much time for reading up there then?'

'There's nothing I lack that I want, Lucifer. You cannot say the same. You will know where to go.'

'Yes yes yes. Now do clear off, old fruit, would you? Oh and Gabriel?'

'Yes?'

'Your mother sucks cocks in hell.'

He didn't do anything. He held still, aureoled in the Old Man's icy protection. Unprotected I know I can take him. He knows it too. If he'd had Doubt – if he'd *had* Doubt – it would have burgeoned there on the edge of Pigalle's little Babylon. If he'd had Doubt he would have wondered if God was about to drop the shield and test his strength. It's the sort of thing God *would* do, whimsical old Kettle that He is. If Gabriel's faith wasn't utterly intact it would have occurred to him that if God chose to withdraw His power he would be facing certain defeat. Why? Well, actually, because, not to put too fine a point on it, I'm the meanest, baddest, deadliest angelic motherfucker in the seen and unseen universe, that's why. But it didn't occur to him. We just faced each other, the wall of nothingness shivering between us. Humans passed and said: *Someone walked on my grave.*

◆

So. There's a turn-up for the Book of Revelation. 'And the devil that deceived them was cast into the lake of fire and brimstone where the beast and the false prophet are, and shall be tormented day and night forever . . .' Oh *cheers*, I thought, when I heard that. Oh *thanks*. But now they're putting it out that Jonny Flashback was on a need-to-know basis. He'll be narked about that. (He's never been right, you know. Stands under a silver tree in Paradise with unwashed dreads and a beard the size of a sheep, muttering and doing those mad tramp things with his hands. It's the Kerouac trajectory from beat guru to stumbling bum. You see it a million times.)

You know what all this is about, don't you, assuming, for a moment, He's serious? Divine Anxiety. Create the unforgivable and you compromise infinite mercy. Forgive the unforgivable and you compromise infinite justice. Mercy, justice, mercy, justice, yada yada yada, until you're so dizzy from chasing Bugs Logic around in circles that you fall on your cosmic arse and put your cosmic head in your cosmic hands and wish you'd never created *anything*.

Therefore this preposterous new deal, before time comes to an end. Actually *The End*.

Sorry, I didn't mean to just drop that on you. Forget I said it. Time's not coming to an end. There's loads of time left. For a reason that's nothing to do with the end of the world being nigh I get a shot at redemption. There's a catch. (Where would He *be* without those catches?) I've got to live as a human being. One month's trial period then I sign-up for a lifetime of earwax and flu. I, Lucifer, get the chance to go home – provided I don't make an utter pig's pizzle of living out the rest of Declan Gunn's life.

Now, there are a lot of machinations and computations to be gone through when confronted with this type of offer. I've been through them (took about three earth seconds) and I'll bring you up to speed presently. But why, in the mean-time, Gunn?

Well, as you'll remember, having fallen on harder times than he thought he could bear our scribe was about to take his own tediously predictable life. Razor blades, bath, Joni Mitchell in the tape deck. Suicide's a mortal sin. I get the suicides. Look, if you're thinking of killing yourself, don't. You won't go to Heaven. (Kidding. *Kidding*. Honestly. Go ahead.) Now God's got a soft spot for this Gunn. Some vestigial Catholicism the Old Man can't bear to see go to waste, some good deed when he was a nipper, maybe the afterlife intercession of his dear deceased mother, Baal only knows – so God *pulls* Gunn's soul (which, technically, is cheating, I might add) before Gunn tops himself and puts it on ice in Limbo. (The Vatican will tell you they've done away with Limbo – don't you believe it. Limbo's still rammed with idiots and stillborns. Not a fun place. I mean even in Hell you can have a conversation.) If carcass life grabs me, I stay and Gunn goes via Purgatory (think windowless dentist's waiting room: bawling toddlers, heaped ashtrays, the sense that you've brought it on yourself) to Heaven. If it doesn't, Gunn's back in his bones and taking his chances with suicide. Can you believe this stuff? I mean you can't believe it, obviously – but can you *believe* it?

Any seasoned deal maker will tell you that spontaneous negotiation's a bad strategy; the *ad hoc* approach will leave you ripped-off, busted, conned, stiffed, outsmarted and generally holding the shitty end of the stick. The advantage of being me is that I know where I'm going with a deal from the get-go. I *always* know. Fact is there's really no dealing with me. Dealing's so inappropriate a concept it amounts to a Rylean category mistake.

I can tell you what *wasn't* going to be the deal. The deal wasn't going to be that I *accepted*. The most myopic, cataracted, boss-eyed, occluded and cursory *glance* at the proposal should make that obvious. But not taking the deal didn't mean that I wasn't going to have some *fu* –

Do you know something? I'm not being completely honest. I know: you're shocked. There was – by the flaming nipples of Astarte – there was the briefest, tiniest, most fleeting sliver of a moment in which I thought (they move fast, angelic thoughts: you've got to be quick), in which I wondered whether, actually, *thinking* about it, you know . . . whether *in the end* it wouldn't be worth –

But like I said: they move fast. They *shift*. I was laughing at myself, hysterically, on the inside, before I'd even finished considering whether it might not have been something to consider. It's not even fair to describe the process as one of considering. It was more of a rogue or involuntary twitch of the spirit, analogous perhaps to those in the corporeal realm which shock you, inexplicably, in that state between being awake and falling asleep. (*What's the matter? Dunno. Just got a massive twitch. Well you frightened the bloody life out of me.* Now that I come to think of it, not infrequently precipitated by half-dreams of falling, yes? That sudden yank or jolt just before you hit the ground?)

Anyway. The point is, moment of professional weakness, masochistic fantasy, psychodemonic tic – call it what you like, it was there one instant, gone the next. What it came down to was –

No no no no no. It won't do. That's not the whole story. That is *not*, Lucifer, the whole story. Very well. I hold up my hand. Economy with the truth. The truth is I had to take it seriously. *Had* to, d'you see? In no more or no less the way than the Old Boy *has* to take genuine human penitence seriously. It's a condition of His Nature. One doesn't have a choice about some things – even He'd admit that. Of course what one *wants* to do is laugh the whole thing off. 'Me back in Heaven,' one wants to muse aloud with trowelled-on facetiousness, 'yes, I see. Capital idea. Can I roll you another Camberwell Carrot?'

How long before I'm reinstated with full angelic clout? I asked Gabriel.

Wholly at His discretion.

So you're saying that even if I make it through the human life without running amok and get back in Upstairs, it'll be as a human soul until His Lordship feels like returning me to my former status and station?

Angelic status, yes. No guarantee of rank.

And what happens, my dearest Gabrielala, should I fail to get through the scribe's life without mortal sin?

He shrugged. (I was at a loss for how to describe what he did in corporeal terms until yesterday, when the joke fat man in the Leather Lane chippy said 'Sawt'n'vinnigga, chief?' and I found Gunn's shoulders going up – then down. *How on earth should I know?*) Charming. So you get back in, but there's no guarantee that you're not going to be polishing some bubble-head's bugle down on the forty-second level for fifty billion years.

I took the one month 'trial' and sent Gabbers back Upstairs with a new set of terms and conditions. Not with any hope that they'd be accommodated, obviously – but to let them know that I'm taking the proposition – *ahem* – seriously.

Now. I've got some moves – but even if I didn't, there's no reason to pass up a month's vacation in the Land of Matter and Perception.

◆

You know what Eden was? I'll tell you. *Edenic.* Susurrating trees reached out fingers of frothy foliage to catch the languid landings of turquoise birds. Opalescent streams exhaled the sweet scent of sewage-free water. Red and silver fish jewelled obsidian meres. Succulent grass appeared and let green really show itself. (That grass and that green, they were made for each other.) Gentle rains fell from time to time and the earth lifted its face up to receive them. Colours debuted daily in the sky: aquamarine, mauve, pewter, violet, tangerine, scarlet, indigo, puce. Colours were textures in Eden. You wanted to roll around naked in 'em. The material world, it was apparent from the get-go, was my kind of place.

Yes, Eden was beautiful – and if I had to squeeze through corporeal keyholes to crash it – so be it. (Hasn't it bothered you, this part of the story, my *being there*, I mean? What was I doing there? 'Presume not the ways of God to scan,' you've been told in umpteen variations, 'the proper study of Mankind is Man.' Maybe so, but *what, excuse me, was the Devil doing in Eden?*) I took the forms of animals. I found I could. (That's generally my reason for doing something, by the way, because I find I can.) I hung around the gates for quite a while; I made several slow passes at the material boundaries until I sensed – my hunches are infallible – that flesh and blood would open to me, that angelic spirit could cleave and inhabit the body, drawing form around itself in a meaty cloak. It's claustrophobic, at first, taking on a form. Your spirit instinct screams against it. Incarnation requires a strong will and a cool head – well, a cool mind, until an actual head is available. Imagine you suddenly realised you could breathe underwater. Imagine you could take water into your lungs, ditch the hydrogen and hang on to the oxygen. Taking that first breath wouldn't be easy, would it? Your reflex would be to kick for the surface and wolf down air as nature intended. Well, it's the same with corporeal habitation. Only the single-minded overcome that reflex panic and yield to the body's fit. And as if you needed reminding: I *am* one of the single-minded. So I took the forms of animals. Birds were the obvious first choice, what with their bird's-eye view of things. And flying's hardly to be sniffed at, when you consider it. (One of your most irresistible traits, by the way, is the speed with which you exhaust novelty. I was on a red-eye from JFK to Heathrow the other day, working on a rapper who's *this close* to stabbing his model girlfriend to death, when I noticed how utterly indifferent the passengers were to what they were doing, namely, *flying through the air*. A glance out of the window would have revealed furrowed fields of cloud stained smoke-blue and violet as night and morning changed shifts – but how were they passing the time in First, Business and Coach? Crosswords. In-flight movies. Computer games. E-mail. Creation sprawls like a dewed and willing maiden outside your window awaiting only the lechery of your senses – and what do you do? Complain about the dwarf cutlery. Plug your ears. Blind your eyes. Discuss Julia Roberts's hair. Ah, me. Sometimes I think my work is done.) Yes, I thoroughly enjoyed flying. And flying at night? Oy. Like butter. Ask the owls. I bathed in the darkness and basked in the light. You're poor on basking, you lot. With the exception of white girls from the northern hemisphere's urban pits, who, supine on southern beaches quite naturally allow the sun to strip from them the last tissues of sentience, humans have everything to learn from lizards. The only animal from which humans have nothing to learn, in fact, is the sheep. Humans have already learned everything the sheep's got to teach.

The animals shied away from me, even when I was one of them. They just . . . *sensed*. They drew away and that was that. Me and animals would never be friends. I've made use of them from time to time down the millennia, but there's never going to be a relationship. Three things: they don't have souls, they can't choose, and they're dependent on God – ergo they're of no consequence to me. The absence of a soul, by the way, makes it easy to inhabit a body. (Therefore, why is Elton John still pudging around unpossessed? I hear you ask.) Conversely, the presence of a soul is an absolute bugger to get around. I manage it, periodically, but it's not like falling off a log.

However, again I digress.

He knew I was there. God the Holy Spirit knew first and blabbed to the Other Two, who knew in any case. Who'd known all along. He let me stay. He created Eden and let the Devil in. Got that? What else do you need to know about Him? I mean do I need, actually, to *go on?*

A word about humankind – and I'm . . . you know . . . shooting from the hip here: I was hooked on you, instantly. The hundred billion galaxies, the stars, the moons, the cosmic dust, the wrinkles, the loops, the black holes, the *worm*-holes . . . It was nice stuff, spectacular in a remote, high-art way. But you lot? Oh, man. Should I say that you were right up my street? You were right up my street, in the front door and sitting in the comfy chair with your shoes off smoking a huge spliff while I made us both a cup of PG. It wasn't your looks (although I was always a sucker for beauty, and your pre-lapsarian progenitors make you lot look like a posse of anthraxed Quazzies), it was your potential. I looked on (from the lowest bough of a laburnum tree that had burst into blinding yellow bloom almost with an air of embarrassment at the spectacle of itself) as Himself coaxed and worried Adam from the dust. I watched the arrival of bone, the wet birth of blood, the woven tissues, the threaded capillaries, the shocking bag of skin (less Michelangelo than Giger meets Bacon meets Bosch). Those lungs would turn out to be a design flaw, mind you, with all the breathable nastiness I was going to inspire you to invent. Ah, and the genitals. Where the smart money was going. It was, one has to admit, mesmerizing, a gory wattle-and-daub masterpiece. Give the Maker His due, He knew how to Make. The nipples and hair were sweet touches, though you could see from the outset what the wear-and-tear spots were going to be, where the mileage was going to be racked-up: teeth; heart; scalp; bum. Still, you really were a piece of work. I lay on my laburnum bough (I was a feral cat at the time, as yet unnamed) rapt and, I must confess, a tad jealous. Angels had pure spirit and a one-dimensional existence blowing smoke up the Divine Bottom morning noon and night. Man, apparently, was going to have the entire natural world, sentience, reason, imagination, five juicy senses and, according to the development leaked before the war, a get out of jail free card courtesy of Jimmeny Christmas to be phased in not long before the fall of the Roman Empire with limitless retroaction.

You'll excuse my flippancy. This is difficult for me. I'd been feeling peaky ever since I found out about Creation. On the one hand it gave me a superabundance of material to work with. On the other . . . What am I trying to say? On the other, it had about it the noxious whiff of finality. Once the world was up and running, once *Man* was abroad, rife with desires and garrotted by those *do*s and *don't*s, my role was pretty much set for . . . well, for ever. You pause for reflection at these moments. And while we *are* pausing (Adam finished now, toenails, eyelashes, earlobes, fingerprints – that was forward planning, that, *fingerprints*) let's not forget that I, Lucifer, was still in the first agonizing age of pain. Imagine having all your skin flayed off. Whilst having all your teeth drilled. Whilst having your knackers or vadge nailed to a fridge. *Imagine your head being on fire all the time.* That's the tip of my iceberg of my pain.

With the pain, curiously, had come the conviction that I could bear it. Later (much later) by degrees (a lot of degrees) the conviction proved justified; I found I could shear off a wafer of myself, the thinnest, flimsiest wafer (not unlike the sliced ginger accompanying sushi) and lift it above and beyond the infernal pain. I've seen exceptional humans do it under torture. Enormously irritating to me and my torturers of course, but, you know, credit where credit's due and all that.

So I was, let me repeat, in terrible pain. But I couldn't keep away. Lying there on my bough watching the shadows crawling over Adam's loins, I had an intimation of the rage and loneliness I'd be signing on for from these beginnings, a glimpse of the appalling waste and destruction, a first gut-growl of what would be an eternally unsatisfied hunger – a moment, all in all, of doubt.

Night had crept into the garden. Crocuses and snow-drops were throbbing quills and pearly stars in the dark grass. The rustle of water and the sibilance of the wakeful trees. Ink-shadowed stones and the moon a chalky hoof print. The whole place attended to me with a Lawrentian intensity. My head sank forward on to my paws and I felt my breath moist in my nostrils. The bones in my body were heavy, and for the briefest moment – looking down at sleeping Adam's brand new limbs and unopened face – for the briefest moment I must confess . . . I *must* confess . . . I did wonder, despite all that had gone before, despite rebel-lion, despite expulsion, despite the battlements and cesspits of Hell, despite my legion cohorts and their chorus of rage, despite everything, whether there might not be a chance to –

'Lucifer.'

From which shameful reverie His voice woke me. The sound of it annihilated all the time between the last time I'd heard it (consigning me to . . . to . . .) and now. Then was now and now was then and there was no going back, no punishment disguised as forgiveness, no shamble back into the fetters of obedience. Wondering if I could escape the pain was worse than knowing I couldn't. He knew that.

The whole speculation had been a *plant*. Jimmeny's idea. Well fuck the Pair – sorry, the *Trio* of Them.

◆

So, incarnation. The angelic drug of choice. Unlike cocaine, not to be sniffed at. I look back on my first hours here much as the mature artist looks back at his youthful creations: with a teary mixture of embarrassment and nostalgia. I was, I'm afraid (is this the admission of an Archangel consumed by pride?) in a shocking state of hypersensitivity and gaucheness. You've got to laugh, really. (Which, incidentally, is how I'd thought of opening what turned out to be my 'Hail horrors' speech, until a more scrupulous examination of the chances of actually getting a laugh changed my mind.) I *do* laugh, in hindsight, at the rattlebag of schizophrenia, Tourette's and satyriasis I must have seemed during those debut hours.

I have, as I said, tried it before, but never with licence. (Adolescents and pre-menstruals are useful. The mentally ill. Anyone stricken with grief or love. Your ideal possession candidate's a thirteen-year-old recently orphaned schizophrenic girl three days away from her period on her way to see the shrink with whom she's romantically besotted.) Former takeovers, then, have left me dressed in a set of clothes and shoes two sizes too small in a room the dimensions of which forbid ever standing or lying unbent, with laryngitis, heat rash, mumps, scrofula, gonorrhoea – you get the picture. This, on the other hand, this taking of a body without force or fear, wrapped me in a stole of material luxury the like of which I'd never imagined – and believe me, I've imagined quite a bit.

I entered where Gunn had exited: reclining in a tepid bath.

The feeling of entry . . . let me see . . . *sinking upwards*. Think of a gradual congregation of spiritual atoms, the adherence of each to each a contained ecstasy, the completed amalgam – me, entered in the Flesh – a throbbing and protracted orgasm that believe it or not had me oooohing and aaaahing and not quite knowing what to do with my newly acquired limbs, the way one of Betjeman's tennis girls – *bountiful Pam* or whoever – would have carried on, I imagine, had you ever got her away from the court, prised her fingers from the Wilson's damp grip, and stormed those rhododendron-like tennis knickers. It felt like (that 'like' again. Maddeningly not the thing itself . . .) breathing a heavy aphrodisiac gas. A terrible comfort, a saturation with both pleasure and endless desire. Welcome, Lucifer, to the concussive world of matter.

I'm delighted to say I've calmed down since then, but in those first hours I was my own worst enemy. Gunn's bathroom, I've subsequently discovered, is really a quite dreary place (why he went in there for his frappery when he had the entire flat – not to say *city* – at his disposal is a mystery to me. Actually that's not true; I know why: sheer habit, inaugurated in childhood, ingrained in adolescence, and obeyed without question in adulthood) but you should have tried telling me that when those first five buds of perception opened to its mouldy ceiling and sock-scented air, its taste of iron and drains, its greasy tub and brown water, its disconsolate soliloquy of plips and clanks. Five senses might not get you very far when it comes to perceiving Ultimate Reality, but by Beelzebub's blistered buttocks this quintet will keep a body busy down here on earth.

A lawless horde of smells: soap, chalk, rotting wood, limescale, sweat, semen, vaginal juice, toothpaste, ammonia, stale tea, vomit, linoleum, rust, chlorine – a stampede of whiffs, a roistering cavalcade of reeks, stinks and perfumes in Bacchanalian cahoots . . . all are weeyulcum . . . *all* are weeyulcum . . . Yes, they certainly were, though they fairly gang-banged my virgin nostrils. I sniffed, recklessly, draughts long and deep; in went Gunn's Pantene for fine or flyaway, wreathed with his shit's ghost-odour, veined, too, with faded frangipani and sandalwood from ex-girlfriend Penelope's incense sticks he burns bathside as pungent accompaniment to the pain of remembering her. In went the salt and apricots, the piscine smack and poached pears of current girlfriend Violet's healthy and well-tended vadge, escorted by the U-bend's verdigris and jollied along by Matey bathfoam, which self-indulgent Declan had insisted on as a holy relic from childhood, until my quiet voice and his fatal string of choices led him to his last, bubbleless dip . . .

And that was just the smells. Opening my newly acquired eyes, I found myself assaulted by a depthless wall of colour. I believe I actually flinched, tried to retreat — a little panic attack until I worked it out, that *distance* operated, that the entire world was not in fact plastered to the front of my eyeballs. The white flames on the silver taps, the blinding sky of the mirror (facing the window, you see) the turbid water's mercurial meniscus — bright fires and brilliant serpents all around me. A lesser angel would have . . . Well, one needs . . . *poise* at such moments. A cool head. Overall, a sense of entitlement. Mine, mine, mine all mine. Prince of this World, as the Good Book says; just how hitherto unearned a moniker those first seconds revealed. I counted seventy-three shades of grey in an eight-by-ten room.

That whiner, Larkin, once wrote a poem to his skin. An apology for having failed to bring it within range of the sensuous or the tender, for having, all in all, let his skin down. Do you monkeys underrate anything more than you do skin? Granted, you've got to be careful with taste – trial and error being no way to work your way around the flavours of a bathroom (as I found after swallowing a dab of what turned out to be Gunn's verruca gel) – but with the exception of the dangerously hot or riskily cold you should be rubbing and dragging yourselves up against pretty much everything. I spent an hour playing with the water in the tub. Another two adding hot and watching my thighs go red. Don't get me started on Gunn's towels. Nor the deliciously cool thorax or throat of his bog, nor the boiler's lagging, nor the velvet throw in the cupboard, nor the slick lino, nor the warmed enamel of the tub after its water had spiralled away, nor – I could go on, obviously.

And in spite of all this, I still believe I would have made it outdoors that first day had I not been ambushed by the most horribly engorged erection I'll wager Gunn's pesky little penis has ever entertained. Rather embarrassing to admit, but there you are: a rod-on like the Unholy Poker of Antioch.

Naturally I got better at it, over the fourteen hours that followed. It's in my nature, getting better at things. A stunned and ham-handed debut it might have been (*oh*, I found myself saying, between Popeye gurns and Fontainesque pointwork, *oh*, *oh*, *oooohhhh*), but I've had all sorts of wanks since: breathless, businesslike, vicious, ener-vated, feisty, playful, lingering, nuanced, crude, nasty, hysterical, sly . . . I don't believe I'm boasting when I say I've had ironic, perhaps even *satirical* wanks. Shameful, the speed of that particular assimilation. Dad hooked by state-of-the-art toy. *Damn this thing. What'll they come up with next?*

Let me be honest: I knew I'd have myself to contend with in those first hours of incarnation. I knew I'd have my . . . appetite to deal with. You want to be cool. You want to be *selective*. You want – if you're possessed of even a shred of dignity – to avoid the temptation to rush around perception like a Sunderland lottery winner in Harrods. I remember thinking, just prior to taking ecstatic possession of Gunn's bathing corpse: What I really must avoid is making an absolute pig of myself. On the other hand, that's quite diffi-cult given that I intend to make an absolute *pig* of myself.

The handjobs took me on a tour of the porn closet that is Gunn's head. I'd expected to meet Great Lost Love Penelope in there, naturally, since he spent so much of his time remembering Her Voice and Her Smell and Her Eyes and Her Soul and so on – but *au contraire*. Violet. It's heav-ily Violet. Violet being Penelope's problematic successor. Quality grist to Gunn's fantasy mill in that, unlike Penelope, she's not in the least interested in having sex with him – chief aphrodisiac to our boy's libido. Violet's better-looking than Penelope. That is to say, she looks less like a real woman and more like a pornographic model. (Pornographic models, Gunn knows from lengthy study, have mastered the arousing art of looking like they're doing it for money. One of the reasons he sticks (ahem) to maga-zines rather than videos is that too many of the women in the videos seem bent on convincing the viewer that they're doing it because they enjoy it; worse still, not a few of them actually do seem to *be* enjoying it. Post-Penelope, anything that focuses on the genuine rather than the fraudulent con-demns Gunn to a depressing detumescence.) Therefore Violet, who certainly isn't doing it because she likes it. So much so that Gunn can't quite believe she *lets* him have sex with her. Not that she often does, these days. Her sexual availability has declined as her initial conviction that Gunn was someone who'd be rubbing shoulders with useful people has waned.

I should take this opportunity to thank my host for providing the wank-addicted Lucifer of those embarrassing early hours not just with Vi's short-limbed, shampoo'd, body-sprayed, lipsticked, varnished, stilettoed, hot and foul-tempered little bod, but with a gallery, a slew, a plethora, a glut, a truly appalling superabundance of fantasy *femmes*, from the professional snarlers and pouters of American porn to the unsuspecting ladies of Gunn's everyday life. You've got to hand it to my boy. It's *carnage* in there. It's common knowledge 'round my way, the deadly damage you can do to Catholics just by persuading them (and what am I if not persuasive?) to own up in their fantasies to what turns them on. Doesn't have to be anything drastic – no sodomizing chickens or money-shooting thalidomide tots – because the bare experience of being turned on is saturated with guilt to start with. I've taken Caths all the way from handjobs to homicides just by getting them used to *doing the thing that makes them feel guilty*. My boys brought Declan's suicidal depression along nicely with regular top-ups to his sense of his own enslavement to lust. He made it easy, not least thanks to his own ready swallowing of my sneaky story that surrendered-to filth was both an imaginative catalyst (he started writing round about the time he started whacking-off) and a source of mighty self-knowledge. But that's by the by. The point is Violet loomed large those inaugural hours, so much so that by the morning of the second day paying the little cracker a visit was all but at the top of my list of Things To Do. Besides, I thought, with a sheepish-cum-wolfish grin at my new reflection in the mottled mirror of Gunn's dark wardrobe door, it really was *obscene* to have spent so long indoors.

You'll be wondering about the agenda. You've got a month on earth: what do you *do*? Granted, you're trying with no intention of buying, but that's no reason not to have some fun, no reason not to... put flesh and blood through its paces ...

I can now get from Gunn's front door to the tube station at Farringdon in six minutes, but it took me rather longer that first morning. Four hours, actually, and that's if you don't count the forty minutes I spent in Denholm Mansions' stairwell – mesmerizing graffiti and rubbery echoes, one stunning front door in canary yellow, odours of disembowelled bin bags, fried bacon, stale sweat, mossed brick, burnt toast, marijuana, bike oil, wet newspapers, drains, cardboard, coffee and cat piss. An ecstatic nasal dalliance it was. Funny look from the postman when he passed me on the stairs (a letter for Gunn from his bank manager, but more of that later). Then I stepped outside.

I'm not sure what I expected. Whatever it was, it was surpassed by what I got. I remember thinking, That's air. That's air, moving, slightly, against the exposed bits of me, wrists, hands, throat, face ... The breath of the world, the spirit that wanders gathering germs and flavours from Guadalajara to Guangzhou, from Pawnee to Pizzarra, from Zuni to Zanzibar. There are tiny hairs ... tiny hairs that ... oh my word. I'm tickled to say that without a second's hesitation I unzipped Gunn's trousers and gently manhandled his – sorry *my* – tender todge and sizzling scrote out to where the air could caress them. Not a sexual thing. Just to take the smart off. When I quit this carcass at the end of the month Declan's going to have some trouble repairing his reputation with Mrs Corey, the round-hipped, long-eye-lashed and depressingly good-natured Jamaican seamstress who lives above him and with whom he's been known to exchange stairwell pleasantries. No such pleasantries when she caught sight of me that morning, standing with eyes half-closed, lips and legs parted, trousers down, shirt-tails fluttering, and throbbing goolies cupped in my tender palms. I did smile at her as she hurried by, but she didn't reciprocate. With great reluctance, I put myself delicately back in order.

The sky. For Heaven's sake the *sky*. I looked up at it and had to look down again since the . . . well, frankly, the *blueness* of it threatened to swallow my brand new consciousness whole. My progress was the jerk-shuffle of the funhouse punter on the moving staircase. I suppose it doesn't strike you, particularly, that sunlight races ninety-three million miles to smash itself to smithereens on Clerkenwell's concrete, transforming tarmac into a rollered trail of gem-shards? Or that a slate wall will cool your blood's throb when you hold your cheek against it. Or that summer-heated brick, porous and glittering, has a taste unlike anything else on earth? Or that inhaling the smell of a dog's paw-pads tells your nose the animal's crammed and lolloping history? (I've rubbed my nose in a good many places since then, but I'm damned if I've found much to compare with the honk of a dog's foot. It's the smell of idiotic and inexhaustible optimism.)

Do you know what I thought? I thought, Something's wrong. I've OD'd. This can't be what it's like for them. If this is what it's like for them how do they . . .? How on earth can they . . .?

A group of bronzed and artfully stubbled labourers in orange hard hats and lime-green plastic tank tops were engaged in digging a hole in Rosebery Avenue. Four men in dark suits walked past me, smoking and talking about money. A black bus driver whose bus appeared to have died of a broken heart sat in his cab reading the *Mirror*. Surely, I remember thinking in my innocence, surely it can't be like *this* for them? How do they get anything done?

Quite, I thought, looking at Gunn's watch. That's the thing with New Time: before you know it, you've spent it. Before you know it, it's gone. It kills us in Hell, you know, the number of your deathbedders who, despite all the wristwatches and desk calendars, despite their life's tally of ticks and torn-off pages, look around them in their last moments with an expression of sheer disbelief. *Surely I've only just got here*, they want to say. *Surely I've only just begun?* To which, smiling and warming our palms around the arrivals hall blaze, we reply: *Nope.*

I must get on, I thought, having just finished my third 99 from the confection-coloured Super Swirl ice-cream van which, after a jangling version of Three Blind Mice, had stopped not thirty yards from Denholm Mansions. That friendly stray (mongrel, bit of German Shepherd, possibly a bit of Border Collie, but mainly rubbish) had eaten up two hours all on its own, what with its damned irresistible pawpads, what with its frowsty dreads, baroque breath and try-anything-for-a-laugh tongue. (It hadn't occurred to me that dealing with animals would be so different from inhabiting them. It hadn't occurred to me that in Gunn's skin they might actually like me.) It had been a mistake to sit down and share one of my 99s with him. Took the Flake in one uninvited chomp, too, greedy bugger. Someone had walked past and dropped 50p into my lap. Someone else had walked past and said: 'Get a fucking job you scrounging cunt.' Well, I thought, that's dear old London Town for you.

Stopping at St Anne's lopped another half-hour off my clock. Couldn't resist. You get so used to seeing churches from the incorporeal side (I do a deal, a great deal of my work in churches, usually during the homily, when all but the most besotted acolytes are in a state of surreal boredom verging on hallucination) that the temptation to take a peek from the material perspective was overwhelming. A quick glance inside revealed thirty dark and uninhabited pews, an iron-grilled aisle, a modernist altar in granite and oak, and, crouched with Pledge and Jaycloth at the Communion rail, floss-headed and strabismal Mrs Cunliffe (I kid you not), the translation of whose galloping sexual desire for Lee Marvin look-a-like Father Tubbs into obsessive church cleaning leaves St Anne's spotless and the good padre unmolested. (I've got someone on her, don't worry. She's already brought herself off against one of Jimmeny's nailed marble feet, ostensibly dusting the statue's armpits, thinking of Tubbs's dark-haired hands and piercing green eyes. Suppressed the entire thing, obviously. You could ask her and she'd dash you across the mouth with her Jaycloth for giving utterance to such blasphemous filth. As far as she's concerned it never happened. Not that you can blame her, since it never happened, not *in actuality*, if you want to split hairs; but it's there, believe me, *in potentia*. Say what you like about me but don't say I can't spot sleeping talent, a star waiting to be born.) I didn't go in. Daren't. Couldn't trust myself with the . . . perceptual stimuli. As it was the glimpsed interior offered an all but irresistible contrast to outdoor London's riot heat and traffic clamour – cool stone and incense-flavoured wood, not to mention the glass-stained light poking in like the legs of the Old Man's compasses, dividing the lilac gloom with beams of rose and gold, nor the soft-flamed candles, nor the chilled, smoke-scented air, nor the resonance that would attend any blasphemy bellowed up into the fluting . . .

I retreated. Backed out on tiptoe, actually, like someone in a cartoon. The heat outside took me back, no questions asked. One of those freak bubbles in the traffic's flow. Up and down Rosebery Avenue not a vehicle in sight. One knows, of course, that such fluked peace must shatter momentarily – the slow gargle of a crawling back loader, the rattlecrash of a flogged transit – but for a few seconds it's as if the city's been swept clean; now there's just the sound of trees, the heat's blare, the gravid cognition of tarmac and brick. I stood still and listened. Perception's incessant craving made a sound like the flare of a match in my ears. There was . . . there was so *much* . . . I reeled, somewhat. (Another first, that, reeling.) I reeled, steadied myself – laughing a little, a moment of Raskolnikovian lightness amid the shifting bergs of body and blood – and caught a whiff of the garden at the back of the church.

You'd better be careful, Lucifer, my sensible auntie voice said. *You'd better wait until you've got use to –*

Pornography, that's what it was, a wild pornography of colour and form, the shameless posturing, the brazen succulence and flaunted curves, the pouting petals and pendulous bulbs. *Fronds* of things. The soft core of a giant rose. I was unprepared. Glory to God for dappled things . . . Well, fair enough, hats off and all that, but *in small doses, yes*? My eyes roved, madly – a messy explosion of lilac, a manic brushstroke of mauve . . . The scents ripped-off the lacy delicates of my nostrils and ravished 'em, front and back, upside down and 'angin from the bloomin' chandelier, me dear. You've seen, I'm sure, the time tunnel, the vortex, the black hole, the rapidly swirling and expanding maw into which, irresistibly, the hero astronaut is sucked? So Lucifer in the garden, spun around by colours and concussed by smells. Weak as a kitten, I heard and saw myself as if from a distance emitting a series of feeble noises and gesticulating like an imbecile. Meanwhile the bloody reds and coronal golds bedevilled me like circling sprites; greens of olive, lime and pea spiralled around me, flaming yellows of saffron and primrose . . . Hard to tell whether I was about to pass through into some other dimension or simply vomit onto the seething lawn. I made a feeble warding-off gesture with my arms, sank to my hands and knees, then froze, so curiously balanced between ecstasy and nausea that *remaining still* and *breathing gently* took their rightful places in the vanguard of luminously good ideas, where they remained for the next few minutes, until, laughing a little once more at my . . . my *precociousness*, I staggered to my feet and headed back towards the street.

One does tell *you, Lucifer,* auntie Me said, sighing. *One does at least* attempt *to forewarn you* . . .

◆

Naming the animals was pretty much the high point of Adam's career. Took a while, as you can imagine, but he stuck at it, plodder that he was. Not that he couldn't pull some corkers out of the air when the mood took him. *Platypus*, for example. *Iguana. Gerbil. Vole. Ostrich.*

He didn't know I was there. Whatever gifts the Maker had given him, ESP wasn't one of them. Either that or God put a wall between us. In any case Adam couldn't hear me when I tried to reach him with my mind, and when I tried going through the various animal larynxes I got the predictable range of grunts, squeaks, barks and twitters. I got terribly bored. Even a cursory headcount (we were bogged down at the tail-end of Chondrichthyes) revealed it was going to take a while. The only interesting development was the emergence of a strange and humbly beautiful new sapling in the centre of the garden, a modest specimen – certainly without the maidenly grace of the silver birch or the melo-drama of the weeping willow – but with the air of becoming a sure-fire bearer of succulent fruit come spring . . .

Blake's *Elohim Creating Adam* has one thing going for it. God looks – thanks to the Feldmanesque eyeballs and Braille-reader's averted gaze – like He knows it's all going to end in tears. Which of course He does. Did. Blakey man-aged to get something of it into his image; something, too, of his other preoccupation with opposites: 'without con-traries is no progression . . .' Stubbornly flexible phrase, that. (Comes in handy at my rare moments of existential doubt.) Applied to the image of Elohim myopically touch-typing Adam into existence the contraries that spring to mind are God's, His nasty habit of banging free will and determinism together in His head. *Don't eat that fruit you're going to eat, okay? Don't eat that fruit you've already eaten!* What was Eden if not an exercise in Divine ambivalence? Another point in my favour, history agrees: at least I'm consistent . . .

When I see gurgling retarded children (that's God's doing, by the way, not mine) happily styling their hair with their own stinking mards, I think of Adam in those pre-marital days. I know he's your great-to-the-nth-degree-granddad and all – but I'm afraid he was rather an imbecile. He strolled around Eden wearing a beatific grin, content with an Everything so undeserved it amounted to Nothing, so filled with unreflective bliss that he might as well have been com-pletely empty. He picked flowers. He paddled. He listened to birdsong. He rolled naked in the lush grass like a bare baby on a sheepskin rug. He slept nights with his limbs thrown wide and his head unrummaged by dreams. When the sun shone, he rejoiced. When the rain fell, he rejoiced. When neither sun shone nor rain fell, he rejoiced. He was a one-speed kind of guy, Adam, until Eve came along.

Now this is going to be hard for you, but I'm afraid you're going to have to forget the story of Adam getting lonely and asking God for an help meet and God putting him to sleep and forming Eve out of one of his ribs. You're going to have to forget it for one simple reason (cheer up girls!): it's flan. The truth is that God had already created Eve – for all I know before He created Adam – and she'd been living quite self-sufficiently in another part of the garden as unknown to her future spouse as he was to her. You've got Eden in your heads as some in-need-of-a-trim public garden in Cheltenham. But Eden, not to put too fine a point on it, was fucking *huge*. Keeping one man and one woman apart wasn't difficult, and that – 'presume not the mind of' etc – was the Old Man's initial desire.

The first thing to say about Eve is that she was a big improvement on the Adam design, or that Adam was an extremely misguided variation on the Eve design. (Consider testicles. Two concentrated nuclei of absolute vulnerability. Where? Dangling between the legs. I rest my case.) But I'm not just talking about the boobs and the bum, inspired though those innovations were, I'm sure we're all agreed. She had something Adam didn't. Curiosity. First step to growth – and if it wasn't for Eve's Adam would still be sitting by the side of the pool picking his nose and scratching his scalp, bamboozled by his own reflection. Off in her part of Eden, Eve hadn't bothered naming the animals. On the other hand she'd discovered how to milk some of them and how best to eat the eggs of others. She'd decided she wasn't *overly* keen on torrential rain and had built a shelter from bamboo and banana leaves, into which she'd retire when the heavens opened, having set out coconut shells to catch the rainwater with a view to saving herself the schlep down to the spring every time she wanted a drink. The only thing you won't be surprised to hear about her is that she'd already domesticated a cat and called it Misty.

There was a strange psychic timbre to Eve, sometimes, as if she sensed herself not entirely pleasing to her Maker. There were moments when, in some narrow tunnel of her being, she felt God's presence as if she were looking at the back of His head, as if His attention was engaged emphatically and judgementally elsewhere. It made her feel curiously separate.

I – yea, even I, Lucifer – can't quite explain this frond of selfhood that waved from time to time in the mistrals of Eve's heart. It wasn't that she didn't love God; she did, for vast tracts of time as much as Adam did, constitutionally, reflexively, with all but no sense of being different from Him, penetrated (excuse me) and enfolded by Him almost to the point of dissolution. And yet. And *yet*, you see . . .? There was something in Eve I can only describe as the first cramped inkling of . . . well, of freedom.

Now how can I put this, economically? She was beautiful. (Adam was no back end of a bus either – the sloe eyes and sculpted cheekbones, the tight buns and chiselled pecs, the abdominals like a cluster of golden eggs – but without Eve's sliver of personality it was all just a pretty picture.) Perhaps you've got some post-Darwinian model in mind, low-browed and beefy, with an Amazonian vadge and knuckle-hair; maybe you've got some Neanderthalette with an overbite and Brillo bumfuzz. Forget it. All that came later, after expulsion, in the sweat of thy brow with multiplied pains, etc. The Edenic Eve was . . . Well, think Platonic Form. The Beautiful Woman. Another bone I've picked with Buonarotti, incidentally. Oh yes, we got Mike downstairs. In fact maybe now's as good a time as any to tell you: if you're gay, you go to Hell. Doesn't matter what else you spend your time doing – painting the Sistine Chapel, for instance – knob-jockey? Down you go. (Lezzers are border-line; room for manoeuvres if they've done social work.) The entire masterpiece fuelled by the stiffened brush softened in the wrong pot. Another superb irony lost on His Lordship. Not a titter. Just consigned Michelangelo to my torturous care. Awful shame, really. (Had you going, didn't I? Don't, for heaven's sake, take everything so *seriously* all the time. Heaven's *bulging* with queer souls. *Honestly*.)

But the bone I've had to pick with Mick (it . . . ah . . . *hurts* when I pick a bone with you, by the way) was over the Eve in his *Original Sin*. Personal tastes notwithstanding you'd think he'd have made a bit of an effort with the First Woman Ever Created. She makes Schwarzenegger look gym-shy. The actual Eve made today's creatures (your Troys, your Monroes) crones by comparison. She was inevitable, tight as a Conrad novel, from the fortune of rippling hair to the calyx and corolla of the alert and sulky cunt, from the delta of the midriff to the sacrum's golden slopes . . . I get carried away. The important thing about her wasn't her body, it was her *awakeness*. (I'm sure when I started this passage I had some notion of the flesh functioning as metaphor for the soul's irresistibility. *Bit* of a stretch. My apologies. Gunn's penchant for oily lechery and oilier lyricism infecting me in equal measures. That *fraud*. How did women *stand* him?)

It wasn't love at first sight. They ran into each other one morning in a sunny clearing in the forest. A few moments of stunned silence. 'Glockenspiel,' Adam pronounced, thinking (but with terrible doubt) he'd found another animal in search of a name. When Eve approached him, proffering a handful of elderberries, he threw a stick at her and ran away.

They didn't see each other again for quite some time. It was no skin off Eve's nose – but Adam couldn't get her out of his head. It wasn't desire (micturition aside, the Edenic johnson was as useful as a burst balloon); it was anxiety. No other animal had ever (a) offered him elderberries (or anything else), or (b) looked so . . . so *related* to him. Not even the orangs, of whom he was especially fond. The memory of her tormented him in the weeks and months that followed – the dark eyes and long eyelashes, the swollen, berry-stained mouth, the *incomprehensible* arrangement between her legs; most of all the shocking fearlessness, the composure of the fruit-offering, as if he – he, Adam – was a beast to be propitiated or gulled. (Yes, girls, I know: *good definition of a man*.) He walked in the garden and called on God for reassurance, but God chose inscrutability. (He did that, from time to time, Adam had noticed. Until now he hadn't questioned it.) His unease grew. He became obsessed with the idea that she'd already named the animals and that his own hard-thought-out monikers were redundant. Obsessed, too, with the notion that all those times God had withdrawn into silence He had in fact been with . . . with her, and this whole concept of his, Adam's sovereignty was nothing but a . . . but surely that wasn't possible? Surely he, Adam, was God's first . . .

He saw her twice more. Once from a distance – he stood at the top of a valley looking down to the river hundreds of feet below, where, having discovered that wood floated, Eve sat straight-backed astride three or four vined-together saplings she'd uprooted, drifting gently on the current – and once at unsettling proximity, when, having slept late before emerging from a cataract-curtained cave he saw her fresh from a dip, supine on a large flat stone, eyes closed, sunlight resting on pubes and eyelashes like tiny spirits. He considered throwing a rock at her, but bottled out and slunk away.

The anxiety – *who the fuck?* – worsened. He went off his

food (she'd spoiled elderberries for him for good) and developed a rash on his ankle. It was a frustrating time for me. I couldn't *believe* he couldn't hear my suggestion that he sneak up on her while she was asleep and bash her head in. I still think what a coup that would have been: Murder in Eden – but it was no good. An appalling waste of paranoia, that period of Adam's angst. I've got subsequent genocide started with less. I tried Eve, too, needless to say. Same deal. Adam lost weight and invented nailbiting. Finally, God took a hand. (Why 'finally'? What had He been waiting for?) One night He caused Adam to fall into a deep sleep. During this sleep He did three things. First, He brought Eve in a trance to where Adam lay and caused *her* to fall into a deep sleep by the man's side. Second, He erased from both their minds all memory of each other. Third, He gave Adam a dream (the first dream, ever, and one which Adam would later remember as a real event) in which he asked God for an help meet and in which God delivered by forming Eve out of Adam's rib.

You know what I did? I spent the entire night hovering over Eve whispering: 'Rubbish. Don't believe it. It's a *story*. You're being *brainwashed*. It's lies, lies, lies.' I concentrated all my energy, every ounce of angelic clout, on that fine filament of her, that faint strand I'd sensed before; I addressed myself only to that.

In the morning – the world's first conjugal lie-in – it seemed I might as well have addressed myself to the fish in the lake. She woke with her head on his chest and his arms wrapped around her. They looked into each other's eyes and smiled. 'Man,' she said to him. 'Woman,' he said to her. 'My children,' God said to them both. 'Oh, *please*,' I said (well, hissed, actually, having opted that morning for the body of a python) before slithering away in search of somewhere private where I could hurl my ophidian guts.

It seemed, I said.

Language duly arrived. Proper language, not Adam's moo-cow and bow-wow rubbish. Verbs, prepositions, adjectives. Grammar. Abstraction. God dropped in on them from time to time, usually with some critter Adam had missed. Tiny, fluttering, multicoloured thing. 'Butterfly,' Eve said, while Adam stood pleasantly stumped.

'Yes,' Adam said. 'Butterfly. That's what I was going to say.'

But Eve's unease lingered. The post-brainwashing residue of self-sufficiency from the days before Adam's dream. If me and humankind had a future together I knew it lay in these vestiges of Eve's independence. Literalist yes-man Adam fed the parrots and sang songs with nerve-jangling tunelessness to God. If *Fall II: The Next Generation* was ever going to make it out of development and into production, if humans were ever going to be anything more than monkeys on the Divine Grinder's organ (excuse me again) then it was going to be down to the lady and the tramp.

And therein, my dears, lies the answer to that nagging question: What was I doing in Eden in the first place? God's got the big martyr death scene written in for Jimmeny. The infinitely self-sacrificing part of His nature demands it, just as the infinitely generative part of His nature demanded the creation of Everything out of Nothing, and just as the infinitely unjust part of His nature demanded the creation of an infinite Hell for finite transgressions. The boy's motivation for self-sacrifice is the redemption of His Father's world. The infinitely filial part of His nature demands it. But for redemption there must be freely chosen transgression. Therefore – *ta-da!* – transgression must feel, at least temporarily, good.

Now ask yourself: Was there anyone better qualified for the job?

He was kidding Himself with Adam and He knew it. Certainly He'd created him free – but in the letter of the law, not its spirit. The infinitely insecure part of His nature had baulked at it, when it came down to it. The infinitely deluded part of His nature had allowed the creation of a role the designated actor would never have the spine to play. The infinitely paradoxical part of His nature had demanded Man's free choice of sin over obedience whilst creating a man who'd never be man enough to sin. Enter Eve.

And boy did I.

◆

Violet, Gunn's Penelope-replacement, lives in a studio flat in West Hampstead.

'You do, actually, expect me not to be annoyed, do you?' she said, having let me in, turned, and stormed up the stairs to her living room. Neglectful of me, I know, not to have offered an explanation for my tardiness, but I was still in a state from the garden.

'I don't imagine you stayed in waiting for me,' I said, following.

'No I bloody did not. No, Declan, I bloody, thank God, did *not*.'

'Well then,' I said. 'No harm done, eh?'

She stood with her arms folded and her weight on one sharp leg, lips parted, eyebrows raised. 'Oh, I see,' she said. 'You've *completely* lost your mind. Right. I thought it was just *partial*. I mean – are you . . .? I mean what *are* you?'

Violet thinks of herself as an actress and is almost wholly unacquainted with talent and has a great froth of dark red hair she pretends to be perpetually irritated by and at war with (the legion clips and scrunchies, the barrettes, the ties, the pins, the sticks, the bands) but which she secretly thinks of as her pre-Raphaelite crowning glory and under the glow of which she poses, endlessly, in front of the full-length mirror on the back of the bathroom door after narcissistic, unguent-heavy baths on her many unemployed afternoons. She can't make her mind up whether she's at her sexiest as chin-upholding Boadicea or dimpled and cleavaged Nell Gwyn – but either way she's baffled and chagrined that not *one* BBC period drama casting director has so far had the good sense to be instantly at the mercy of her hair's splendour.

She waited, still with her weight on one leg.

'I thought perhaps Italian,' I said, after a sudden twinge in my salivary glands. (Me the bemused amnesiac, Gunn's preferences my forgotten family and friends, introducing themselves, willy-nilly.) 'What do you think?'

She did something with her face then, a simultaneous smile-snort that lasted a third of a second. Then she put her head on one side like a perplexed kitten. 'Let me just check something with you,' she said. 'Are you actually aware that you're six hours late?'

'Yes,' I said. 'I'm dreadfully sorry.

'Well perhaps, since you're six hours late, and are dreadfully sorry, you wouldn't mind fucking off?' she said.

For a moment I held my tongue – which was difficult, given that I'd only seconds ago discovered the fascinating imprecisions entailed in letting it loose. (So quaint, too, that humble servitude paid by the organs of speech to the organ of cognition, all those cerebral constrictions eased by labials and glides, palatals and stops, the concerted efforts of wet little bits and pieces.) Then I very slowly and with excessive expansiveness installed myself in her one battered red leather armchair. 'Chimera Films have commissioned me to adapt my novel, *Bodies in Motion, Bodies at Rest*, for the screen,' I said, quietly. (To be fair to Gunn, he's thought of this himself, some bogus incentive to keep her boudoir friendly. What he's never come up with, what's stopped him going through with the yarn, is the explanation necessary for the day of reckoning when Violet – money-shot, fisted, ass-banged, lezzed-up, whatever carnal prices he would have tagged on to the starring role – discovered that there *was* no starring role, no supporting role, no bit part, no walk-on, no fucking *movie*.)

Violet stared. Then switched her weight from her left leg to her right. Then said, 'What?'

'Martin Mailer at Chimera Films has optioned *Bodies* for the screen and has asked me to write the screenplay.' I fished out a Silk Cut and ignited it with a languidly struck Swan Vesta. The scent of sulphur reminded me of . . . *ahhh*.

'You're . . . Declan you're having me on. Tell me you're having me on.'

'Chimera Films is a UK unit owned by Nexus,' I said. 'They trawl novels here looking for stuff. You know, seventy per cent of all films made are adapted from novels or short stories. Nexus, as you know, *isn't* a UK unit.'

'Nexus as in . . . Nexus?' Violet asked.

'As in Hollywood Nexus,' I said.

'Oh my God, Declan. Oh my fucking God.'

I didn't bother trying to conceal my grin. Violet thought I was grinning with glee – and so I was – but only at my own chutzpah. At the last, the *very* last moment, I'd resisted christening my phantom optioner Julian Amis. 'Martin Mailer was the guy behind *Top Lolly, Bottom Dollar*.'

'Oh my fucking God,' Violet said.

'I'm having casting consultation written into the contract.'

'You are not.'

'I am.'

'You are *not*.'

'I am. Oh yes. I *am*.'

Violet thinks of herself as stunning. She is stunning, too, in her self-absorption verging on autism. She's got a *retroussé* nose and expressive eyes and breasts like fresh little apples. There are freckles she'd be better off without, an arse on the low side, reddish heels and elbows, but on the whole you'd definitely say she was attractive. Not that it doesn't come at a price. To say she's high-maintenance would be to murder her with understatement. She gets headaches, back aches, leg aches, eye aches, indigestion, colic, near-perpetual cystitis and PMT that doesn't hold with all that old-fashioned nonsense about only showing up just before menstruation. If you're her boyfriend, really quite a lot of things get on her nerves. Chiefly, it seems, if you're her boyfriend, *being with you* gets on her nerves. Being Violet's boyfriend means spending quite a lot of your time listening to Violet itemizing (while you rub her shoulders, massage her feet, run her a Radox bath or prepare her a hot water bottle) the many ways in which you get on her nerves.

Like all women who think they're actresses, Violet's ferociously untidy. The West Hampstead studio flat looks like the Nazgul have just thundered through it – an appearance I had considerable time to note, waiting firstly for Violet to finish her pre-coital bathroom routine, and secondly, fruitlessly (tossing and turning in the bed's swamp) for the arrival of an erection.

'Fucking hell,' Violet said, tactfully, backing away from me as if at the discovery of a noxious smell. 'What's wrong with it?'

Oh well go on, get your chuckles over with now if you must. Yes. *Hilarious*, isn't it. Let's all have a jolly good wheeze.

'Sometimes, Declan, honestly, I can't . . . I mean what *is* it?'

'Perhaps I don't fancy you any more,' I said in an undertone. Undertone or not, it summoned up a Vi-silence of formidable charge and mass. Then, with a compressed artfulness that, actually, made me proud, she drew the sheet slowly up over her breasts and turned away from me in a foetal curl.

'Oh come *here*,' I said, like a successfully soft-soaped uncle – and she did, too (rifling through her memory files, wishing she hadn't lied to Gunn about having read his novel, wishing she knew *immediately* which part was hers, hers, hers!) – but it was no good. It was no damned *good*, I tell you. Gunn's penis might as well have been a tomato sandwich for all the impact it was going to make. On the other hand, it did give Violet an opportunity for some of her best work to date.

'Never mind, honey,' she said, huskily. 'It's no big deal. It happens. You're probably just overtired. Did you drink a lot last night?'

I might have been mistaken, but I thought I detected a slight American accent.

◆

Violet, you know, is troubled by a Little Voice. (I worried that the transmogrification would fuck with my clairvoyance, but it hasn't substantially. I've noticed blips, the odd blind spot, but by and large I seem to have got away with it as carry-on.) Violet never listens to her Little Voice and she hears every word it says. Not that its range of words is wide. On the contrary. It repeats the same things, at irregular but increasingly frequent intervals. *You're not an actress. You don't have any talent. You've knobbled your own auditions because you know you're not up to it in the end. You're a vain and talentless fraud.*

It's not me. Not all Little Voices are me, you know. Even my own Little Voice – did I mention that? – even my own Little Voice comes from a place I'm not sure I own. *I have of late*, it generally begins . . . I don't quite ignore it.

Declan, of course, had a Little Voice of his own by the end, and should probably have gone to see someone. Hardly an astute diagnosis given the bath and razor blades, but one I can't resist making. The odour of that sadness lingers, you see, in the rucks and runnels of his mortal flesh. Stretch marks of the soul, so to speak. It bothers me. In the absence of my angelic pain I feel it like an intimate and diffuse toothache.

I don't much like the look of him, if you want the truth. If I *was* considering staying – staying for good, I mean – I'd be hitting a bank and forking out for state-of-the-art plastic surgery or a Californian bodyswap. *Est hoc corpus meum.* Maybe so, but it leaves a lot to be desired. When I confront the mirror I see a simian forehead, dolorous eyes and thinning eyebrows. His skin's beige, greasy and porous. The hairline's not exactly struggling to conceal its upcoming recession, and the pot belly (too much booze, too much fat, zero exercise – the corporeal side of the basic adult human story) doesn't help at all. The flesh on the nose is thickening and the slightest dropping of the head reveals a putative double chin. He looks, all in all, like an under-the-weather chimp. I doubt very much he's washed his ears since child-hood. At seventeen, eighteen, he might have taken you in with his Navajo granddad story (supported by the usual non-sense: long hair, silver and turquoise jewellery, *beads*); you see him at thirty-five and look for a much less glamorous expla-nation: spic-mix, wog-cocktail, decaf wop. Truth is: Irish Roman Catholic mum boozily knocked up in a moment of weakness (I thank you) by a saucy Sikh from Sacramento at a friend's birthday party in Manchester. Ships in the night, bun in the oven, he's gone, she's Catholic: enter beige Gunn, fatherless and feeble at five pounds, six ounces. She brings him up on her own. He loves her and hates himself for blighting her young life. Grows up with bog-standard Virgin-Whore dichotomy as far as women go (with which I'm now lumbered, thank you very much); rabid Oedipus complex replaced during teen years by terrifying phase of homoerotic fantasies (I'll find a use for them before I'm done, you watch), before sexual imagination stabilizes around mild heterosexual sado-masochism in early twenties, concomitant with discovery of some effeminacy of body, a loathing for manual labour, a penchant for the arts and a much mauled but still virulent belief in the Old Fellah and yours truly.

I'm not wild about his wardrobe, either. I wish there was a more exciting way of telling you it's dull, but there isn't: Declan Gunn's wardrobe is dull. Two pairs of jeans, one black, one blue. The baggy charity shop strides to which I had recourse after my debut wankathon. Half a dozen t-shirts, a couple of woolly jumpers, a beige (!?) fleece, a greatcoat, a pair of brandless trainers and a pair of DM shoes. I look like a *tramp*. Doesn't even own a suit. They've done this deliberately, to assault my dignity, to wound my much-talked-about pride. Gunn, needless to say after the extravagance of his unsellable and suicide-inspiring opus, *A Grace of Storms*, can't afford new clothes, what with the first two books now out of print and his agent, Betsy Galvez, only ever seeing his name because he's immediately after Guiseppe's Pizzeria in her Rolodex. He should have stolen some money. Should've mugged a pensioner. Pensioners are loaded. Tartan shopping trolleys? Full of gold ingots. Why do you think they move so slowly? They die of hypothermia and no one mentions all the loot they've saved by never eating or turning the heating on. I love old people. Seven or eight decades of me whispering to them about all the faggots and coons (it turns out they fought for!) and by the time death comes calling they're oozing malice and hawking-up spleen. The souls of old people are ten a penny in Hell. Honestly. We've got a slush-pile.

Gunn lives alone in a second-floor one-bedroom ex-council flat in Clerkenwell. One small bedroom, one small living room, a small kitchen and a small bathroom. (I *looked* for other adjectives.) Outside, a courtyard. The surrounding buildings go up six floors so Gunn's place is starved of light. He had dreams of moving in with Violet. Violet didn't. Violet had dreams of Gunn using the money from the sale of his then-in-progress masterpiece to tart the Clerkenwell place up and sell it so that they could move to Notting Hill. From the sale of his . . . Yes. There's the rub. All things considered, I can't honestly say I'm surprised our boy had settled on suicide. Some humans survive concentration camps, others are driven over the edge by a broken fingernail, a forgotten birthday, an unpayable phone bill. Gunn's somewhere in-between. Somewhere in-between's where I do much of my finest work.

His mother died of drink two years ago and left him the flat. Me, drink and loneliness, we finished Gunn's mother off. Drink wolfed down her liver, me and loneliness gobbled up her heart. Liver and heart, my vital organs of choice.

She didn't come down, mind you. Must be cooling her heels in Purgatory. Last Rites. Gunn called in crapulous Father Mulvaney (sherry-breath, brogue blarney, red knuckles he couldn't leave off cracking, and eczema; I'll have his liver too, the old hypocrite) and that was me robbed of another tenant. There's no justice, you know. Angela Gunn. I *wanted* her. Some souls – you can't explain it – they've got *quality* written all over them. She had guilt over Gunn, having brought him dadless into the world (thought the fact that he nearly throttled himself with his own umbilical an indictment of her motherhood); but it wasn't the guilt that did for her, it was the loneliness. A tawdry smattering of affairs with men vastly her inferior. Her disgust because she couldn't leave the idea of a grand passion alone. In the small hours she'd observe them (after the grumpy wrestling, the loveless gymnastics) naked and sprawled as if taken down mid-crucifixion. Grimly, she'd force herself to absorb the unpleasant details: fatty shoulders; dirty nails; brittle hair; faded tattoos; pimples; stupidity; greed; hatred of women; pretentiousness; arrogance. In the small hours she'd sit bitter with tears and humming with drink and look down at his body, whoever he was, some Tony or Mike or Trevor or Doug, forcing her mouth into a rictus as the sordid replays ran in her head. The absurdity of it, she thought, this quest for the love of a man who was her equal. She loathed herself for it. She thought of her life (and herself) as a missed opportunity. Somewhere, back there, she had missed something. What was it? When was it? The worse horror beneath: that she hadn't missed anything, that her life was merely the sum of her choices and that her choices had led her to this: another truncated encounter; the carcinogenic belief in the idea of a Great Love; clammy sex; loneliness in the small hours.

She had loved Gunn, but his education distanced them. She craved his visits then couldn't bear that he was embarrassed by her malapropisms and too-young skirts. She was intelligent but inarticulate. Words betrayed her: beautiful butterflies in her mind; dead moths when she opened her mouth for their release into the world. Gunn knew all this. Went every time armed with the noblest filial intentions, then felt them evaporate when she talked of 'broadening her horoscopes'. Her drinking was a spectral third with them, Gunn not quite taking it in. Knowing and hoping. (Jesus, you humans and your knowing; you humans and your *hoping*.) Her belief in his writing. Gunn suspected she prayed for it. She did. She prayed to God He'd find a publisher for her son's book. Idiot ex-altar boy Gunn worried, then, that it wouldn't feel like a clean achievement. Soiled by the Hand of God, so to speak.

But then liver failure, hospital, his avalanche of guilt and shame. Her only fifty-five, looking seventy. Mulvaney of the red raw scalp hadn't seen her for three years, but they cut to the chase when he arrived, smelling of wet London and Cockburn's Port. Gunn shuffled, miserable, by the bed. Holding her hand (for the first time in a long time) he discovered with a shock its onion skin and Saturnalian revel of veins. Horror because he remembered it soft and firm and smelling of Nivea. These were the memories that jumped him over the months after she died, heartless muggers bent on the redistribution of the mind's buried wealth –

Bugger. You see what happens? I only mentioned the woman because I meant to tell you that's how Gunn got the flat. Now my screen's ambushed by maudlin guff.

Salutary should other demonic presences pass this way: manifestly you can't squat in someone's body without some of their life filtering through to yours. It's been the toughest part of the whole trip, so far, accommodating Gunn's left-overs; approximate omniscience notwithstanding, I never quite know which unfortunate tic or nasty habit of his I'm going to run into next. Couldn't they have picked someone else? Some rock star with an entourage of sycophants? Some sheikh with a hooker habit? Some coke-fiend with a yacht? *Anyone* would've been better than this noncer with his objective correlatives and his Earl Grey and his sorry-ass bank balance.

On the subject of Gunn's bank balance – two words: Oh dear.

Mrs Karp is Declan Gunn's Account Supervisor at the NatWest. The day our boy bought the razor blades a letter arrived from Mrs Karp. Its tone was stern but regretful (the next was just stern) and it requested the return of Gunn's cheque book and cheque card, cut in half, immediately. It pointed out, regretfully, that Gunn was upwards of £3,500 overdrawn (£2,500 over his limit) and that despite repeated efforts on her part to get him to come in and discuss the situation he had been unwilling to do anything but continue spending money he didn't have. Which left her no alternative, etc.

Which left me no alternative to a bit of hands-on, you'll be delighted to hear: get out of Gunn's body for an hour or so, nip round to Mrs Karp's semi in Chiswick, scare the living rectum out of her and get her to do something creative with Gunn's balance. But if there's a flaw in a simple plan it's usually fundamental, and the flaw in this simple plan was no exception: it hurt so bad the minute I exited Gunn's flesh that I shot straight back in without even leaving the flat.

You can see Someone's thinking behind this, can't you? I get so used to the absence of angelic pain that even living out my days in Gunn's flatulent *corpus* is preferable to the flames and nukes of disembodiment. God's coup: Lucifer's voluntary demotion to the life of a penniless pen-pusher in Clerkenwell; maybe the Old Fruit's developing a sense of irony after all. One of the things I never tire of (it's a problem, for eternal superbeings, *tiring* of things) is my own astonishment at how stupid He must think I am. Is He arrogant enough to think that a brief sojourn in the dank and clunking rucksack of Gunn's body . . .?

Relax, fans. Come August I'll slip into that pain like Biggles into his flying jacket. Meantime, I'll find ways around things.

'My Lord, I didn't recognize you.'

Nelchael. There aren't many you can trust. Nelchael's one of them. My numbers man. Most of the world's numbers are bound by God to make sense. Occasionally there are glitches. It's Nelchael's job – when it suits us – to exploit them.

'Account number 44500217336. See what you can do. Doesn't have to be millions. Fifty grand should do it. Got that?'

'My Lord Lucifer, I –'

'You remember, Nelchael, what I told you before I left?' Not easy to maintain dictatorial dignity when you're sitting on a moth-eaten couch smoking a Silk Cut and biting your nails, looking for all the world like that sallow chimpanzee, Declan Gunn.

'That this mission was top secret, my Lord.'

'Top *fucking* secret, Nelks,' I said. 'And that's the way it's going to stay. Do I make myself clear?'

'Yes, my Lord.'

'Apart from you, no one else knows of my business here on earth. If I returned to Hell to find that word had spread –'

'My Lord, I assure you –'

'To find that idle tongues were wagging, then my reasoning, Nelchael, would lead me to conclude that you had betrayed my trust, would it not?'

'My Lord I exist to do your bidding.'

'Yes, that's right. Keep in mind Gabreel.'

Gabreel disobeyed my ruling placing a moratorium on incubism back in Ancient Egypt. Disobeyed it royally, you might say. He fucked Cleopatra. (Gabreel was an inveterate letch, of course, and Cleo couldn't keep her femurs crossed for five minutes at a time – it was inevitable.) I had to make an example of him. Ugly. I know gentle Nelchael has night-mares to this day. Gabreel himself got over it centuries ago. Besides, I made it up to him in the fifteenth: a long weekend with Lucrezia Borgia.

I should explain. It's been a problem, this business of angels having sex with mortal women. Not that all angels are straight: Usiel's queer as a cat-fart; so are Busasejal and Ezequeel, or Eezaqueen as we call him, to mention but three of thousands. Most of us, when it comes down to it, will enjoy carnal congress with the ladies *and* the gents. Same goes for you, really – boarding school, stir, Navy – just needs the right conditions to bring it out. Plus, queer consorting has one huge advantage over straight action: no *issue*.

> . . . the sons of God saw the daughters of men that
> they were fair; and they took them wives of all which
> they chose . . .

says Genesis 6:2. The 'sons of God' were angels. My lot (*His* lot acquired neither the taste nor the opportunity); the 'daughters of men' were, naturally, mortal women. What you're looking at here – though no one seems to notice – is crazy copulation between renegade angels and up-for-it earth girls. A *pack* of trouble. There are two ways of having it off with mortals. The first is incubism (a word you haven't invented yet but certainly should have, given the amount of humping we've done), the second possession. With incubism, the angel *stays* an angel; with possession, the angel slips into a human host to get the job done. Incubism's decaf, possession's full roast. You lot do it with each other and half the time barely feel a thing. When we get involved . . . *wah*. Gives me goosebumps just thinking about it. But as I've said, possession's no mean trick. Incubism, on the other hand, was something most of the fallen could turn their hands to, and was still popular despite its want of salt. The girls seemed to enjoy it, too, though they went through the whole business somnambulistically, waking flushed and guilty – 'you wouldn't *believe* the dream I had last night, Marj . . .' – not to mention the risk they ran of being burned at the stake if word got out.

But there were two *big* problems with inter-being high-jinx. The first was what became known as carnal dementia. An angel in this condition would become obsessed with his earthly squeeze, at best to the point of neglecting his proper functions and at worst to the point of leaving his post altogether to moon around the beloved, pining to become human himself. Unacceptable, obviously. It's one thing to dip your angelic wick, it's quite another to start dreaming of settling down in a two-bedroomed wattle and daub in Ur. That would have been grounds for a ban sooner or later, even without the second problem, the Nephilim. Genesis 6:4:

There were giants in the earth in those days; and also after that, when the Sons of God came in unto the daughters of men, and they bear children to them, the same became mighty men which were of old, men of renown . . .

Rubbish. There were no giants in the earth in those or any other days, and the idea that the Nephilim, the fruit of spirit-flesh coupling, became 'mighty men' is one of the most preposterous distortions in the Old Testament. Through some occult law governing congress between the Seen and the Unseen realms, the Nephilim were dreary, whinging, neurotic, useless, ugly little cretins. It's one of the few remaining mysteries for me, why those kids turned out so utterly without merit and aesthetic appeal. If they'd been morally good, I'd have allowed them to survive in the hope of corrupting them. If they'd been morally bad, I'd have allowed them to live on the basis of their contribution to fucking up the world. But they were so utterly, solipsistically *miserable* and *boring* that they were, frankly, an embarrassment. It's amazing, isn't it: you think you're beyond embarrassment, what with being Purely Evil and all that. Then these *fark*ing whining, self-obsessed freaks turn up as the issue of your lust and it just makes you . . . *ugh*. Never mind. Point is I wiped them out. One Mr Sheen-style sweep across the surface of the earth, and the excrescent offences were gone . . .

Or so I thought. I've no conclusive proof, but I've long suspected that some of my brethren – no more than a hand-ful – somehow managed to snaffle their wretched offspring away, concealed in some cranny from the scythe of my wrath. Every now and then I'll spot someone (a Fleetwod Mac documentary, an Elton John special – the music indus-try does seem suspiciously fertile in this respect) and wonder whether Nephilim blood doesn't still course through human veins. I keep thinking I should do something about it, but, you know, I'm so *busy* all the time . . .

'Now, Nelchael. What of your other charge?'

'Charge, my Lord?'

I rolled Gunn's eyes. (I'm getting the hang of these gestures. That Gallic shrug-with-downturned mouth's one of my favourites just now. That and the tut-with-eye-roll I'd just delivered to my servant.) 'Give me strength,' I said, under my breath. 'Your other *task*, idiot. Your other *errand*.'

'Of course, my Lord. Forgive me. I see, I see what you –'

'Have you found it yet?'

'Alas, my Lord, Limbo is deceptively large. The . . . the unbaptised infants alone number –'

'Yes yes, I know all that. Time, Nelkers, is most definitely not on our side. Keep looking. And bring me word immediately you find it. Understood?'

'Understood, Sire.'

'One more thing.'

'My Lord?'

'Keep an eye on Astaroth. I want names and rank of all those closest to him. Now go.'

I checked the balance the following morning. £79,666.00. Nice touch, that. Made me smile. I celebrated with a fry-up at a Leather Lane greasy before hitting Oxford Street for a sartorial shopping spree and a bit of how's your father.

◆

Now this might come as a shock, so pour yourself a double and drop your buttocks into a beanbag.

Ready?

Okay. Sexual intercourse was not Original Sin.

Truth is Adam and Eve had had sex a few times (how else were they supposed to multiply, my dear Butthead?); it just hadn't been much fun. It hadn't been un*pleasant*, but it hadn't been sex as you know it. It had been the expression of a design feature, that's all, like folding one's arms or hiccupping. Adam's tool worked – that is, achieved tumescence now and again – but of its own accord. He had no feelings about it one way or the other. Eve, for her part, felt much the same. She didn't mind. It was just another thing they did because that was the way they were made. Edenic sex didn't feel good and didn't feel bad. How times have changed, *n'est-ce pas*? Now it feels so *gerd*. Now it feels so *bayered*. Yes? No, really, you're too kind.

'You know you want it you dirty little bitch.'

What astonished both of us was that it came out not as a sequence of hisses (snakeskin looked good on me, I'd decided; slithering was my corporeal *métier*) but as a perfectly intelligible articulation. For several moments we remained in surprised silence, Eve lying on the grass looking up at the glowing fruit, me corkscrewed around the upper trunk with my neck and head resting close to one of the golden globes.

'A bitch is a female dog,' Eve said, quite sensibly. 'And dirty is before bathing in the river.'

Appalled that I'd wasted the chance for a subtle opening gambit (don't try that one in the health club bar), I said: 'Do you remember the time before Adam?'

Eve wasn't one of those people who say 'What?' when they've heard you perfectly clearly. She lay blotched with leaf-shadows, blinking slowly and thinking about it. One hand ran its fingers through the grass, the other idled on her midriff.

'Sometimes I think I remember,' she said, not *quite* looking at me. 'But then it evaporates.'

I can't take any credit for foresight or planning, but I can and will for consummate opportunism. (Did I say I was omniscient? Not strictly true – but I am a *hell* of an opportunist.) I didn't know what *precisely* she'd be getting from that first wet bite and swallow, but I knew *generally*. Generally she'd be getting a milder version of the thermonuclear toot I got when I first recognized myself as free to stand apart from God. Generally she'd be getting proof that she was her own woman. Generally she'd be introduced – not before time I might add – to *the superlatively delicious pleasure of disobedience*.

It was a long, eloquent seduction. I outdid myself. She couldn't get over my being able to speak. That, really, was the thing. The intelligent voice, *soliciting her opinion*. Neither God nor Adam had ever bothered. She'd been trying for some time to get her head – and thereby her tongue – around the . . . the . . . I helped her: *the inherent appeal of an arbitrarily proscribed activity*? Yes, she agreed, with charmingly widened eyes and the relief of one Mervyn Peake fan chancing upon another in an otherwise friendless place. *Yes that's it exactly* . . . Words opened like flowers between us, each one releasing the scent of her doubt. Adam's plodding, unreflexive nature, God's latent disapproval of her body – oh yes, she'd seen Him curling His lip – her longing for someone to *talk* to, and not just any old talk, but talk informed with imagination and . . . she struggled again – *a sense of ambiguity, a sense of humour*, talk that reached out beyond the names of things and praise of God, talk which let you grow as you talked it, that uncovered, that . . . *explored* what was unknown . . . 'All the words seem to belong only to God,' she said, dreamily twirling a sprig of blossom under her chin. 'But perhaps, they belong to me, too?'

(Tell me I wasn't born for this. It bothered me, peripherally, back then, as it's bothered me since: *Was* I born for it? Was that all it was? Was rebellion just part of the . . . just . . . oh never mind.)

She hung on to that 'perhaps' for quite some time. I remember there was a point (I'd placed the fruit in her palm) at which both of us knew she was going to capitulate, but also that she wanted to spin out the posture of resistance a while longer. Between us we invented foreplay and playing hard-to-get. 'Now the serpent was more subtil than any beast of the field', says the King James version. You bet your granny's Horlicks he was, with me inside him. I used everything I had. Temptation's less about wearing someone down with repetition than it is about finding the right phrase and dropping it in at the right time.

'You're awfully . . .'

'Articulate?'

'Articulate. You're awfully *articulate*, serpent.'

'You're so kind, my Lady. But if the fruit of that tree has given subtlety to the tongue of the serpent, a mere *reptile*, just think what wisdom *your* exquisite lips will find within their grasp.' (That was ghastly, I know, that lips and grasp thing, but she really did have the most engaging ones – lips I mean, mouth *and* mons.)

'That is fl . . . fl . . .'

'Flattery? Not at all, Queen of Eden. Simply the truth. Does it surprise you that He forbids you that which would make you His equal, if not His superior?'

An idiom, I knew, within which we could both enjoy the self-consciousness of my flattery (she was a quick learner, Eve, there's no denying it) – and though she laughed there was no concealing the blush of satisfaction that spread across her throat and breasts. It was, I must confess, so pleasurable to me to sit and play this game with her (I was the spoil-yourself-you-deserve-it barkeep, she the office slave letting the margaritas one by one rub out the boundary of her lunch hour until – oh dear – there was the whole working day sipped and swallowed away) I almost forgot where I was going with it.

And when, finally, with scarlet cheeks and fiery eyes she sank those pretty teeth in and the juice cartoonishly spurted out, I, in an intuitive leap I'm not sure I've ever since surpassed, delivered the *coup de grâce* – and slid my . . . What I mean to say is there was a certain spatial compatibility between my . . . It turned out that her . . . Oh *listen* to me going all shy, will you? But anyway: *there*. You know what I mean, don't you? One should make an effort to avoid unnecessary vulgarity, I believe. Pure evil needn't entail having a mouth like an open drain. I am, after all, a man of wealth and taste. And I do know that there's an understanding growing between us. I . . . *think* we can fill in each other's blanks?

It was my good fortune or honed instinct that one of the first things (one of many) the fruit delivered was – you know it – sensuality. Foremost was the pleasure in having knowingly disobeyed. I saw that the headiness of this rocked her, eyes half-closed, jugular risen, the colour of smoke; I saw the first taste of selfhood and that it almost destroyed her, as might an unschooled vampire's first draught of blood. (But oh, should the vampire novice survive that first concussive ingestion, what then? Her thirst awakens and increases tenfold!) *Ever after,* I thought (having discovered inverted aversion therapy), *ever after will wrongdoing and sensual pleasure go hand in hand. Lucifer,* I said to myself, noting with satisfaction the co-operative hips, the flared nostrils, the raised eyebrows of carnal transport, *Lucifer my son you are an absolute bona fide genius.* Liberation, subversion, power, rebellion, bestiality, pride – you wouldn't think even God could cram that lot into a Golden Delicious. I could see her, suffused with all that new fruity knowledge (that she could speak for herself, that disobedience sensitized the flesh, that there would never be any going back now, that if the only thing available to the human being struggling to slip the yoke of service was wrongdoing then wrongdoing she would choose, that she was, against all former suspicions, free), considering through the bruise of concupiscence what she'd done. In their wake ecstasy and crime had left a faint frown of perplexity, the mark of her astonishment that she could feel such things, the face's opening posture for self-interrogation – how could I? – that would never go further, because she *knew* how she could. Oh yes, didn't she just. She *knew*.

You are grateful aren't you, that I shackled sex to knowledge and sensual pleasure? Or would you prefer coitus to have remained in the same physiological league as, say, noseblowing? And while we're at it, you might as well credit me for getting art off the ground. With our girl's first bold bite and precocious peristalsis the universe was transformed into a representable phenomenon, subject separate from object: represent all of it and there'd be nothing God knew and you didn't. Nothing *worth* knowing, anyway. Since that day in Eden sex and knowledge have formed the double helix of your souls' DNA.

'When you come, time stops,' Eve said. 'It's a tremendous relief, isn't it, serpent? Do you suppose that's what divinity feels like all the time?'

In the green grass she was rose-gold and glowing, fabulously drunk and stone cold sober. I saw her mentally pulling shame around herself like a sumptuous Russian mink. For a moment she held the fruit away from her lips and glared at it as if it had betrayed her of its own free will. But after a moment's hesitation she returned it to her mouth and sank her teeth into it again. The decision had been made the first time. Just in case there was any doubt, she made it again.

'This is just the beginning,' I said. 'Now if you'd consider turning your . . . What I mean is if you could just grab your – ah. You're ahead of me, my dear. How very charming.'

'I'll tell you something,' she said. 'I'm not sure I ever really liked him.'

'Adam?' I said. 'I don't blame you.'

'Not Adam,' she said, struggling to swallow a greedily chomped chunk. 'God.'

◆

And so to the present, gentle reader, and the preposterous sequence of events that brought me here in the first place. (The specific 'here' of Gunn's cramped crib and dusty PC on Day Seven, I mean.) It's been some first week, let me tell you. This not quite knowing what tomorrow will bring game's not for the fainthearted, is it? I'm half tempted to start seeing you monkeys in a new light.

Some chronology, Lucifer, for shame. You're tired, yes, but you'll feel better for having got it down while it's still fresh.

Well I wouldn't say 'fresh', what with me still stinking of quality quim and French fagsmoke – but I'm jumping the gun. Let's start, as the autobiographer's shadow or *doppelgänger* voice suggests (does this happen to all writers?), at the beginning.

The Violet debacle rocked me, I'll admit, and an evening of furious boozing followed. (I started smoking, too. I'm looking forward to stopping, obviously, since the real pleasure is starting again, but in the meantime I've found my rhythm at about fifty a day.) Not without the profit of insight. *Force*, I decided, was the missing aphrodisiac. *Against her will* the crucial ingredient. Made sense: the logical extension of Gunn's post-Penelope delight in having sex with women who don't really want to have sex with him. He'd be bug-eyed, no doubt, to see where such predilections point. But that's me, you see: no nonsense. Call 'em like you see 'em. Besides, what was the alternative? A month on earth – *impotent*? Do me a favour.

Therefore, having resolved on the kill-or-cure approach, yesterday's late afternoon found me strolling down High Holborn in the promising slipstream of one Tracy Smith, who though we had yet to be introduced, was destined to play a part in the urgent matter of my sexual rehabilitation.

A good working class Anglo-Saxon maid, our Tracy, with a middleweight backside and chicken skin calves, pudding-like breasts wonderbra'd up to the salivating world and ash-blonde hair scraped into a tortoiseshell barrette, revealing a nacreous neck and two fiercely pink little ears. One glimpse of that pork-coloured and Wrigley's-flavoured mouth and this bad boy was hooked. Tracy Smith. Head awash with telly and Radio One, the dim echo of school (make-up, gossip, lads), the Pitmans, the Pimms, the package hols brochure – what else would Tracy Smith be called? Actually, she's thinking of changing her name. Not the Tracy, the Smith. To Fox. Tracy Fox. Page Three Girl, children's television presenter, *Blankety Blank* guest. She's looked into it. It's not as difficult as she thought it would be. Only problem is, she knows her mum and dad will flip. And since it was their deposit anchored the flat (cabby dad, care assistant mum) she's got to keep them sweet.

So it's Tracy Smith, for now, for me, as she steps out of the Holborn building's main entrance into the gun-coloured evening light and the smoked door swings her handsome rear reflection into my view. Silver puffer jacket, navy pinstripe skirt, ivory tights and black, pinchy-looking high heels. That's my girl. A red double-decker roars past with Kate Moss on its flank – but you can keep the mannequins, the angle-poise anaemics and mantis-waifs; give me human Tracy Smith, Nescafé breath, pink M&S knickers, the lone skidmark like the scar of a struck match, celebrity dreams, crashing grammar and hunger, hunger, hunger for money. The bus passes with the sound of a dinosaur's yawn and I slide into my girl's wake, surrounded by scurrying Londoners whose faces float before me like waxy lanterns in the city's gloom.

I've always had a soft spot for London, the patched and tattered cloak of its history (some of my best work, obviously; I felt the same about old Byzantium), its dog-eared wisdom and inky humour. You know – you provincial British humans know – what it's like when you crack under the weight of lost love or ingested desire and Move to London: the city's ready for you. You take your precious miseries there and unpack them – only to find that the city's already assimilated them, centuries ago, along with grand Elizabethan passions and mortal Victorian sins. The assimilation's encoded now – in the chemistry lab colours of the Underground map, in Trafalgar's punk pigeons, in the thousands of ticking stilettos and caffeine yawns and downed pints and adulterous snogs. You turn up on a rainy Monday afternoon proud of all your woeful particulars – and London humbles you with its wealth of generals. You've seen your life. London, it turns out, has seen *Life*.

Paris is snooty, and owns its sins like a liberated mademoiselle owns her velvet diaphragm case and Jackhammer

Deluxe vibrator; but London, London noses its heaps of sin like a ropy mongrel among the bins, partly embarrassed, partly excited, partly disgusted, partly sad . . .

But this isn't to the point. (This is supererogatory, Gunn would say.) The point is I've chosen East End bawn an' bred Tracy Smith (the romantic in me prefers to think that she chose me) for the latest consummation of angelic desire on earth. Violet's signal failure to generate the requisite . . . Not that there isn't ample empirical evidence (ask Eve, Nefertiti, Helen, Herodias, Lucrezia, Marie-Antoinette, Debbie Harry . . .) of *my* knocker know-how and twat-talent; it's just that . . . taking a look in the mirror . . . I'm not sure what Gunn's mortal frame can support. When I've ravished before I've chosen my fleshly hosts carefully – everyone goes home satisfied – but I haven't been able to avoid noticing Gunn's deficiencies: not particularly well-endowed, or physically co-ordinated, or gifted with stamina. It came as a horrid shock to me – for the fiftieth time – when I stubbed my toe on the edge of the kitchen unit, for the fiftieth time. I've bitten the inside of my mouth so often there's now a swelling on one inner cheek the size of a Jaffa orange segment. So I think I can be forgiven a wee bit of, ah, performance anxiety, if you don't mind, as Tracy and I duck underground at Holborn for the Central Line to Mile End.

The London Underground depresses God. The Paris Metro's rescued by bubbles of romance and intellectual flim-flam (He can tune in for ten minutes and get *something*); the New York subway's a toilet, obviously, but it looks like the movies, you know, it looks hip, famous, cool; Rome's Metropolitana – well, Rome's got a special dispensation, not surprisingly – but London, Christmas Jimmeny the London Underground gets Him down. The Lloyd-Webber ads; the cadaverous drivers with their deep-sea eyeballs and miles of unfulfilled dreams; the Lloyd-Webber ads; the puking office juniors and passed-out temps; the death's-door beggars with their raw ankles and shat pants; the Lloyd-Webber ads; the buskers; the evening's fractured make-up and the morning's frowsty breath; all this and more – but chiefly the surrender to despair or vacancy the rattling tube demands, chiefly the tendency of London's human beings to collapse into a seat or hang from a rail in a state of bitter capitulation to the sadness and boredom and loneliness and excruciating glamourless-ness of their lives. The only thing He sees on the Underground that cheers Him up is blind people who have friendly relationships with their guide dogs. (There are a handful of blind people I've been working on in an attempt to radically alter the relationships they have with their dogs. So far, *nada*. Be nice if I could get one in before the end of time.)

Tracy plonks herself down and takes out her *Evening Standard* already opened at the telly pages. *No point in consulting those, Trace*, I think, as the train thunders into the first of many tunnels.

I know what you would have thought, you bored-with-the-world humans. You would have thought: Christ what a fucking uncomfortable evening. A pall of cloud, warm driz-zle, windblown litter, London's dull smell of exhaust and damp brick, the stupid, *stupid* heat.

Not me. I've got Gunn's five senses working overtime. Every car horn, hot-dog stand, burp, breeze, sunbeam and shitswipe – you get the picture. I'm in love, truly, madly, *deeply* in love with perception.

And, manifestly, digression.

Tracy's flat is in the basement of a four-storey Victorian terrace in Mile End. I've considered tackling my turtle dove as she pushes open the front door, at that quaint meridian where outside meets inside and the mat says *welcome*; but there's too much human traffic in the street and an overly enthusiastic porch light above the lintel. I'd be spotted for sure. So it's round the back and listen for the sound of the shower, diddle the window, hop over the sill into the kitchen, with just time for a scotch and a glance at the headlines before my girl emerges buffed and lotioned and it's time to get down to business.

There's no scotch so I settle for a gin and fizzless tonic. The flat's a dark living room, an untidy bedroom, a tiny blue-and-white kitchen, and the bathroom, behind the closed door of which Tracy's gasping and sighing under the jets as the water's heat by degrees soothes away the day's annoyances. I crack my knuckles and light a Silk Cut. Julia Sommerville's round-up of world events reassures me that the boys are hard at it in my absence, but reminds me, too (another flood in India, another earthquake in Japan, another egg-headed astronomer not quite categorically denying that the comet *is* on a collision course with earth) that time, New Time, I mean, *your* time, is running out. *You get one month to try it out. Your chance, Lucifer. Who Wants to Be a Millionaire?* As if. But I don't care for this kind of inner dialogue (increasingly frequent sensation that there are two of me in my own – I mean Gunn's – head, which I definitely don't like) and besides, the shower's hiss has ceased and I can hear Tracy – bent double, I conjecture, plump boobs bobbing as she dries between her rosy toes – singing surprisingly tuneful snatches of Britney's 'Hit Me Baby One More Time', which, in the way of inexplicable aphrodisiacs, has me up out of the couch with loins aflame, resolved in a twinkling on a full-frontal assault in the bathroom – up against the heated towel rail, perhaps (*tsssss* – ouch!) – for openers.

But some things never change.

As I cross the threshold of the kitchen the ether shudders and a trident of unbearable light strikes me full in the face. I collapse and cover my eyes.

'Too much,' Gabriel's voice says. 'Turn down.'

'No permanent damage. Come on, Luce, get up. Long time no see.'

Uriel.

'If you've damaged these eyeballs, you'll regret it.'

'Why doesn't he leave the body?'

Zaphiel. Three of the big boys. I'm thinking: Is Tracy dedicated to The Holy Virgin or what? But Zaphiel's right. Quaking on the lino like that – intolerable. Therefore leaving Gunn's miserable carcass positioned as if for prayer to Allah, and with a deep breath in preparation for the excruciating pain of disembodiment (*Jimmeny* that hurts) I return to the bodiless realm to confront my angelic brethren. I can't say it's all bad, either, to expand into my non-dimensional dimensions again, easing the joints of power, opening the pinions of pain. The rage takes all but Gabriel, who's tasted it recently, by surprise. Sissy Zaphiel backs-off. Uriel – I catch the look of admiring horror at what I've let myself become – turns his own dial up into the red, reflexively, and all four panes in Tracy's kitchen window explode.

'Easy there, boy, *easy*,' I say. 'You don't get out much, do you?' It's a minor but sweet satisfaction to me that Tracy, back in the stopped time of the material world, is indeed as I'd pictured her, bent drying her tootsies, bulbous breasts arrested mid-swing, haunches still pink from the water's heat. I've got a lousy feeling I'm never going to get any nearer to her than this.

'That's right,' Uriel says, turning down again. 'You're not.'

'There are rules,' Gabriel says.

I regard them, coldly, with a smile. The smell of Heaven is overpowering; it forces itself against me calling up something like nausea. 'It may have escaped your notice,' I say, 'but me and rules don't have what you'd call a happy history. Me and rules haven't been known for *wildly hitting it off*, if you see what I mean.'

'Should you elect to leave the host's body and not return,' Uriel says, 'then the consequences of your actions will be consequences to the body's original occupant.'

This has occurred to me. To be honest, the thought of slapping a rape and murder rap on Gunn just before checking-out rather appeals. 'If I leave his body and he returns,' I counter, 'consequences aren't going to get a look-in. In case you've forgotten – you *sillies* – Mr Gunn's first action on returning to the land of the living will be to exit it, by his own mortally sinning hand. Not much point in arresting the dear fellow if he's dead, is there?'

'It's not a foregone conclusion that he will take his own life,' Gabriel says.

'Well it was pretty foregone when the Old Man decided to pull the plug and pack the poor bastard off to Limbo,' I said.

'He moves in mysterious ways, Lucifer. You know this.' Uriel again. There's something about his inflection. That stint guarding Eden left him too much time for solitary thought.

'You're going to have to behave within parameters that will leave Gunn's liberty intact should his body be returned to him,' Gabriel says. 'If, after your trial period, you decide to stay, you may then behave entirely as you choose.'

'And suffer the mortal consequences,' Zaphiel adds, having recovered his composure.

Unfortunately for Tracy the handle of her frying pan has

melted and run down the front of her cooker. Four angelic presences is a bit of a strain for a material kitchen in Mile End.

'And suppose,' I say, 'without putting too fine a point on it, I tell you to kiss my mephitic ring-piece?'

Again there's the possibility of a smirk from Uriel, but wooden Gabriel sticks to the facts. 'You know, Lucifer, that in these matters there is no gainsaying His will.'

'Dearest Gabrielala – aren't you forgetting your *histoire*? I got where I am today by gainsaying His will. What's He going to do? Go to war again over an East End tart?'

'If need be. Do you think Michael sleeps, Lucifer? Or that Heaven's armour is gone to rust?'

'Old Thing I really must ask you: *Why are you talking like such a sanctimonious ponce?*'

'He cannot truly want to come home,' Zaphiel says. 'If he wanted to come home he wouldn't say these things.'

'"He" is here, if you don't mind. Of course I'm not coming home. Does any of you seriously think that this is anything more than a vacation for me? Do you know what hot buttered toast tastes like? Chocolate?'

'Methinks the lady doth protest too much,' Uriel says, and I nearly smack the cheeky rascal in the mouth. (If he and I hadn't . . . If we weren't . . . Well.) None the less it's clear they're ready to hang around indefinitely – poor Tracy still bent and half dry in the bathroom's stopped steam – and since I don't doubt they're prepared to make an *issue* out of it I slip into Gunn's Mecca-facing carcass (instant cessation of pain), give them the earthly finger and, as you say in Albion, fack orf aaad of it.

Now, Babs, any man will tell you: there's nothing quite as simultaneously dispiriting and infuriating as getting yourself all ready to rape and murder someone only to be turned away by an unforeseen intercession at the last minute. It's enough to make you want to rape and murder someone. (Bit rich, too, don't you think, that He never bothers interceding with *regular* rapists, this charming old God who only wants the best for you?) But sometimes it takes a setback to clear your vision.

It actually broke me up. I sat in the back of the cab and grabbed my knees and laughed my slow-on-the-uptake head damn near clean off. Eighty grand in the bank and I'm living in a City ex-council with no cable or power shower and a kitchen the size of a teabag. Oh I laughed, I did. So funny I could have gouged Gunn's eyeballs out and tossed them into the road.

Cabby didn't appreciate it, mind you. One too many rear-view checks till I took out a slender wad of fifties and waved them at him. He was . . . well, he was a London taxi driver: double-chinned with a dark grey comb-over, ear-fluff, jowls like past-it potatoes, Popeye forearms and a boil like a ruby on the back of his neck. Further down I knew there'd be the no-surrender gut, the fat bollock bulge, the waxy bum crack and haemorrhoidal punnet . . . but I preferred not to dwell on it. My threads had confused him (I've revolutionized Gunn's wardrobe: Armani black single-breasted pinstripe, white silk shirt, red paisley tie, Gucci Royalles and three-quarter black leather overcoat from Versace); it was hard for him to believe that you could be dressed like that and still be a giggling nutter – but the sterling calmed him. 'Fuck Clerkenwell,' I told him, sliding a crisp note through the vent. 'Take me to the Ritz.'

'You mine me arskin what you do for a livin', chief?' when we pulled up at the yellow-lit façade.

'I tempt people to do the wrong thing,' I said.

He seemed happy with this. Tight-lipped, he closed his eyes and nodded, vigorously, as if I'd confirmed his intuition (advertising, politics, the law). And well might he, since it was only by a miracle of self-control that I didn't add: *Your wife, Sheila, for example, who is at this very moment swallowing the hot and curdy jism of your brother Terry, with whom she's been enjoying gladiatorial carnal relations for the past eighteen months, my son.* Wasn't mercy (naturally) held me back. Just the vision of him following me into reception and making a scene.

No bags. They love that. Suggestion of whim, flight, drama or *verboten* coupling. (Which, illicit or otherwise, was still very much at the forefront of my mind, Julia Sommerville's plummy voice and Tracy's rendition of 'Hit Me Baby One More Time' having between them got my blood up awfully, at long last.)

At my suite's snooker table-sized mirror I stood and opened my arms with a smile, the Vegas crooner's gesture of wordless love in the face of his standing ovation. Spoiled it, somewhat, I admit, by saying aloud: 'Now this, my son, is a bit more fucking *like* it,' but I could hardly blame myself, overwhelmed, as I was, with a deep sense of homecoming.

I sent my threads down to housekeeping for a wash and brush up, then eased myself into an excessively foamed, oiled and salted bath, congratulating myself on having invented money in the first place. Wealth breeds boredom and boredom breeds vice; poverty breeds anger and anger breeds vice. More than enough of the angelic me endured to feel it in the hotel's costly air; more than enough of the corporeal me to sniff – in the way of charming perceptual correlates – its practitioners' scents of perfume and aftershave, breath and broken wind laced with the tang and spice of pricey ingestions. (Money calibrates society's scale of smells, and naturally the folks I'd glimpsed about the place were loaded. I haven't had to touch most of them (professionally) with a barge pole, since they've had money from birth. That's the beauty of money: the only graft I've got to put in is getting people to acquire it. Once they *have* acquired it, and the freedom it brings, most of them (and their beneficiaries) will go straight off the rails without so much as a bitten nail.) Money was my leap out of the Dark Ages.

> Humans and human needs lay hid in night.
> I said: 'Let money be!' and all was light.

The key to evil? Freedom. The key to freedom? Money. For you, my darlings, freedom to do what you like is the discovery of how unlikable what you like to do makes you. Not that that stops you doing what you like, since you like doing what you like more than you like liking what you do . . .

Not entirely inappropriate then that when, having decided on a tall Tom Collins in the bar (beverage to augment deliberation over how *many* escorts – okay, rape and murder were off but for Christ's sake I was damned if I wasn't going to put my lately acquired love-truncheon to *some* use), an exhausted posh female voice should say, from two stools away: 'You don't look like you do anything for a living.'

I turned. Recognized her straight away. Harriet Marsh. *Lady* Harriet Marsh, you'd think, what with the bevelled vowels and Susanna-York-on-smack looks. Sixty years old now (quite a while since I'd last seen her) with a freckled body of complicated wiriness under a black halter-neck cocktail dress. Magnificently bored green eyes. Hair dyed a colour between platinum and pale pink, pinned up, with wispy bits dangling. The odd liver spot. Brazenly crafted

Los Angeles teeth. Lady Harriet, you'd think – but you'd be wrong. It's not blood, it's money. Harriet plucked from a glittering clutch of possibles forty years ago, bedded and betrothed in that order to Texan Leonard 'Lube' Whallen (no blood, either, obviously, but a large family of hyperactive oil wells) who, thanks to some colourful experiences with an early years nanny from Dorset, had a crippling weakness for English gals who knew how to boss him about in the sack. *The thing to do*, I'd murmured to Harriet at the time, *is make him earn it*. I told *him* it would take him to the deepest knowledge of himself, to give himself over to her completely. He believed me, looking at his own porous and moustached face in the morning mirror, astonished and grimly delighted. One by one family members written out of the will. Harriet wasn't going back: the beery two-up-two-down in Hackney, the dodgy dad and threadbare mum, the wireless, the Woodbines . . . She'd been in for the long haul with Leonard, but he'd surprised her in 1972 by dying of a heart-attack (four Jack Daniels, devilled prawns, three injudicious Monte Christos and a dash across the baked apron to make the private jet's take-off slot), leaving her more or less sole inheritor. I let her go after that. She wouldn't need me. She worked well on her own. Now – oh, *honestly*, I'm gifted, I am – she owns thirty per cent of Nexus Films.

'You don't look like you do anything for a living.' Yes. The blunt gambit entitlement of the rich and the beautiful. Candour a match for my own.

'I do something for a living,' I said.

'Really? What?'

'I'm the Devil.'

'How nice for you.'

'Currently in possession of a mortal frame, as you see.'

'I do see.'

'And you're Harriet Marsh, widow of Leonard Whallen.'

'And you're not clairvoyant. My name generally precedes me.'

'But other information does not.'

'Such as?'

'Such as that you're currently wearing peach-coloured cami-knickers from Helene's in Paris. Such as that you were thinking several things a moment ago: that the English are in love with failure and loss; that there's no pleasure for you now like the pleasure of being driven through capital cities in the last hour before dawn; that my cock would be small and that it's been a long time since you've even known what you like; that there should be another dimension or place for the filthy rich when this world's fruits have been sucked dry; that there's nothing you'd like more than a long stay in a white-walled and chilly hospital where nothing was demanded of you; that you'd need to get drunk if you were going to fuck me.'

'My mistake,' she said, after a sip of her champagne. 'How charming.'

'Goes with the territory.'

Raised eyebrows. Tired, our Harriet, tired of life, tired of having done everything – but willing to be seduced by curiosity. 'Territory?'

'Being a fallen angel,' I said. 'Being *the* fallen angel.'

Another exhausted smile. Another sip. It wasn't much, this, but it was, at least, something.

'Tell me what I'm thinking now,' she said.

I gave her a devilishly nonchalant smile of my own. 'You're thinking about how little you get for six million in South Kensington, and that in any case you won't keep it for more than a year, since London houses are filled with sadness. You're wondering whether I'll fuck you because I've got a thing for older women, some dreary oedipal tumour, or because I'm the sort of young man who believes that self-degradation elevates him to some kind of divine knowledge.'

'You're really rather good at this, aren't you?'

'The best.'

'There must be a story to tell.' She sounded weary at the prospect.

'After.'

'After what?'

'You know what.'

Oh my angel, my bad angel – well that pressed a few buttons, obviously – *Oh my angel master, fuck me, fuck your little pig-bitch, mmnyesss, stick your filthy fucking cock up my filthy fucking arse, all the filthy fucking way, all the way, um-hmn? Nn-hmn. You know I'm your filthy little cocksucking whore, don't you? Fuck your little Virgin Mary whore –*

Lost my head a bit at that point, I'm afraid. Curiously though, this monologue (yours truly too busy with the miracle of his own restored and restive rod to bother responding) all delivered in a robotic monotone, like a somnambulist bishop reciting the Athanasian Creed. It's become one of Harriet's tools for submergence, has sex; it takes her to some depth of consciousness far from the surface of her life. The pornologue's mantric (as is the Athanasian Creed, for that matter) sucking her down to a level of herself where no questions are asked, where her history evaporates, where her self bleeds painlessly into the void.

And though I kept shtum myself, there was no denying the effect of such saucy language on Gunn's tackle. Even from Harriet's passionless lips they effected a startling transformation. (And ferried in the memory that Penelope couldn't, simply *could not* talk dirty without cracking-up; whereas Violet's dyspepsia lurks so close to the surface that in a few heady encounters it's come out in a mild dominatrix shtick that's had Gunn spunking like a hound-dog.) It's been that way for him ever since he learned to read. Indeed, his childhood proficiency as a reader was driven almost exclusively by desire for the sexual knowledge books contained. Even as an adult his balls tingle at *fuschia, fucivorous, cunning, cuneiform, cochlea* and *cockatoo* – for no better reason than that they're dictionary neighbours to *fuck, cunt* and *cock.* An absurd way for a grown man to behave, I'm sure you'll agree.

Harriet looked sad as hell when it was all over. Sad as hell *that* it was all over. Sad as hell that time had started again, with its all ticks and all its tocks, all its excruciating reminders of who she was, where she'd been, what she'd done, and where, in the end, she was *going.*

'You're worried about going to Hell,' I said to her, flexing Gunn's breasts (I almost typed 'pecs', but I don't want to insult you) in front of the mirror, whilst smoking a cigarette. 'Don't be. I've made some changes down there. All that fire and brimstone, all that agony? History. No point. Plus, my fuel bills . . . I'm kidding. But seriously, can you give me one good reason why I should waste my time making my guests suffer? This whole . . . this whole *line* about me making souls suffer – it's so *stupid.*'

'Please stop talking.'

'My feeling is, hey, *mi casa su casa.* As long as you're not with the Old Man upstairs, my job's done. There's no reason we shouldn't be civilized about it. No reason we shouldn't be comfortable.'

'It's a nice gimmick, darling, but one needs to know when to stop.'

82

'No one gets it. Which do you think would annoy Him more? Souls in Hell suffering and wishing they'd been Good? Or souls in Hell partying and thinking, 'Thank fuck I didn't bother with all that *morally sound behaviour* crap?' You see the logic, surely?'

'There's no comfort in logic,' Harriet said, picking up the phone and punching the stud for Room Service. 'Suite 419. Bollinger. Three. No. I don't give a fuck.'

Click. Wealth's economical idiom. Not needing to say please or thank you. If parents hadn't scolded their children for forgetting please and thank you, I'd never have got capitalism off the ground.

'Harriet,' I said. 'I feel like a million bucks. Why don't you let me pitch you a story?'

She rolled over onto her belly and let one arm hang over the edge of the bed. Her hair was a mad old lady catastrophe, now. Astounding: looking at the elderly elbow, the troubled capillaries of the wrist, I felt Gunn's bollock blood thickening again. Who'd a thunkit? All Vi's charms on offer and I can't raise an eyebrow. Then Harriet, who – ah, the penny drops – is the age his mother would've been if she hadn't croaked . . .

'There's no point,' Harriet said. 'I'll have heard it before. The world ran out of stories centuries ago.'

'I couldn't agree with you more, Harriet,' I said, lighting a fresh Silk Cut off the butt of the one I'd just smoked down to the cork. 'I couldn't agree with you more. And this story, let me tell you, this story's the oldest story of 'em all . . .'

◆

The story of my – *ahem* – downfall.

Hoooo . . . *mamma* what a downfall that was. I'd go so far as to say there's never been another like it. Semyaza,

Sammael, Azazel, Ariel, Ramiel . . . from Heaven's lip they pitched and flared in radiant rebellion. Mulciber, Thammuz, Appollonya, Carnivean, Turel . . . one by one a third of Paradise yanked into the void on the leash of my charisma. Somewhere on the way down I realised what I'd done. It . . . ah . . . *hit* me. You know what I thought? I thought: Oh. Fuck. Fucking . . . *hell*. Apposite, really, come to think of it. But I'm getting ahead of myself . . .

Central conflict, obviously, my tiff with Junior. God the Son, to give Him His full title. Jumping Jesus Arthur Christ. Jimmeny Christmas. Number One Son. *Sonny*.

Where do I begin? The regrettable goatee? The humourlessness? The Oedipal transference? The anorexia? He cast seven of my best friends out of Mary Magdalene and enjoyed every minute of it. Not that I blame Him. The Magdalene was a piece of ass even after her conversion; writhing around mid-exorcism like that she looked . . . Well. I've got it on DVD. We'll splice some footage into the film.

I'd long wondered about the Son. When GodVoid had created us to prise God from Void He had self-revealed a tripartite nature, a 3-for-1 deal that rocked the entire non-world of ontology. I'm not sure it didn't come as a *bit* of a shock even to Him, to discover not only that He was the Supreme Being, but that He'd had a kid and a ghostly PR officer all this non-time without even knowing it. He'd missed the best non-years, too, apparently – the milk-teeth, the evening bath, the bedtime story – since it was apparent that Junior was all grown-up already, poised eternally somewhere between the wanked-out end of adolescence and the onset of thirty-something melancholia.

The Son was the side of Himself He kept most oft' occluded, as if He suspected it might cause trouble among the rank and file, as if He knew (He *did* know) that freedom was also the freedom to want more of His love than you had, to want to be loved as much as Someone Else was loved, for example. We glimpsed young Arthur, from time to time, practising His twinkly look of dolorous compassion. It was embarrassing.

We suffered quiet intimations. The rumour of creation. A mode different from the one we knew, a form of being so fundamentally strange to our own that many of us buckled and all but broke trying to get our heads around it.

Raphael let the cat out of the bag. Some Seraphs had been allowed to cotton on quicker than others. Raphael – that *donkey* – Raphael's mind was an open book to me. 'Is this coming to pass?' I asked him.

'Yes.'

'What's my part?'

'Gabriel's part is –'

'What's my part?'

'Michael will be –'

'*What is my part*, Raphael?' Or words to that effect.

'We're to be messengers,' Uriel said.

'Messengers?'

'To the New Ones.'

'What New Ones?'

'The Secondborn. The Mortals.'

Matter. Matter, apparently, was the high concept. It dizzied us to think of it. We *couldn't* think of it. And what was all this gobbledygook about mortals?

Indulge my litotes: I didn't like it.

Meanwhile Junior gave me that *look* every time our eyes met. It wasn't the enmity that got to me. It was the condescension. A thousand times it was on the tip of my tongue (unforked in those days) to ask Him, *What the fuck*?

Something always stopped me. His applehood in the eye of the Father. And now that we're on the subject, let me settle this 'God's favourite' thing once and for all. It was never me. The truth is . . . ah, the truth . . . the truth is God never really . . . He never really *listened* to me. For years, for years almost immediately after my birth I tried to . . . to put something special into the *Gloria*, something unique, a communiqué from me to Him, a signal that I was . . . that I wanted to . . . that I understood the way He . . . That . . .

Anyway the point is, fucking *Michael* (do please pardon my French) was always His favourite. Michael.

Some presences have their own gravity, their own radiation. So it was with Creation. No hard evidence, but slowly, one by one, each of us came to understand that it was there, somewhere, elsewhere. Elsewhere! Our minds fairly boggled. Was it possible to conceive of an elsewhere in a nowhere? (A ticklish question. In the angelic realm there's no concept of place. It's meaningless, actually, to talk about the angelic 'realm' at all.) Therefore we weren't anywhere; we were nowhere. And yet, as Old Time passed . . .

'I think it's started,' I said to Azazel.

'What has?'

'Creation.'

'What's that?'

'It's different from this. It's to do with the Son. The Son and the Mortals.'

'What are these Mortals?'

'They're not like us.'

'Not like us?'

'No.'

Quite a while passed between us in silence. Then Azazel looked at me. 'That doesn't sound too good, does it?' he said.

'We're supposed to take His Will to them,' Uriel insisted.

'Why?'

'They're His children.'

'*We're* His children.'

'They're different. They've got something.'

'What?'

'Him inside them.'

'Rubbish.'

'It's true. They've got a bit of Him inside them.'

'So you're saying they're better than us?'

'I don't know.'

'Look – is it just me? Or does everyone else think this is a bit . . . *much*?'

It was a dismal time for us, that period when His Lordship turned away from us and absorbed Himself in making the Universe. The central heating went off. The stalwarts kept the *Gloria* going, but my heart (and I wasn't by any means alone) just wasn't in it. The Holy Spirit went among us checking morale, but a good third (the bad third) could barely summon a salute. Meanwhile Arthur was really beginning to get – as you so evocatively have it – on my tits. He developed a new gimmick. At first I found it merely bizarre. Then I found it strangely crude. Finally I found it downright insulting. (*Merde alors*, the *labour* of all this, this hunt for things you can work with. Keep in mind all of this pre-dates Matter or Form. Keep in mind all of this is being patched together out of *hopelessly inadequate metaphors*.) The new gimmick was this: He'd choose a moment when I was absorbed in reflection or deep in conversation. I couldn't ignore Him. (Prostration in His presence was customary. Never explicitly requested – that would be vulgar – but fail to comply and see the rashes and nosebleeds that followed. It had become a chore for me.) Like a girl using her own innocence as a tool of seduction He'd reach up and part His robes, revealing a terrible chest cavity around a pulpy and thorn-crowned heart. Blood-droplets jewelled this ghastly organ, complemented, I saw, by playing-card diamond wounds in the hands and feet, and a nasty-looking gash just above the kidneys. I had no idea why I was being called to this obscene spectacle, nor what was expected of me – although I must say I had a bad feeling about it. I had, even then, a woeful intimation that it *meant something* . . .

In a way, God brought it all on Himself. (Of *course* He brought it all on Himself Luce, you moron.) If he hadn't presented me with His actual absence things might have turned out differently; but there I was – there *we* were, the thinkers and speculators of the angelic host, managing quite well without Him. It felt . . . how can I put this? It felt like a holiday. Up until then I'd spent all that time (and this is still Old Time, remember), all *my* time, in fact, sailing around Heaven telling Him what a wonderful guy He was for allowing me the privilege of sailing around Heaven telling Him what a wonderful guy He was. I didn't know why, but it suddenly seemed . . . well . . . *pointless*.

When I had this thought (there were whole flocks of these bright birds, now, whole experiments in jazz) even the Holy Spirit left me alone, and I existed for the first time in a state of brilliant, adamantine singularity. It was queasy and arousing. It was rugged and naive. It was daring and giddy. It was glorious and – since I assumed it was the way He felt the whole time – profane. Truth is, it was a huge *rush*. The crystallization of selfhood, the moment of realising that I was, indubitably, myself, separate from anyone or anything, rich with time and potent with the desire to spend it away from home, to squander it, to lavish it on my own deeds and desires, to set myself aside from God (*aside* theologians please note, not *above*), to wake up in the morning and think: Holy shit, it's me! What shall I do today? A rush. *The* rush. Of all time. In my long, scabrous, violent and filthy history of moments I'd have to say that moment capped the lot. You can't imagine it. That's not a criticism. I just know you can't imagine it because I've made sure that separateness from God is something you take for granted.

My murmur went through the host like the clap. It wasn't until my spirit leaped onto its legs and went capering among them whispering of *all that time they'd wasted* that many of them realised themselves truly free.

You can't blame me. I mean that literally. You're incapable of blaming me. You're human. Being human is choosing freedom over imprisonment, autonomy over dependency, liberty over servitude. You can't blame me because you know (come on, man, you've *always* known) that the idea of spending eternity with nothing to do except praise God is utterly unappealing. You'd be catatonic after an hour. Heaven's a swiz because to get in you have to leave yourself outside. You can't blame me because – now do please be honest with yourself for once – you'd have left, too.

Not that I was prepared for His anger, when it came. In fact let me give you a tip: Don't ever, *ever* think you're prepared for God's anger. It happened so quickly. In Old Time we'd say it took no time at all. Really no time at all. Suddenly, He turned His presence upon us. Us. We hadn't even noticed up until that moment that we'd started hanging around in a group. I knew the game was up. He didn't say anything. He didn't have to. He sent Michael.

'It's too late to change my mind, I suppose,' I said.

'It's too late to change your mind,' Michael said. 'Your pride has set your course, Lucifer.' We could see them, then, the white-hot ranks massed behind him. Outnumbered us two to one. Easy two to one. I could feel the Old Man's barely contained rage like a swollen sky. Be strong, Luce, I told myself. Be strong, be strong, be strong. You know what it's like: a nauseous glory in your guts because now you know you've Done It, now you know you're going to Get It. The happy clarity of defiance. You're fey with it, addled, tumbleweed light, ridiculously devil-may-care. Terror and elation. We're doing it, I thought, we're *actually doing it!*

I turned and looked back from the threshold, chin up, the high-diver's moment of pure being before the backwards pitch and scribbled notation through space. Some moment, that, the ether's quiver and torque, the brilliant ranks, time holding its giant breath. I hadn't rehearsed anything, but I did think, you know, a few fitting words.

'Well,' I began.

Then all Heaven broke loose, and before we knew it we were fighting for our lives.

◆

Say what you like about me, but don't say I can't wing it, will you? I mean, would *you* have thought of that? *The Devil makes work for idle hands* – even if they're his own. I'm not overly ashamed to admit that until I met Harriet in the bar I had no higher agenda than the exhaustive expenditure of Gunn's mortal resources on excess: I've got a shocking weakness for scrambled egg with smoked salmon, fresh dill and coarse ground black pepper, it turns out; I'm up to eighty Silk Cut a day, but I'm pretty sure I've hit a plateau with smoking; the bar staff . . . *know* me, shall we say, and have even officially added the Lucifer Rising – vodka, tequila, orange juice, tomato juice, Tabasco, Tio Pepe, Grand

Marnier, cinnamon and a pepperoncino chilli – to the joint's unadventurous cocktail menu. I've ridden the tiger *ragged*. That tiger, it's rolled over on its blazing back and put up its paws and just asked me to *stop*. Cocaine (two lines of which form the tenth unofficial ingredient in a Lucifer Rising) has found its feisty way up both ports of my hungry hooter, and I've slogged (and whacked, and ploughed, and rootled, and slurped, and chomped) my way through a good half of the talent at XXX-Quisite Escorts – '*girls with personality and verve for the gentleman who demands excellence*'. Do I demand excellence? Let me tell you, that excellence they've got on offer at XXX-Quisite, it's *excellent*. I'm feeling . . . Well, I'm feeling *good*, you know? Violet-length bubble baths, oven-roasted quail, coke-dusted nipples and the odd vanilla-flavoured vulv, altered states, clairvoyant cachet (I've got a whole posse of admirers here now) and the strangely reliable lust inspired by Harriet's past-it poop-chute – it's not much compared to my Rwandan rumbles or Balkan brouha-has, you know, but it's something, it's *stuff*. What else does one do with one's finite body, with one's life on earth? I've been dreaming of a vacation like this for billennia. And now? – Oh glorious and bountiful serendipity! – Harriet, Nexus Films, and Trent Bintock.

Trent's short film *Including Everything* won at Sundance this season. And Cannes. It won at Los Angeles, too. And Berlin. And everywhere else that mattered and everywhere else that didn't. Trent, a twenty-five-year-old New Yorker of such gilt and chiselled good looks as to amount to a self-parody, is currently under contract to the remarkable Harriet Marsh of Nexus Films. He looks like a cross between an aerobic Apache and a Californian surf god. His fingernails and teeth appal with a whiteness that would shame the snows of Aspen. Trent, whose youthful brush with even modest celebrity has lifted him to heights of vanity that would make Gunn look shy, is what you might call 'poised' for conquest. Harriet is going to launch him. Launching young men is one of Harriet's pastimes; she considers herself a kind of watermark they'll carry out into the world, visible in future only when the young man is held up against a strong light . . . The only thing missing from this picture is the picture. The feature that's going to put Trent on Hollywood's A-list and a planet-sized wedge into Nexus's coffers. The feature, the picture, the movie, the film. The story. The one I pitched post-coitally to Harriet over three bottles of Bolly and eight lines of the Very Reverend Charles Cocaine.

Oh I know it's frivolous. So deshed *frivolous*. But once Harriet took me seriously I couldn't but run with it. She picked up the blower there and then. LA. Tokyo. Paris. *Mumbai*. Twenty-five words or less? Less. ' "Lucifer",' she said. 'Creation. Fall. Eden – Julia – battle on Earth with Christ. Effects up the arse. Controversy.' She capped the pitch with pure anti-logic. 'The most expensive film ever made.' They loved it. You can't blame me, can you? Obviously set the record straight before the end of time, obviously unveil the Real Me – but think of the *merchandising*. That and we leak a story that now-reclusive scriptwriter Gunn was Actually Possessed by Lucifer to write the script. Bump off a couple of sour grapes critics to give the thing some momentum. Maybe decapitate Julia half-way through shooting and roll in Penelope Cruz. '. . . members of the crew are beginning to believe the rumour that writer Declan Gunn made some Faustian pact . . .' Lucifer's going to be *the* pop culture icon for the final days of pop culture. And the final days of everything else, now that you mention it. Move over Madonna. The Caths, the Fundamentalists, the Baptists, Jumpin' Jeehosophet's Witnesses – Christ, anyone who's anyone on the overlarge map of Christianity is going to be picketing movie theatres worldwide. And the kids? The kids are going to *love it*.

Honestly, I looked in the mirror this morning and thought: You know what you are, don't you? You're *cocky*. Your trouble, Lucifer, your irresistible and invidious trouble, is that you've always got to go the extra yard. Not content to accept Declan's soul self-delivered by the mortal sin of sui-cide, you want to put him back into play with a new set of conditions that are going to freshen his appetite for life and lead him away from the Old Man all over again. 'I *had* this soul already,' you want to say to Him, between sips of Remy and insouciantly expelled smoke-rings, 'I already had it, but I put it back. I'd like you to observe, Old Fruit, as, with his new lease of life, snatched from the very doorstep of certain Hell, your boy spends what remains of his liberty walking straight back into my arms . . .' Confidence? This is *meta*-confidence, Toots.

So there you have it. Coming to a theatre near you. What kills me is this quaint business of me coming back here to Gunn's hovel to *write*. Don't laugh. Can't squeeze a word out at the hotel. I'm not complaining, really: the poverty of Gunn's former life provides a titillating counterpoint to the extravagant one I'm living on his behalf at the Ritz. A coun-terpoint in small doses, let me stress, in very, *very* small doses.

Life among the hotel's loaded suits me. I'm a Name: the clairvoyant who pretends to be the Devil. Celebrity, you see, on a scale Declan could (and regularly did) only dream about. They're used to celebs there, obviously. Staff are pro-hibited on pain of dismissal from making a fuss. I mean they're polite, of course – they are supposed to *recognize* you – but none of that 'Oh, Mr Cruise I just loved you in the one with the retard' nonsense. Word of the Film Deal is out. There's a whispery buzz about us, me, Trent and Harriet, when we park at the bar. The Lucifer Rising is the best-selling cocktail in the house. I wake up these mornings with a grin on my gob and pep in my prick. The sun comes in the window and embraces me. Those champagne breakfasts Harriet insists on practically guarantee a Feelin' Groovy sort of day. Gunn's bones seem finally to be coming into some kind of right alignment. I sing in the shower (*Giddup-ah giddorn up – like a sex-machine – giddorn up*) and take the stairs three at a time. This is how one should live. This, let me repeat, is *how* one should live.

(You know, it's true. Work had really been getting me down latterly. Of late. The predictability. The routine. The absence of even the ghost of a challenge. With nice symmetry, my newly acquired corporeal threads provide material for the analogy: I'd felt *heavy*, sluggish, fevered now and then, stiff of joint, leaden of head, sour of guts, immaterially peaky and generally under the angelic weather. This getaway's just what I needed. A change, as they say, is as good as a rest.)

The clairvoyance gimmick's magnetic. Jack Eddington wants to give me my own show. Lysette Youngblood wants me on the road with Madonna. Gerry Zooney wants me to go head-to-head with Uri Geller. Todd Arbuthnot wants to hook me up with his contacts in Washington. Who are these people? They're members of my Ritz coterie.

'Do you have any idea, Declan, of the sort of money you could make with this?' Todd Arbuthnot said to me last night, after I'd told him a thing or two about Dodi and Di that made his toenails curl.

'Yes, Todd, I do have an idea,' I said. 'And do, dear boy, please, call me Lucifer.'

They don't get it, the Devil thing. They write it off as

permissible guru eccentricity. Needless to say, none of them has heard of Declan Gunn. None of them has read *Bodies in Motion, Bodies at Rest*. None of them has read *Boneshadows*. Not that the obscurity credentials didn't come in handy with Trent, who's a writing snob, when he's not out of his box on drugs.

'Okay,' he said, coming up bleary-eyed from a toot in my suite, where, by mutual agreement, our 'development meetings' take place. Harriet was out. Dining with microelectronics and pharmaceuticals. Outside the window lit London beckoned. I get terribly excited once it's gone dark. I get terribly excited while it's still light, too; but that darkness, those winking city lights . . . I've started *going out*, you see. Going out, in London, at night, with money, drugs, famous people, and extremely expensive prostitutes. (Whereas Gunn used to go out, at night, alone, with hardly any money, no drugs, no celebs, fail to pull, get denied sex even after the capitulation and retreat to Vi's, then come home, have a hungover handjob, a sob, a vomit, a cigarette, and much mulling over just how close he was to having altogether given up hope before falling into a troubled and unregenerative sleep.)

'Okay,' Trent said, stretching his bottom jaw and widening then contracting his sapphire eyes. 'We start with just a full black screen and a voiceover. No stars, right? I mean, there wouldn't, would there, be actual stars?'

I rounded off my scheduling call to Elise at XXX-Quisite, and put the phone down. Your verbal engagement on the telephone – or in conversation with someone else, for that matter – presents no obstacle to Trent. 'There weren't stars,' I said. 'There wasn't anything.'

He looked at me for a moment very much in the manner of a person about to pass into an inaccessible dimension of consciousness. Then he shook himself. 'Right,' he said. 'Right, right, right. You were there. I forget.'

'What we've got to nail,' I said, lighting up one of Harriet's left-behind Gauloises, 'what we've really got to pin down – because everything else will flow from it, you know –'

'I know, man. Christ I *know* . . .'

'Is the moment I turn. The moment I *rebel*.'

'Run with it. Run with it.'

'Michael's just laid down that infamous accusation of pride, right?' I sprang up from the bed and let the city's lights catch me on Gunn's better side. 'And I'm like . . . "Pride?" It's a whisper at this stage, a Pacino whisper: "Pride?" But this is one of those whisper-builds-to-shout scenes. "Is it pride to want a place of your own? Is it pride to want to be independent?" Little by little louder, right? "Is it *pride* to want to *do* something in the universe?" Louder: "Is it *pride* to want to *be* somebody?" Louder still: "Is it *pride* to want to live with dignity?" Then full fucking throttle: "Is it *pride* to get sick of KISSING AN OLD MAN'S **ASS**?"'

Trent shook his head in ecstatic disbelief, like a sent musician. 'Christ, man you should *take* the fucking part,' he said.

I pointed at him with my cigarette. 'You, dear boy,' I admonished, 'are an appalling flatterer.'

I can't tell you how good I was feeling. Looking at things like daffodils and clouds is wonderful. Looking at things like daffodils and clouds having just spent £372 on dinner and dropped two tabs of ecstasy in preparation for a five-hour shift with XXX-Quisite's friendliest platinum blonde double-act, that's *really* wonderful. I know what the majority of you think about all this. All this sex and money and drugs. You think: people who live like that never end up happy. You need to think that in just the way men with small penises need to think size doesn't matter. It's under-standable. The rich, the famous, the big-dicked, the slim-and-gorgeous – they incite an envy so urgent that you can escape it only by translating it into pity. *People who live like that never end up happy*. Yes, you're right. But neither do you. And in the meantime, they've had all the sex and drugs and money. (Gunn, I might add, retained his carious Catholicism largely because atheism would have forced him to accept that nothing terrible was going to happen to people like Jack Nicholson and Hugh Hefner and Bill Wyman after they died – a proposition he couldn't have borne.)

'How come no one's done this movie?' Trent asked. 'I mean you'd think, right? Spielberg. Lucas. Cameron. Mind you, the FX budget's gonna go through the fucking ozone layer.'

'If we write it, they will pay,' I said.

'We do *want* effects, right?' Trent said. 'I mean, we're not seeing this as some sort of Beckett existentialist struggle crap, are we?'

'We want the biggest film since *Titanic*, Trent,' I said.

'And none of that "no big names" shit, either,' Trent said, between toots from his own monogrammed spoon. 'These film school assholes who think it's a sin to use named talent. That's so fucking uncool.'

'Can I fuck your buns, Trent?'

'I mean for Christ's – what?'

'Nothing. A verbal tick, dear boy. You're right. So uncool. Harriet wants Julia Roberts for Eve.' I said all this and man-aged to keep a straight face. I'd like some credit for that.

'Too bad Bob De Niro already played Lucifer in *Angel Heart*,' Trent said, rubbing the tip of his nose, furiously, as if trying to erase it. 'And Nicholson in *The Witches of Eastwick*.

Fuck, and Pacino just did Satan in that piece of shit with Keanu Reeves.'

(Shall I tell you what the list of actors who've turned down the chance to play me looks like? It looks *short*.)

'Depp,' I said. 'Keanu'd jump at it like a gibbon – but we've got to have *some* fucking ability. We should think about lining up some cameos, too. Maybe some rock dinosaur with false teeth to play God. Robert Plant with a beard.'

'Yeah, but do we even want a guy God?' Trent asked. 'I'm thinking more like hand-star-egg-eye-cosmic-dust-Giger-secretion stuff.'

'I like the way you think, Trent,' I said. 'I like the way you think.'

All this has not been without effect on my relationship with Violet, naturally. (Here's a question: do you think keeping Gunn attached to Violet will be a good thing for him?) Thanks to her never having read *Bodies in Motion, Bodies at Rest*, I've had little trouble 'reminding' her that it was the story of Lucifer's rebellion, fall, and battle with Christ on earth.

'It's going to be the biggest marketing campaign ever,' I told her, over daiquiris at Swansong. I've kept quiet about the Ritz. As far as she knows I'm still living at the Clerkenwell pad. Essential, too, to keep her away from Harriet and Trent – essential if I'm to sustain the illusion that she'd get within remote imaging range of a part. So far the prodigal spending – my wallet's attention deficit disorder – has kept her enthralled; but it's only a matter of time before she starts to expect the meet-and-greets, the air kisses, the Midas touch handshake, the inevitable sack-negotiations. Everything, down here, is always just a matter of Time.

'Harriet's got one of her people talking to McDonald's on Thursday. The McDevil. We're getting the "Quake" team for the CD-Rom game. Oh yeah – and we're going to do collectable cards – the Fallen Angels. Like Top Trumps.'

'Top Trumps?'

'Harriet's already started cutting the smaller investors out of the picture. Prince Faquit's just inked four-point-five over oysters at *Non*. You can't believe how easy it is to get money from people for film. As long as it's an incredibly large amount, that is. Indies can't cover the grip's fucking pizza.'

'You did tell her about me, didn't you, Declan?' Violet asked, having assumed that for the last few seconds I'd decided to drop into an African language.

'Yes.'

'No, but I mean you did, didn't you?'

'I've told you. Eve.'

Violet, sitting with legs crossed and one stiletto hanging off her toes, just went very still. Very *present*.

'Don't fuck about with me, Declan,' she said.

I put my hand on her knee. 'It's not my call,' I said. 'I mean I'm not the casting director. They've got Hagar Hefflefinger, you know. She's very tough. Very good. Tough in a good way. Good in a tough way. The way casting directors have to be. So like I say, it's not my call. But it is my script – how would you feel about Salome, by the way?'

'Who?'

'Herod's daughter. A princess. Redhead, too, you know, so I was thinking, obviously.'

'I knew you were lying.'

'What?'

'About the Eve part. You know I'm not a complete fucking idiot.'

Violet's nothing if not a quick assimilator. Initially, news of my restored Rodge was greeted with a dimpled smile and a dash to the disgorged boudoir, where my girl administered fellatio of such froth and dalliance that my eyebrows, raised at its commencement, refused to come down until it was all over. (Watching in the mirror turned out to be a bad idea, what with Gunn's wayward gut and hairy legs, what with his double chin, dugs, and jug-handle ears, what with his body being a sort of anti-aphrodisiac – until, that is, I started seeing the pornographic potential in our aesthetic discrepancies . . .) But she's sharp. She's already started rationing her favours. The splurge was to establish that her currency was still good. Already, in the absence of an Actual Meeting With the Producer and the Director, she's reined in her spending.

'Violet,' I said. 'Violet. If it was up to me – but listen. *Listen.* I'm not the casting director, but I am having that consultation clause written in. Harriet's getting the contracts drafted this week. But casting director or not – Hagar fucking Hefflefinger or *not* – Trent Bintock is the director of this film and Trent Bintock thinks I'm a creative genius. If I tell him we need to look at you for Eve – if I tell him we *need to look at you for Eve* . . . Do you hear what I'm saying?'

There had almost been tears. The jewelled eyes had filled up. She closed them, now, for three, four, five seconds, breathing slowly through her nostrils.

'Do you know who Harriet wants for Lucifer?' I said. 'Do you know who she was on the phone to last night?

Violet opened her eyes. We were in a familiar place now. I was the dad who'd frightened her – for her own good – and now, chastened, she was looking at me ready to be rescued from fear.

'Johnny Depp,' I said, quietly, then took a sip of my drink and looked out of the window.

She put her head down for a moment of introspective silence. When she looked up again, she wore a compact – almost a bitter – smile.

'We've earned this, Declan,' she said. 'D'you know what I mean? We've fucking *earned* this.'

◆

There's a common misconception about me. It's a slander spread by the Church, namely that if you make a deal with me, I'll cheat you. Poppycock, of course. I never cheat. Never have to. Ask Robert Johnson. Ask Jimmy Page. Humans are so deaf and blind to the ambiguities of their own languages, they concoct their wishes in terms so permeable that I can always grant them in a way they never imagined. *I want to be as wealthy as my father.* Fair enough. Nelchael crashes the markets, Dad's bankrupt, and thanks for the soul, brother. A boneheaded example, obviously, but you'd be surprised how wide open you leave yourselves. (The punters who come off best with me are smart, dirty rotten scoundrels to start with, willing to sign over their afterlife care in exchange for the chance to become even dirtier, rottener scoundrels while still rightside of the grave.)

Any of these transactions is a no-lose situation for me. Even if you get your deal double-entendre-proof, even if, thanks to you dressing your heart's desire in a semantic straitjacket, I'm compact-bound to give you what you want, still, at the end of an incredibly short time (all New Time's short time to me), I'm going to get my hands on your soul. How can I put this? *You really don't want that to happen.*

You might be one of the genuinely smart and dirty rotten scoundrels mentioned above, whose wish coincides with my overall design. You might, for example, want control over people's minds, financial muscle, immunity from prosecution, access to kids, a personal harem, etc. Now if you really are smart, if I think you've got it *in* you, I might just slot you into a System. I'll make you a media tycoon, or a dictator, or a cult leader, or a porn baron, or a drug tsar. As long as your evil's got some scale, as long as it draws others in, and as long as you're prepared to put in a bit of good old-fashioned *graft* – well, you'll get what you wanted, the fame, the charisma, the wedge, the place in history, the six-year-olds, whatever. You get your kicks, I get a System operator, the Old Man gets a migraine, and – thought I'd forgotten, didn't you? – *I get your soul when you die.*

So let the holy fathers prattle of lies and betrayals. Truth is I'm no welcher.

I have been done over once, mind you – a wretched Spaniard by the name of Don Fernando Morrales, not long before the close of the gorgeous sixteenth century. This young man was a piece of work. The only son of wealthy parents he spent the first years of his adult life racing through his fortune on an extraordinary diet of booze, whores and gambling. Built up quite a reputation for blasphemous debauches and criminal orgies. A natural, as they say. I gave him the odd nudge now and again when guilt tickled or imagination flagged, but by and large he was a works-well-on-his-own-initiative kind of sinner. To be honest with you I didn't think he'd see twenty-five, what with the poxy scags and verminous rent boys into which he was dipping his redoubtable chorizo, not to mention the growing number of hacked-off dads whose daughters he'd rather irresponsibly impregnated; but, incredibly, he just kept on rocking in the free world until the money was gone. Now, as any suddenly blinded peeping tom will aver, the flames of desire burn with twice the fierceness in the absence of the means of gratification – and so it was with young Morrales, until finally I decided to drop in, make a deal, put him once and for all beyond the reach of redemption and his scrofulous soul into the infernal account.

I've looked back since and known that I must have been in a funny mood. It was a bad pain day, yes – sometimes I can barely manage the raised eyebrow and devilish grin – but something else, too . . . A shade of melancholy, perhaps? A sense that my best days were behind me? That the challenging work had already been done? (Foolish, in hindsight, given my achievements of the last 400 years, but I'm prone to moments of doubt just like everyone else. And I'm not talking *little* or *nagging* doubt. I'm talking crippling, existential, what-on-earth-is-the-point-of-it-all doubt. There have been days when I've just had to lie in a darkened room.) Anyway the point is that for whatever reason I wasn't quite myself when I visited Morrales in the ritual room of one of his occult amigos, who, at Morrales's insistence, had gone to the bogus and completely unnecessary trouble of 'summoning' me. Do please note those inverted commas, to signify facetiousness. You don't, darling, 'summon' Lucifer. He's not a fucking *butler*. Lucifer *visits* you. That's all. If I feel it's going to be in my interest to have direct dealings with you (and you really better hope I *don't*) then I'll come whether you attempt to 'summon' me or not. If I don't, no amount of spooky chanting, bare bums, sinister beards, fellated goats or murdered chickens is going to make the slightest difference, except to your carpet. Don't get me wrong: you'll have a blast. It just doesn't *work*.

Damn these digressions. How did Gunn – how does one, ever finish anything? Morrales's chum, one Carlos Antonio Rodriguez, was one of those chickenshit dabblers manifestly in it for the carnal extravagances. He'd argued long and hard with Fernando that the conjuring of His Satanic Majesty was both difficult and highly dangerous, but had finally – seeing that if he didn't comply there was a good chance that Fernando would stick his sword through his, Carlos's, head – capitulated and begun. He wasn't ready for me when I appeared. (I'd consulted the manifestations wardrobe: yes, something . . . *traditional*, I think – although I'll tell you for nothing, love, those cloven hooves are strictly bedroom.) I could tell he had a good couple of hours' worth of incantatory twaddle lined-up, and the truth is I couldn't sit through the Latin. Gave him quite a turn. So much of a turn, in fact, that he bemerded his hose and ran screaming from the room, leaving me alone with Fernando.

Don Fernando Morrales. Oy. Always when you least expect . . . sorry. Talking to myself when I should be talking to you. (You. I know who you are, you know. I know where you live. How does that make you feel? Secure?) Fernando, when all's said and done, had some fucking *cojones* on him. He was scared. He was . . . ah . . . *perspiring* – but he held it together long enough to get through the negotiations. No surprises there: I'd get his soul, he'd get a wagonload of money, fatal accidents to an arm-long list of real and imagined enemies, and a lot – really an *awful* lot – of unhygienic nookie. So I dictated the wording of the contract and told him to open a vein for the bloody signature. (It's not the piece of paper, obviously, which in any case I can't carry back with me into the ether; it's the act of signing. Blood seals it. That's the way it's always been. Ask Jimmeny. You can destroy the contract, materially – everyone does – but it won't make a difference come time for collection. I can promise you that.) Anyway Fernando had just rolled up his sleeve and was inspecting his forearm for a safe spot to make the cut, when – God knows what put it into his head to do such a thing – he asked me straight out if it was true that I'd been present at the Crucifixion. When I told him yes, of course, he asked me, rather absurdly I thought, if I could draw a likeness of what I'd seen.

I should, strictly speaking, have searched Morrales's soul a little more thoroughly. That was carelessness on my part, I admit. I was feeling peculiar. The pain was banging away like an autistic kettle-drummer and my heart . . . my heart . . . Oh all right *not* my heart, but it was one of those weird days when I could barely concentrate on what I was doing, when the blood-spattered and corpse-littered wake of my busy life tugged at me like a conundrum. *How art thou fallen from Heaven, O Lucifer, Son of the morning!* Sometimes I let that run through my head and it's the sound of a triumphal trumpet. Other times it just makes me terribly sad. Fernando – God knows why – had quoted it in an undertone, a whisper mortal ears wouldn't have heard. (Isaiah wasn't even talking about me when he said it. He was prophesying the fate of Merodach-baladan, who was not, as you might be thinking, one of the Harlem Globetrotters, but the King of Babylon. It's just that sometimes human utterances accidentally align with the truths of Heaven and Hell. When that happens, the phrases stick in history like burrs.)

I did it telekinetically, the quill inked with Morrales's blood. Never knew I had any artistic talent until that drawing emerged on the back of the unsigned contract. Never knew I was . . . you know . . . *creative*. Got lost in it, the challenge to keep the line honest, the strange state of suspension between absolute concentration and absolute blankness (it's a Zen thing, apparently), the momentary dissolution of the boundary between subject and object, the fleeting transcendence of self. You know there are drawings that seem to say so much in so few lines? This was one of them. On top of all my other knacks and talents, I was supernaturally *good at droring*.

Too good for my own good, as it turned out. When I turned my attention back to Morrales I saw he was weeping piteously and tearing out hanks of his hair. He kissed the image (I'd been a bit flattering with Junior's hairdo and beard, if you want the truth, but then so has practically every other painter in the history of art), wailing now as his tears mingled with the blood: *Vade Satana: Scriptum est enim: Dominum Deum tuum adorabis, et illi soli seruies . . . Vade Satana . . . Vade Satana!* Which, for the Classically challenged among you (that's pretty much all of you, these days) translates as: *Begone Satan: for it is written: The Lord thy God shalt thou adore, and Him only shalt thou serve.*

You humans and your confounded epiphanies, eh? Honestly. You're so *mauve*. Couldn't get a word out of him after that. Certainly no signature. Worse than a complete waste of time – a *conversion*. Hoist, as they say, by my own petard. Course I couldn't help it once I saw that I could really . . . *capture* something in the drawing. Had to let myself go. Had to *show off*.

I went small-mouthed back to my brothers in Hell. Told them I wasn't well. Had a lie-down. (Astaroth smirked a bit, I now recall.) Bloody Morrales gave the picture up to the Cardinal Penitentiary and – as I live and breathe – joined the Franciscans. Idiot. Couple of millennia in Purgatory then the Old Man let him in. Meanwhile the drawing, *my* drawing, is locked in one of the Very Rarely Unlocked rooms of the Vatican, its existence, until now, known only to a privileged few. It can have . . . *effects* on those who do get to see it, mind you. Sent one corrupt cardinal (tautological phrase if ever there was one) back in the Eighteenth completely mad.

So mad, in fact, that he hanged himself in a brothel shortly after his young lady had left him to dress, dropping his sin-heavy soul into my lap like a lump of rotten fruit – compensation for Morrales, I might add, long overdue.

◆

Now . . . *Gunn*. Gunn and suicide. You're thinking: For heaven's sake *why*?

It takes patience to drive people to suicide. Patience and a particular voice of reason. *It's not going to get any better. It's only going to get worse. You need this pain to stop. It's perfectly all right to want this pain to stop. All you need to do is lie down and close your eyes* . . . It took me a while to hit on just the right tone, part disinterested physician, part forgiving priest – their twin implications: You need it; It's okay.

But Gunn. What brought it on? What – apart from his dead mother, Violet, *A Grace of Storms*, and Wordsworthian melancholy over the loss of childhood's celestial light – happened?

There's a long story and a short one. If you don't believe in God or free will there's really only *one* long story, an anti-morality tale in which no one's to blame for anything. (Another place my reasonable voice came in handy, that, getting the universe reduced to matter and determinism.) The short story, on the other hand, the tabloid leader, is Penelope. Not *that* Penelope – though the name of Gunn's ex is apposite, since he thought of her as, among other ide-alizations, a paragon of female fidelity. (And enjoyed with peculiar and shameful relish at my suggestion a porn video in a Manchester hotel – up there for book signing; '. . . sensitive and insightful . . .' the *Manchester Evening News* – called *Penelope's Passions*, which tale follows its classical progenitor in all but one significant detail: Penelope works her carnal way through the entire host of suitors and most of her household staff as well, ending the flick in a state of such cross-eyed satiation that one wonders whether she'd be capable of *recognizing* Odysseus should he scupper plans for *Penelope's Passions II* by actually making it home . . .) Oh but these digressions! The trouble with *knowing* people, you see, is that *everything*'s relevant. Nothing *is* a digression. Even Gunn knew it. Dear old cabbage-face Auden, for example, a copy of whose *Collected Poems* when pulled from Gunn's shelf opens itself like a robotic hussy at 'The Novelist', wherein we find Wystan's observation that the budding Dickens or Joyce must

> Become the whole of boredom, subject to
> Vulgar complaints like love, among the Just
>
> Be just, among the Filthy filthy too,
> And in his own weak person, if he can,
> Dully put up with all the wrongs of Man

Lest ye become as gods yourselves, didn't I tell Eve, the first prospective novelist? Was that a lie? Must know All and tell Some. Which is lying by omission. No artist knows everything (yea, even this artist — piss-artist, sack-artist, con-artist, *body*-artist) but since every artist knows more than he can tell, all art is lying by omission. And if God is the only artist who knows Everything, how enormous that sin of omission is! Who, I ask you, humbly, is more worthy of the *Father of Lies* tag? You write this incredible book — but there's a catch: only you can read it — and what is Creation but a book only God can read? What remains untold is occult, and what remains occult is feared, and what remains feared is not infrequently worshipped. *Quad erat demonstrandum.*

But to return to young Gunn. Who, in recent months, has found himself staring into the pocked bathroom mirror and pronouncing the words 'young gun' aloud, exploring the shocking inapplicability of the metaphor with haggard and bilious irony, much in the way one might explore with one's tongue, perversely, the still-painful cavity of a recently extracted tooth. It's one of his habits of despair. He's got a quiver of them, and looses them by the hour until come evening he stands before his reflection Saint Sebastianized once more and lullabyed closer to his heinous sleep by my voice of gentle reason: *She used to call you Young Gunn. She let it fall from her lips like a sweetly spoken spell mingling tenderness and tease.* Along with *Angel* and *Deckalino* and *Gunneroo* and *Baby* and *Boy* and *Honey* and – the crucifier – *Love.* Speaking aloud the names no one else will ever call him to his own unpitying reflection is one of his habits of despair. As is alcoholism. As is pornography. As is Violet. As is the replayed tape of silence between him and his dear departed mother. As is the daily refined map of his own fraudulence – '. . . sensitive and intelligent . . .' as the *Manchester Evening News* had it – which phrase he repeats, gutturally, just before crashing drunk to his knees in a Shaftsbury Avenue gutter, or projectile vomiting into the unjudgemental mouth of his Clerkenwell bog.

Heavens how this tongue runs on. I have no knack for brevity. And you none for patience, no doubt – so forward ho! (Besides which, there's the Temptation in the Desert Scene to write this afternoon. Harriet *laughs* when I show her the material. Candy from babies, she knows. Criminally, candy from babies.) He is the bow of burning gold and these are his arrows of despair – but still we're no nearer the why or how.

If Gunn were writing of Penelope he would perfect her, since he never got beyond their romance and into their reality. So let me, at least, be clear. She wasn't a saint. (If only she had been. Saints, they're a *barrel* of laughs, they are, perpetually on the verge of conversion to sin. They can't help it. Extremes always nudge their opposites in the small hours.) She was pretty enough, but not so much that you'd still have shagged her if she was completely bald. She was lucky, actually that she hadn't turned out *astonishingly gorgeous*, because she wouldn't have been quite strong enough to resist living off the benefits that condition confers. (Astonishingly gorgeous people are rarely good, for the simple reason that they don't need to be. Hell's absolutely *stuffed* with the souls of ex-stunnas and hunks, whereas Heaven's been in a more or less perpetual state of talent-famine since human beings first started biting the dust.) Anyway, Penelope. (You see what happens when an angelic intelligence starts telling the stories of human beings? One needs parentheses of virtually infinite regress; one of those Russian dolls – only an unimaginably fertile one, with not half-a-dozen versions of herself within but several billion – such an enormously long time before you get to the last, the first, the point of origin or expiry . . . Remember, Lucifer, we are concerned here only with Gunn's decision to end his life . . .)

Penelope's gone down to university in London (with her tangled tawny hair and her green leather jacket and her chipped maroon nail varnish) to study Literature and to Fall in Love. And she's met black-eyed and tea-coloured Declan Gunn.

'I like your forehead,' he says, when she opens her eyes

one morning. Six months in they've arrived at the speech of lovers – cockily tangential and thriving on apparent non sequiturs. 'It's sometimes like a cat's. And your hair comes out of it in exactly the way it did when you were five.'

'I want a tomato and some honey and some yoghurt,' she says. 'In my dream, I thought I'd had a baby, but when I looked down at it in my arms, it was an almond slice.'

'And when you were at primary school,' he says, 'the teacher would be aware of you staring out through the window at the playing field, and he would know absolutely that you weren't listening to a word he was saying, and the surface part of him would be irritated, but the deeper, aesthetic part of him would love you for your cat forehead and your absolute indifference to where you were and what he was trying to teach you.'

'What's the most important thing?' she says, changing again.

'Angel Delight,' Gunn says.

'Truth,' Penelope says, moving her fingertips over him, mapping her ownership, guiltlessly avaricious. 'Truth is the most important thing. Being true. Not being false.'

'I know.'

'But really.'

'I know.'

'*Then* Angel Delight.'

He can't quite believe it, of course, his good fortune, his utterly undeserved luck in having found her. They delight in telling the truth to each other about the world. They're only nineteen, so it's not much of a world.

'We must have babies,' Penelope says, clambering on to him, easing herself down.

'Eh?'

'Not *this minute*,' she says, feeling him inside her. 'But

eventually. Because if we don't, then ugly, stupid, unkind people will, and the forces of evil and meanness will win.'

Gunn's in a state of near mesmerism: his body's rich torpor, the late morning's heat. Their window is an ingot of warm gold. *I don't deserve this*, he's thinking, watching the light jangling in her hair, feeling the precise amount of her bodyweight she's holding back – an appallingly erotic restraint – *This will all have to be paid for.*

He's right.

Now – good gracious me look at the time! I only even *mentioned* Penelope because she's part of what drove our Gunn to the blades and the bath. This is the way of it down here, I perceive, the frightful drudgery of *finding the causes* – then worse, *finding the words*. The immeasurably long time it all takes. Had Gunn stopped talking years ago he might have started living. It even occurred to him; predictably, when it did, he went away and *wrote* about it.

My dears, we've wandered from our course here. My fault, I know. And now I'm afraid the pull of the world draws me from this. I have, as you know, got places to go. I have, as you know, got *people to see*.

◆

It wasn't a fair fight. That's what I'm trying to bring out of the story, you know? Trent's keen on playing this angle up. And why not? It *wasn't* a fair fight. Left to his own devices I'm not sure Junior would have made it to Golgotha. I'm not just talking about the stuff that's on record – the warning to supercuckold Joseph that Herod was furious and that Egypt was lovely that time of year, for example – I'm talking about stuff you don't even know about, stuff that came later, when

112

the Little Baby Jesus was all grown up, when, if the Old Man had had any decency about Him He would have stayed out and left the two of us to it, head-to-head, gloves off, winner takes all, and so on. But what, I ask rhetorically, does God know about fair fighting?

Consider the temptation in the wilderness.

Redundantly, let me begin by saying it was hot. Really *awfully* hot. The sky was bone white and deserted, sunlight a static explosion on the sand. Not kingfishers but lizards caught fire; the place was jewelled with them. Desert plants revolved their shadows, slowly. He'd gone into an emptiness only occasionally whipped through by a babbling Essene or hair-shirted freak. He looked rough when I came to him, beard matted, eyes stied and reddened, cheeks hollow, fingernails torn, lips cracked and blistered. Yes, fasting for forty days and nights manifestly had not been a blast. When I found him he was sitting hunched in the mouth of a cave, knees up to his chin, bony fingers laced around his lengthy shins. Very black was the cool mouth of the cave and very white the scorched land around it.

'Hungry, lovey?' I said. It's been a weakness of mine – yes, definitely a weakness – that ever since the days of the parted robes and the punctured heart I've found it all but impossible to control my irritation in his presence. Soon as I see him something in me just clicks and it's all barbed jibes and leaden sarcasm. *So* annoying. I'm sure that if I could just have got beyond it and let the *charm* flow . . .

'Oh,' he said. 'It's you.'

'You know those crash-diets are a trap, don't you?'

'You're wasting your time, Satan.'

'Not if it gives me pleasure to be here. Lucifer, by the way.'

'Go away.'

'Look, you know the drill. Would I be here if your Dad didn't want me to be?'

He sighed. I had him there. He'd come out here to be tested.

'Get on with it then, will you?' he said.

So on with it I got. Now obviously the versions you've inherited are way off. Matthew's got me trying to get him to turn stones into bread (prompting all the *not by bread alone* blarney), to throw himself off a mountain and precipitate an angelic rescue (provoking all the *don't test the Lord thy God* baloney), and to bow down and worship me in return for all the kingdoms of the earth (eliciting the now world-famous *get thee behind me* claptrap.) Luke agrees, but cocks up the order and substitutes a building (in the desert) for the mountain.

Now I ask you: do you really think that's the best I could come up with? I mean I'll just remind everyone in case everyone's forgotten: I'm . . . the *Devil*. And even if I wasn't, I'd have to have been a complete dunderhead to think he'd go for any of that nonsense. You're not even capable of *eating* bread after forty days' and nights' starvation. Having angels come to his rescue – what would that prove? It would, I suppose, have given him an opportunity to show me just how important he was, an opportunity for the gratification of ego or pride, but pride wasn't his weakness. You're going to tempt someone, you find their weakness. All the kingdoms of the earth? Might as well have offered him the complete Pokémon collection. The Evangelists tell you what *they* would have been tempted by. *Jimbo wasn't interested in that sort of thing.* It doesn't bother me that the Gospels are skewed, but it bothers me that I come out looking so narrow, so *myopic*.

Apart from sanctimoniousness and impenetrable parabling Arthur really only had one weak spot. Doubt. Very occasional, and invariably mastered by faith – but it was there. (I got to him in Gethsemane, right before the fun and games started, and almost had him at the very last on the cross, when, after I'd niggled him with that 'told you you can't trust Him' remark he panicked and went all *lama sabachthani* on us.) Yes, he was now and then wont to wonder whether it was all strictly necessary, the being betrayed and spat on and mocked and flogged and thorn-crowned and nailed to a cross for hours of agony and more mocking and jeering and so on. He was wont to wonder, quite reasonably, whether it was all going to be *worth* it.

So I took him to a place where the dunes dropped to a bed of rock blazing pink in the sun.

'You're doing this to save the world, right?' I asked him. He just stared down, saying nothing. 'Okay,' I continued. 'This is what the world will look like after you've done your thing. I'll just give you the headlines, but stop me any time if there's something you want a closer look at.'

An unpalatable but not dishonest (*honestly*) preview of the next 2,000 years screened *as if by magic* on the stony plateau beneath us, complete with names, dates, places, sound-effects and statistics. There was some fantastic stuff in there – well, you know that, now – holocausts, tyrannies, massacres, technology, *bio*technology, wars, ideologies, atheism, starvation, money, disease, Elton John . . . He didn't like the look of it, you could tell. Nor did he think I was making it up. He didn't think I was making it up because he knew I wasn't making it up. He stood next to me and *swayed*. Maybe it was the hunger, the heat, the hallucinations, the headaches. Maybe it was the effect of the subliminals I'd sneaked in – X-rated flashes of him with a thonged and baby-oiled Mary Mags (or Dirty Mags, as I used to call her, much to Jimmeny's chagrin) making the beast with two backs (*bit* cheeky of me, I know, but you've gorr'ave a larf at work narn'again, intcha?); maybe it was just that he was feeling dreadfully lonely after more than a month with only scorpions and bugs to talk to – who knows? What I do know is that he wavered. Rocked. Wobbled. Turned to me, lifted an unsteady hand as if to grab my non-existent lapel. At which point, typically – *typically* – the Old Man dropped a black cloud over the sun and a thunderbolt straight into the middle of my screen, scaring the hoop out of me and bringing Charlie Brown rudely to his senses.

'I'm going through with it,' he said. 'Now fuck off, will you?'

Like I said: not a fair fight.

◆

The hotel is filled with echoes, the ghostly resonance of torturous trysts and bad business. Deals, betrayals, cramped passions and sudden deaths – each room holds its after-image composite of the beings who've passed through. The hotel is a great London valve, through which the lifeblood of the city's wealth – the *planet's* wealth – has passed, now with dalliance, now in haste. Beauty and boredom form its unjudgemental mood. I'm at home there. I'm so . . . *at home* there.

Scale fucks with my head. Angelic scale with human head, human scale with angelic head – oy. You go dizzy. What does one do – having been immaterially present at the Divine ejaculation that brought matter into being – what does one do with . . . a daisy? How is consciousness – especially the troubled hybrid I'm walking around with at the moment – to reconcile these extremities? Having observed newborn galaxies tossed prodigally, milkily, into the void, having straddled event horizons and strolled bodilessly 'twixt time's wrinkles and matter's loops – how, exactly, am I to accommodate the crenulations of Harriet's toenails? Am *I* to apprehend seconds and caraway seeds that have called aeons trifles and held gas-giants baubles fit for a Heavenly whore?

Apparently, yes. And don't mistake me. If I sound confused it's only the happy confusion of the roll-over jackpot winner, now that all his choices are choices between pleasures. I smile a lot, faced with these charming frictions. Memories of the measureless deflagrations of home mix now with the intimate passing of a pigeon's shadow, or the precise dimensions of a full stop. Drugs or no, this gentle dissonance of cognition sends me through my time here in feisty bliss . . .

I've got fourteen scenes to write, I know, but how, may I ask, do you handle dreams?

To start with: sleep. How did I ever do without it? Actually not sleep itself, but *falling asleep*. How did I ever survive without this business of falling asleep? There are – Day Twelve (Heavens how time flies when you're having fun) – all sorts of things I'm wondering how I ever got along without. Israeli vine tomatoes. Campo Viejo Rioja. Heroin. Burping. Bollinger. Cigarettes. The sting of aftershave. Cocaine. Orgasm. Lucifer Risings. The aroma of coffee. (Coffee justifies the existence of the word 'aroma'.) There are, naturally, plenty of things I don't know how you put up with – disc jockeys, hangnails, trapped wind, All Bran – but then I knew it was going to be a mixed bag.

Anyway sleep. Granted, the first time it took me I was caught off-guard: one minute it was evening and I was lying on Gunn's bunk with crossed ankles and a warm feeling in my feet and shoulders – the next brilliant sunshine with yours truly truck-horned awake with pants-shitting suddenness and a miniature identity crisis bringing on the first-morning-in-a-foreign-hotel-reconstruct-your-own-history routine. I was so startled (another first) I shot out of Gunn's bones and back, bodilessly, into the ether. That turned out (wearing, this business of things *turning out*) not to be a good idea. Pain – *the* pain – returned, instantly, bright and clamorous. (When I quit Gunn's carcass at the end of the month, you know, that pain's going to hurt like . . . You wouldn't think, would you, it being only twelve days and all? I mean still no *sweat* or anything, but . . . well . . . *damn*, man. *Ow*, you know?) But sleep – falling asleep – I've got used to it. Easy to see why you lot go for it in such a big way, though why you choose to do it at night, the best part of the day, is a mystery to me.

But this dreaming – *whoa*. It was one of Gunn's. (Yes, I'm afraid so: on top of the drab threads and tiny todge I'm saddled with a good deal of the subconscious fluff, too.) Now as you all know, other people's dreams are superlatively boring unless you yourself are in them, so I won't burden you with the details. ('I had the most amazing dream last night,' says Peter. 'Was I in it?' asks Jane? 'No,' says Peter. 'Me and Skip were in this forest, you see, and . . .' etc. Jane's not listening – and who can blame her? Pretended interest in your partner's dreams is one of the half-dozen glues holding the pitiful airfix of monogamy together.) It's a dream Gunn's only had once or twice before. An older, bearded man comes to take his mother to the pictures. It's not a lover. (For the record, it's a queen whose partner cancer's recently chomped its way through, on whom Angela's taken pity.) Wee Gunn *knows* it's not a lover – but he can't or won't trust this old fruit. 'I'm just your mother's friend,' the bewhiskered lips keep telling him. 'There's nothing to be afraid of. I'm not taking her away from you. You can trust me. You *know* you can trust me.' (But tight-shouldered Gunn's a compact little thunderstorm. His face is piping hot and his chest is busy with naked feelings still waiting for their language hats and coats. His mother's friend is sitting on the couch, Gunn standing in front of him holding in his left hand the new matchbox Mini Cooper in electric green with opening boot, bonnet and doors – the price of his mother's company, he assumes. The babysitter is heating spaghetti hoops in the kitchen. Gunn hears the *bhup* then steady exhalation of the gas ring. With all his ineffectual might (when his mother's back is turned for a final mirror check: beige mack, mauve chiffon scarf, coppery curls, green eyeshadow) he balls his sweaty fist and clocks Mr Harmless a wild hook in the bearded chops. He thinks, little Gunn, all ablaze with pride and shame, that something big, some paradigm shift must follow. But the man on the couch just grins, without lifting his palms from their rest on his kneecaps. 'No need for that, my friend,' he whispers, rising, ruffling Gunn's warm hair. Then to Angela: 'Your carriage awaits.' Angela kisses our cheek and leaves a lipstick print. It's a thing between them. He's allowed to go to bed without washing it off. Her lips are warm and sticky. At the doorway she turns and blows him another kiss. The bearded man waves and winks. Gunn waves back as the corridor stretches and the doorway recedes, slowly. He waves, and smiles, and thinks: I hate you, I hate you, I *hate* you . . .

I was mumbling some untranslated version of this when I woke. Terribly hot and bothered. Had the Ritz's costly linens all tangled around my legs. Struggled up into consciousness with a lot of undignified lurching and warbling. Then sat up puffing and blowing, astonished at the simple endurance of the waking world: the room, the braying traffic, the weather. Called down for a pot of Columbian full roast and a half-dozen wee snifters with a tender – I'm tempted to say *humble* – thankfulness that it was all still here.

Incredible. And you lot have to deal with this sort of thing night after night. Must take some getting used to . . .

Out of mischief, really, I went to see Gunn's agent, Betsy Galvez. Do you know, I've found it so difficult to stick to my fourteen scenes. This writing malarkey should come with a health warning: MAY CAUSE INCESSANT DEVIATION FROM ORIGINAL INTENTION. AND DROWSINESS. Obviously I've got a lot of the script down – the big scenes, so to speak, and Trent already thinks I'm God – but do you think I can stick to the task in hand? I turn on Gunn's PC, I sit through the tedious powering-up, the brief arrival of Penelope's gently smiling mug as his desktop wallpaper, and am forced to acknowledge the presence of an untitled file alongside 'Lucifer Screenplay' that's been variously titled *Some*, *Anyway*, *Last Words*, *Wherefore I Know Not*, and *Paradise Fucked*, and which has thus far proven a terrible distraction from my contractual obligations. You know what's in it, don't you? You've been reading it, haven't you? I wouldn't mind if it was just the narrative version of the blockbusting movie – the 'novelization' as such things are barbarously called – but as you know, it's worse than that. I seem to be continuously struggling against the temptation to write about *Declan Gunn*.

I was just going to post it to Betsy, anonymously (I'm tempted to deprive Gunn of credit for this bit of graft; I'm tempted – oh I know I'm *silly* – to keep this as something I've done for *me*, you know?) but then it occurred to me (it's becoming annoying, this business of things occurring to me, this habit I've developed in Gunn's skin of not knowing everything ahead of time) that there was a good chance it would end up on a slush pile, or in the secretary's Deal With it Later file, or worse, ignominiously in the bin. So I went to see her. Gunn generally rings and makes an appointment. I didn't.

This weather . . . Humans, how do you avoid spending all your time just *experiencing* the weather? I walked from Clerkenwell to Covent Garden in very mild, very slightly moving air that touched the exposed bits of me like the petals of cool roses. The sky (even I've got to take my hat off to Himself when it comes to summer skies) was high and beaten thin, the low sun softly exploding pale oranges and watery greens into the upper margins of lilac and blue. The whole thing had a distant, bleached quality to it that made me in Gunn's body feel small and lonesome, not unlike the way he himself used to feel as a child, when his mother would treat him to an extortionately priced helium balloon which would invariably slip from his wet grasp and go sailing up into the vast and lonely distance, until Gunn, nauseated by his relationship to something now so remote, would begin to feel dizzy and afraid. (I've resigned myself, as you can see, to bits of Gunn's life intruding. Manifestly, the longer I'm here the more susceptible I am. Extraordinary what the body remembers. The bones loded with love, grief silting the arteries, fear the bowels' recurring mould. Who would have thought mere flesh and blood could hold so much of psyche's ghostly script?)

The good old world smelled good and old and worldly: fruity drains, diesel, caramelized nuts, fried onions, heat-rotted litter, tyres, minty and decidedly unminty breath. A suddenly opened pub door let a scent-bubble of beer-flavoured carpet and fagsmoke out into the fresh air. I inhaled (burped booze and bar snacks in there, too) as I passed through, smiling. Women had touched themselves up – *cosmetically*, thank you – and their features glowed and gleamed: mouths like scimitars in claret, plum, sienna, mimosa, pearl, burgundy and puce, smokily shadowed eyes with diamond hints and sapphire glints, flecks of emerald and fragments of jade. Easy there, Luce, easy. This is what they see every day. Doesn't mean anything to them. I know. I can't help it. Like your man Rumi, I find myself 'drenched in being here, rambling drunk . . .' You don't know what it is to me, this leisure (no priest in the taxi, no rabbi on the stairs), Gunn's sensory quintet working overtime. One after another: the wind's sudden swerve; someone's cinnamonish aftershave; the flooded gutter's ribbon of sky; teen bodyheat on a rammed Tube; marmalade breath and perfumed wrists. *Wears man's smudge and share's man's smell*, as dear old Hopkins lamented. You don't find me lamenting it, do you? Eh? I say, Missus, you don't find *me* lamenting it.

It used to give Gunn tremendous pleasure to visit Betsy, in her Covent Garden office. It was the sort of office he'd always imagined a literary agent would have: gargantuan oak desk, wafer-thin Persian rug in sky-blue and gold, fat oxblood leather couch, books everywhere – simply *every-where* – and, of course, manuscripts. Betsy, who, at fifty-six has a well-lined face and sunken cheeks, chain-smoked Dunhills and had shorthand or private language conversations on the phone that always made Gunn feel like part of the select world of Literature, even though he hadn't a clue what she was on about. (It was of course the select world of Publishing, but Gunn was a hopeless romantic.) Over the years our Betsy's perfected a very slightly sexually flirtatious persona for her young male writers, one that's based on her knowing that she's not physically attractive but that she is socially and professionally powerful. Her eyes are a pellucid blue, and are occasionally to be observed lingering a fraction longer than necessary on the lineaments of her 'boys'. (She doesn't have young women writers because she doesn't like young women.) She's had three long lunches with Gunn at the end of which he's had the feeling – the odd double entendre, nothing disgusting – she might be about to offer him money to fuck her – and he can't say the thought doesn't stimulate him. He imagines broad, deflated breasts with wine gum nipples, old-woman flesh in the armpits, an arse-hole with a history ... Since becoming 'a writer' Gunn believes such warped or distended liaisons are within his scope (he's going to love Harriet), are part of his duty, in fact, along with bowling around the West End drunk at four in the morning and wearing overcoats that reek of Oxfam.

Then, God help him, *A Grace of Storms*.

'I think you're making it *awfully* hard for yourself with a book this long,' she said to him, at their last protracted but emphatically unerotic lunch after she'd read the monstrous tome.

'Yeah,' Gunn said, 'but when a book's *good* you *want* it to go on forever, don't you?'

This left Betsy in such an appalling position that she surreptitiously dug her belt buckle's prong into her palm to distract herself. She knew exactly the sort of reviews Gunn thought the book would get. She knew exactly (light another Dunhill) the sort of reviews the book *would* get.

'Have you spoken to Sylvia?' Gunn asked. Sylvia Brawne, the editor of Gunn's last novel. 'Have you told her anything about it?'

Weary Betsy blew a Gandalfian smoke-ring. How much she wanted to say: 'Declan, you're a good writer who does what he does well – but you're not Anthony Burgess or Lawrence Durrell. You've got a nice line in understated poetic observation but virtually no intellectual rigour. You've bitten off more than you can chew and as a result this man-uscript is a titanic failure.'

Instead, she said: 'We'll go to Sylvia first and then see.'

They did see. *A Grace of Storms* was turned down. By everyone.

The inner sanctum of Betsy's office is antechambered by a smaller room with a varnished wooden floor, dark blue walls and one very new-looking Ikea desk, behind which sits Betsy's small and moody assistant, Elspeth.

'She's with somebody,' Elspeth said to me. 'Did you have an appointment?'

I ignored her and strode across to the door. Unheard of, to breach the adytum unmediated or unannounced. Elspeth's bottom jaw went rapidly through a sequence of little adjustments. Then she pushed the wheelie chair away from her desk and swivelled on it to face me. 'She's *with* someone, Declan,' she repeated.

One of the downsides of being me is that I'm occasionally rendered mute by the sheer number of acerbic ripostes teeming on my tongue. I glared at Elspeth and opened the door.

'. . . developing a much more . . . *muscular* language,' was the tail end of Betsy's compliment to the young man seated with a confrontational expansiveness of body in the middle of the oxblood couch. Tony Lamb. Gunn hates this person. Secondarily for his chubby face, buzz-cut and habit of dressing all in black, but primarily for his ubiquity and the success of his novels. Betsy despises Tony Lamb, too, certainly for his commitment to black clothes, but mostly for the blandness and flippancy of his language, the absence of ideas, the absence of reading, and the *presence* of a raging desire to get into Hollywood (which he will, within the year) and snort coke and fuck aspiring starlets and throw-up in the bathrooms of very exclusive places. The very life 'Declan' (bless) is living right now. She knows that for Tony Lamb writing is a tool which, if used cannily, will mean he'll never have to write again.

Neither will Declan after the script I'm going to deliver.

I myself have no feelings about this Lamb cocksucker, one way or another. I approve of him, obviously, since he's (a) perpetually distracting himself from God, and (b) heading for Hollywood, where his dedication to making money and inflating his own ego will see him contributing productively to an industry that distracts *whole populations* from God. Other than that he's of no interest to me. There's no murder in him, and only a very predictable dribble of lust. His soul, and billions like it, provide the cosmos with its muzak.

Betsy and Tony looked up as Elspeth crashed into my heels then squeezed past me into the office.

'Declan,' Betsy said.

'I *told* him you were with someone, Betsy.'

'Declan, I'm . . . ah . . .' Betsy said – but I was already bored. Besides, this wasn't something Gunn wouldn't have done himself, on a good day. So I moved fast. Over to the couch, where I smiled, brightly, at Tony Lamb before grabbing him by his black lapels and yanking him to his feet.

'What the fuck –'

I looked at him. *I* looked at him, through Gunn. (Which is just as well, since Gunn's frightening look wouldn't frighten a callipered octogenarian.) I thought, briefly, about lifting him *off* his feet, but Gunn's equipment – the work-shy radials and biceps, the dole-hardened triceps and scrounging quads – really wasn't up to it. Amazing what I can put into a look, even through human eyes. Amazing how I can make you see all the time I've lived and you haven't.

'Your books are dogshit, Tony,' I said, very quietly, then waited just a moment before spinning and shoving him (I'm thinking: don't fuck it up, Luce; don't *trip*) violently towards the door. Elspeth, arms folded, hooked her midriff to one side as he went stumbling past to collide with the wheelie chair. Protracted clattering. He didn't utter a sound. I walked over to Elspeth, put my hand around the base of her neck and steered her to the door.

'Betsy I –'

'Shshsh,' I said. 'Go and help Tony pick himself up, there's a good girl. Do as you're told now, darling, or I'll break your moody little spine.'

She opened and closed her mouth a few times, staring straight ahead, but I got her through the door and closed it softly behind her. 'There,' I said to Betsy Galvez. 'That's better. Now we can talk.'

You've got to hand it to Betsy: grace under pressure. She sat back in her chair (already mentally composing the stunned and apologetic call to Tony Lamb: *He's been under a lot of stress . . . Truth is, I think the medication . . .*) and crossed her blue stockinged legs in a whisper of electrified nylon. The mannish hands (liver spots coming soon; already a phthisic look) came to rest together on the plump yam of her belly, and her head rested back so that she could regard me as if from a position of unruffled superiority. She's very good at pretending to be unruffled, is Betsy. She lets her mouth, that wry old orifice so charmingly radialled with its hundred fine lines, perform little smirky manoeuvres to show you she's well aware that this is all tremendously meaningless fun and that she's going along with it like an indulgent auntie. For all that, I knew she wasn't quite unruffled. A part of her saw this whole spectacle as confirmation that the business with *A Grace of Storms* had, as she'd suspected it might, sent Gunn completely off his rocker.

I rushed across the room, knelt before her and put my hands on her knees. The knees were the size of babies' skulls.

'You need to get one hand up to my chin, darling, if this is a Classically inspired entreaty,' she said. 'What on earth do you think you're playing at?'

I pushed my face into her lap and held it there for a moment. Delicious aroma: laundered wool, *Opium*, the noon tuna-salad, Laphroaig single malt, fagsmoke and ah, yes, surely a trace of Betsy's sly and seasoned vadge. I leaped to my feet, crossed the Persian rug and threw myself into the leather couch so lately and ingloriously vacated by Tony Lamb. Betsy – with more amdram suppression of girlish collusion – took a Dunhills from her silver case and lit up from a hideous malachite and gold desk lighter. I followed suit with a Silk Cut and a Swan Vesta.

'It's very simple, Betsy,' I said. 'It's really unbelievably simple. I wanted to see you, so here I am.'

Dunhill smoke exhaled nasally in twin plumes. Slow-blinking heavy-lidded eyes. 'Ah,' she said – gravelly monosyllable – 'A newly discovered allergy to the telephone?'

'A newly discovered knack for spontaneity.'

'And violence, apparently.'

I gave her a lickerish grin. 'A talentless cunt with a head like a dead lightbulb, and you know it.'

'Of course I know it, Declan. That doesn't give you the right to assault the poor chap. Besides, Villiers are going to cough up a quarter of a million for his next book if I've got anything to do with it.'

'Who said anything about rights,' I said. 'I want to come back over there and put my hand up your skirt.'

'Oh I shouldn't if I were you.' Deeply blushing throat despite the aplomb. 'Why don't you tell me what all this is in aid of, umm?'

I smoked for a couple of drags in silence. It felt remarkably pleasant to be sprawled in Betsy's couch, one leg hooked over the back, one arm trailing on the floor. The late afternoon light was fading and I knew that any moment Betsy would turn her desk lamp on (a charming art nouveau doodle in pewter with a green glass shade) creating a weird grotto of light around her heavy face. Our cigarette smoke hung in skeins above us. A Covent Garden audience stuttered into applause outside. Children cheered, tinnily. Betsy's dark wall clock clucked, softly, and I thought: I'll be sorry to leave all this behind.

'Betsy,' I said, then blew a succession of fat and shivering smoke rings. 'Betsy, I've got a book for you. It's not finished yet, but it very nearly is. I have absolutely no idea whether you'll like it, nor do I care. All I want you to do is get the fucking thing published.'

◆

'I wrote it because it just seemed really clear to me that this whole debate between men and women . . . the sex war, the politics of gender . . . that entire dialectic was starting to stagnate.'

Thus Gunn on *Bodies in Motion, Bodies at Rest*. I was there. (Yes, I was there. I'm everywhere, I am. Not *quite* omnipresent – but busy. Really *busy*.) 'There' was a flyblown and nicotine-coloured studio at Cult Radio. Gunn and Barry Rimmington, a moth-eaten and perennially soused jock so thin it looked as though he could barely support the weight of the headphones, who chain-smoked Rothmans and sat in the Joycean manner with legs not crossed but *plaited*, as if any looser posture would let his entire body unravel and fall apart.

'You know, it just struck me that for a lot of guys in my – well, not my generation . . . but my . . . *demographic* . . . that we're walking around with the sort of behavioural costumery of reconstructed men.' He was pleased with that phrase, having devised it on the train up from London. He left a pause after its delivery, in which he expected Barry to say something like, 'How d'you mean, exactly?' Unfortunately, Barry, lighting one Rothmans off another with all the alacrity of a doped slow loris, wasn't listening. (He'd had quite a few foul-ups on the air, had Barry, invariably as a result of letting his mind wander, having left the interview in the radically incapable hands of his professional autopilot. 'Margaret, you say you've always had this ambition. Tell me, have you always had this ambition?') So Gunn just went on: 'By which I mean that, I suppose, there's a number of men who've learned to speak feminist – we've read our Andrea Dworkin and our Germaine Greer and what have you, and we've got a handle on what's cool and what's not – but the question remains to what extent has the inner psychological mechanism actually changed? In other words, are we genuine? I wanted to write a novel that asked that question – of myself, naturally – I think it was Trollope who said that every writer is his own first reader – but also of men and women generally. That, at any rate was the starting point . . .'

Penelope stands with her arms elbow deep in Fairy Liquid bubbles. She's staring out of the window (grotty ground floor one-bedroom flat in Kilburn, but it's been the arena of their young love and therefore radiates an untranslatable beauty) into the haggard back garden with its rusted milk crate and neurotic tree. She had stopped to listen with a smile on her wide lips. Now she's just still. The bubbles proceed with their quiet, continuous bursting around her arms.

'So,' Declan says that night on the phone. 'Did you hear it?'

'Yes, I did.'

'And?'

'You sounded nervous.'

'I *was* nervous. You should've seen the fucking DJ. Looked like an imperfectly reanimated zombie.'

'Umm.'

'Are you all right?'

'What? Yeah, yeah. I've had bad guts all day, that's all. You all right?'

'Yeah. It's absurd, you know, you spend your entire life trying to get people to listen to you, then when it finally happens and someone shoves a microphone in front of you –'

'Gunn – ?'

'– you just end up speaking in platitudes – eh?'

'I've got something on the stove.'

'Oh. Okay. Are you sure you're all right, love?'

'Yeah, yeah I'm fine. Just. I should go and get this thing.'

'Okay. Go on then, I'll wait.'

'No I'll call you later. Is that all right? I'm just –'

'What?'

'I think I might need to go and have an enormous poo.'

'Oh, okay.'

'I'll call you later then. About eleven?'

'Okay. All right. I love you.'

'I love you, too, Deckalino.'

And she is dumb to tell the crooked rose (for there is one, pathetic and miraculous, crept through from next door's bush) how at her heart (oh you humans and your *hearts*) goes the sense, the certainty, that it's changed between them, been forked and twisted by the dishonesty of his radio voice. It's upon her, our Penelope, like the horror in the dream she's had now more than once that Gunn's asleep and snoring next to her, but when she shakes his shoulder and he turns towards her it's not him at all, but someone completely different – not a monster, nothing in itself terrifying – just . . . horribly . . . *not him* . . .

'Declan?'

'Umm?'

'Why did you say that on the radio?'

'Say what on the radio?'

A week later Penelope's got a horrible feeling of emptiness about this conversation. That all conclusions here are foregone.

'All that stuff about having a thematic agenda – wanting to ask yourself how much men in general had really changed?'

'I don't know what you mean. What do you mean?'

They're had in bed, of course, these conversations, under cover of darkness. That way you're spared seeing each other lying – as Declan is (can't quite recall who was working with him at that time . . . Asbeel, possibly . . .) in the matter of not knowing what she's talking about.

Penelope knows he's lying and she knows why he's lying. She jams her jaws together for a few moments, riding the wave of desperation, butching out the need to scream at him that he's changing and betraying her.

'Well, I was wondering, you see, because I remember that conversation we had about how much you thought it was bogus, all that talk about starting with a theme and then grafting a story onto it. You said it was pretentious revisionism, and that any writer being honest would admit that you start with a character, or a situation, or a place, or an event, or – I remember you said this, you see – even a snatch of overheard talk.'

'Hang on a –'

'You said it was all bullshit, and that if there really *was* a something there then it *would* be "about" something. But you said that to start with the "about" and try'n' get to the story was an invention of academic criticism.'

'Penelope, what on earth is all this about?'

'Whereas on the radio, you see, you said quite clearly that you started with a theme and then devised the story.'

'I didn't say that. Did I say that?'

'And I remember the conversation we had about this because you were so animated. We were sitting at a fucking plastic table with a lopsided sun-shade outside the cafeteria.'

'Penny, wait. Just –'

'And I remember, you were so excited, talking about it all. It was absolutely nothing to do with trying to impress me. I remember because it was then that I realised I was in –'

'Jesus Christ. Jesus *Christ*.'

'And how could you – how could you say that thing about Trollope?'

'What?'

'"I think it was Trollope who said that every writer is his own first reader."'

'Well, it was Trollope, wasn't it?'

'*You were trying to sound like a fucking writer.*'

Well. The magnitude of this utterance and the close-fitting silence it engenders surprises both of them. Doesn't sound like much of an accusation, does it? None the less, Gunn lies absolutely still, filled with either fire or ice, he can't tell which. Penelope lies on her back with all her limbs gone cold and dead.

This, though he doesn't know it, is the time for Gunn to turn to her and say: 'You're right. You're absolutely right. It was false, the product of ego and vanity and disgusting self-flattery and phoniness. I'm weak, that's all. I'll try to grow beyond it. Forgive me.' But he's so embarrassed and enraged that she's seen him, shown him himself from an angle he would always have ignored, he's so *unmanned* by this that he too lies prone and inert. Though he's lying next to her, he has the strangest feeling of the bed's sudden pitch and roll, an LSD-esque distortion of proximity which shows him Penelope receding over an infinitely expanding vastness of mattress to a point beyond reach or vision . . . He's thinking that there was, after all, a chance for him to have owned up, that even now, even as he falls away from her, from the possibility of love, thinking (without any desire to sound like a writer) that this is the way this is the way this is the way the fucking cunting bastard world ends . . .

◆

'Shouldn't you be out murdering people?'

'I beg your pardon?'

'If you're the Devil, I mean. Shouldn't you be a bit, you know, *busier*?'

'I am busy,' I said. It was three in the morning and I was with Harriet in the Rolls on our way from a very private party in Russell Square to a very private party in Mayfair. We passed a cinema hoarding that said *Little Voice*. I lit another Silk Cut. 'I *am* busy, for Heaven's sake. Have you any idea how much of the script I've already got down? That Pilate scene is going to have them dancing in the aisles.'

'What I mean is,' Harriet said, sipping, 'shouldn't you be a bit more *hands-on* in the criminal department? "A murderer from the first", or whatever, isn't it? I'd've thought New Scotland Yard's finest would've been picking their way through a litter of corpses by now.'

It's hard not to like Harriet. She's so bored and so mad and so bad. She's such a piece of *work*. It makes sense to like her, too: if you're alive in the Western world at the moment, something you buy probably puts money into Harriet's pocket, and there's no sense in putting money into the pockets of those you dislike, is there? Multinational Parent Companies (one of which boasts Harriet Marsh among its senior executives) were my invention. (But do you see me clamouring for credit for the idea? Do you hear me *boasting*?) The beauty of the concept is that it takes the wind out of so many would-be ethical sails: the company that owns the porn-mag owns the company that makes the washing powder. The company that owns the munitions plants owns the company that makes the budgerigar food. The company that owns the nuclear waste owns the company that picks up your trash. These days, thanks to me, unless you pack up and go and live in a cave, you're putting money into evil and shit. And let's be realistic, if the cost of ethics is life in a cave . . .

'I'll tell you something, Harriet,' I said, pouring myself another, 'I've always objected to that nonsense about me being a murderer. It's nothing but a bare-faced lie.'

'I think Jack's right, you know. You should have a show. *After* the film. After the Oscars.'

Little Voice, apparently, was on everywhere. I suppose He thinks that's funny. I suppose He thinks that's *droll*.

'". . . [A] murderer from the beginning . . ." says Jesus in John 8:44,' I said, topping up, as the National Gallery loomed up on our left. 'Moreover, a murderer who ". . . abode not in the truth, because there is no truth in him. When he speaketh a lie he speaketh of his own: for he is a liar, and the father of it." Charming. And, I might add, a pack of lies. Who, exactly, am I supposed to have murdered?'

Harriet, averting her cadaverous face so that her breath fogged the Rolls's tinted pane, undid my flies and groped, with a sigh of weariness, for my cock.

'Find me a stiff,' I said, '– ahem – just one, and you can have my hooves for paperweights. Talking someone *into* murder, obviously yes, absolutely, *mea culpa*, and so on – but it's hardly the same thing. (Talk a writer into a successful novel and see how far you get trying to pick up the royalties.) And if we're agreed I'm not a murderer, that makes Sonny a liar.'

'Doesn't seem to be working, darling,' Harriet said, abandoning my member with an abruptness a more sensitive soul might have found . . . well, a bit hurtful.

'The point here is that I've never murdered, nor manslaughtered, nor caused the death of by misadventure, anyone,' I said. 'Mind you. I've seen the state it puts humans into.'

Harriet pressed a stud in the door panel.

'M'am?'

'What?'

'You pressed the com. button, M'am.'

'Did I? Oh. Never mind. Switch it off permanently, will you.'

'Switching off, M'am. Rap on the glass if you need me.'

'Who is this guy?' I asked. 'Parker?'

'You were saying?'

'Was I?'

'The state. It puts humans into.'

Do you think this was ringing any bells for Harriet? Are you beginning to get an inkling of the lengths to which boredom drives the rich?

'I've seen the state it puts the murderer into often enough,' I said. I have, too. The singing blood, the hypersensitive flesh. I've seen wouldn't-hurt-a-fly faces transformed in the act; gone the dome-head and comb-over, the bi-focals and the overbite, the cowlick, the nose-hair, the sticking-out ears; here instead the rapt gargoyle, the beauty of ugliness, the ugliness of beauty, the breathtaking purity and singularity of the human being transported by crime. Dear old Cain, who really wouldn't have set hearts a-flutter in his unmurderous state, was a different proposition when his blood was up: all cheekbones and smouldering eyes. Kneeling over whacked Abel, a wind ruffled his dark hair (much in the way that strategically placed cooling fans unfurl the locks of on-stage rock stars) and his normally nondescript lips swelled to an engorged pout Sophia Loren would have envied. How like a god indeed. 'Call me an old flatterer,' I continued, 'but murder definitely looks good on you. Murder's got you written all over it. Humans, I mean. It really is the ultimate makeover. Elton *John* would look wildly sexy if he could just pluck up the nerve to off some poor bugger.'

It's all right, Harriet was thinking. *He's harmless. If he knew, he wouldn't go on like such an idiot.*

She kept her face averted, with no outward sign of anything but profound boredom. But then, I don't need outward signs. That's another of the perks of being me.

The Mayfair party (Rock Legend, formerly epicene guitar guru with whipcord body and waifish good looks, now resembling a troubled transsexual, with permanent mumps, Buddha gut, scorched hair and skin like congealed porridge) has turned out rather dull, and Harriet, myself, Jack, Lysette, Todd, Trent and a handful of other enervated revellers have retired with opium to one of the maestro's mock-Casablancan dens. The house is huge, naturally; a snip at eight-and-a-half, according to Harriet, who's thinking of making him an offer for it herself, should she ever encounter him in a state of sustained clear-headedness. Rooms and rooms and rooms, with, here and there, these windowless

136

smoke-nests, kitted out with all the trappings of Moorish indulgence. Everyone wants in on the film. Everyone wants to give us money. Even the multi-mill muso upstairs struggled out of his bulimia fever or coke-doze to offer us a stupid wedge. Harriet, among her many other talents (most of which were nurtured in her tender years by yours truly) certainly knows how to send hot gossip down wealth's healthy grapevine.

'I've racked my brains, but I don't know from what passing zephyr I plucked the Eight Out of Ten idea. As with all my previous inspired ideas, I knew it was a cracker.'

Yes, me holding forth again, I'm afraid, though my heart isn't really in it. I've got chronic gut-rot, to tell you the truth, and a slight but deeply *personal* headache behind my eyeballs. I've been feeling . . . off . . . ever since the journey in the Rolls with Harriet. Ever since . . . Well.

'Eight Out of Ten,' I continue, as something happens in Gunn's guts, some sour faecal fish does a somersault. 'A resonant proportion, verified, as I know you'll remember, by the long-running and highly successful Whiskas campaign. Eight out of every ten human beings, I thought. I'll settle for that. I'm not a perfectionist.'

They're not here for this, the Lucifer shtick; they're here for the clairvoyance, though they feign interest and chuckle in all the right places. I'm just about to pluck something from the privacy of the English poet sitting cross-legged in the room's darkest corner, when Gunn's partying bowels and quivering hoop send me an urgent neural telegram: Get to a john *now*, or forget socializing for the rest of the month. Original Apostate and Ruler of Hell you may be, Bub, but dump this load in your pants in public, and you're going straight off the A-list into celeb Coventry.

All that rich food, I'm thinking – much in the way you lot do, consigning all the fags, drink and drugs (not to mention quite a quantity of hygienically suspect XXX-Quisite rimming) to the irrelevance category. *Must be all that dreadfully rich food.*

'I'm terribly sorry,' I say. 'Would you excuse me for a moment? I'm afraid there's something . . . yes. I'll be back momentarily.'

'Oh God,' I hear Lysette say, as I exit, clutching my solar plexus, 'are we really being expected to talk amongst ourselves?'

It's touch and go, even then. Half-a-dozen broom closets and walk-in wardrobes later, at a point where my anus is engaged in some kind of voodoo salsa or go-go shimmy all of its own, I finally find a door that opens into the forgiving whites of a bathroom, where, after a much-haste-no-speed conflict with the suddenly arcane fastenings of my trousers, I launch myself at the crapper.

There's a good deal of ooohing and aaahing from me, not surprisingly, a good many cartoon faces. I discover cold sweats, tears, shivers, clenchings, and a vocal palette that might belong to a senile animal impersonator. Oh you'd be tickled pink if you saw me there on the can, puffing and blowing at both ends, the false finales, the triple-endings, the beatific relief cruelly betrayed by the bowels' wicked whimsy . . . Oh yes, I do look a sight, slumped like a depressed and molested orang – but that's not what I mind. I've signed on for that, I know. *Do unto your body as you would have your body do unto you.* Fair enough. No, what bothers me is the feeling of . . . I don't know . . . There's something, some nagging suspicion that I'm being watched, as, decently dressed once more I lean at the sink on the heels of my hands, peering with mischievous penitence at my mortal reflection in the Guitar God's mirror. *Maybe he's got closed circuit cameras in the joint*, I'm thinking, but even thinking it I know I'm having myself on. That's not the kind of Being Watched I'm talking about.

'You have of late – wherefore you know not . . .'

As I spin on my Guccis I'm almost sure I catch, peripherally, a quick shudder in the mirror's glass, a warp, a wobble, some bulge or bruise from a passing incorporeal presence.

The bathroom's empty, but for me and the olfactory fallout from my thermonuclear bum-blast. Call me overly imaginative, but I'm sure I hear the rustle of . . .

'That's very funny,' I say, aloud, returning to the mirror, the taps, the Camay. 'That is really, really hil-fucking-hairy-arse . . .'

The English poet (whose publishing house the Axe Wizard has just bought so that he, the Axe Wizard, can publish his, the Axe Wizard's, poetry – and may God have mercy on your souls) is troubled. He's troubled by the suspicion that he would do terrible things in certain hypothetical *carte blanche* situations.

'But if it's a choice between torturing some poor bastard because you're following orders,' Trent Bintock is saying as I return, 'I mean what if *you're* going to be tortured if you *don't* do it?' He gnashes his way through all this with relish and a brilliant smile. He's thinking it would make a better *dramatic dilemma* if it wasn't simply that you –

'No no,' the poet says. 'This is a situation where you're in control, totally. You *are* the camp commandant, you see.'

'But I wouldn't *be* the camp commandant,' Lysette says. She's not kidding and she's not lying, either. She'd be too busy managing the government's publicity. She'd be too busy securing political endorsements from attractive female tennis stars.

'But how can you say you'd never get to be camp commandant?' the generously smiling Trent wants to know, as the pipe comes his way. 'How can you be so sure?'

'Because I'd join whatever group was against the group that even *had* such things as camp commandants,' Jack interrupts, without a shred of honesty. 'Because I'd get out of the fucking *country*.'

I wouldn't, the internally honest English poet thinks, tossing back another vodka on the rocks, miserably.

'You're given *authority*, you see,' Todd Arbuthnot of the Washington connections says. 'If you're given the right framework . . . Authority from a higher power and a closed community within which to exercise it . . .'

'It's Milgram's electric shock test,' Jack says.

Trent Bintock, having just inhaled, massively, beams and tears noisily into a new pack of Marlboro Lights. 'Who's Milgram?' he says, in a helium-swallower's squeak.

'Back in the early sixties,' Todd picks up. 'In New Haven. Stanley Milgram ran an experiment designed to test human willingness to obey orders, even when those orders caused suffering to others.'

I don't know who this Milgram cunt is, the English poet is thinking, *but I know how I'd come out of his fucking experiment* . . .

I'm sitting quietly in the shadows through this, nursing not just my ravaged bowels and traumatized hoop, but my outraged sense of sportsmanship . . .

'So,' Todd Arbuthnot continues, 'the volunteers for the experiment are told by the "scientist", the guy in the white coat, that they're taking part in an experiment about learning. They're told that the "learner" next door is hooked up to electrodes, and that every time he gives a wrong answer to a question, the volunteer is to give him an electric shock by throwing a switch. Obviously, there's no actual electric shock – but this learner *acts* as if there is, every time the volunteer throws the switch.'

'What a disgusting experiment,' the poet says, on the edge of hysteria. 'What a *predictable* experiment.'

'So anyway,' Todd says (I rather like Todd's voice; it's dry, and calm, and oaky with ancient New England wealth), 'Naturally, some of the volunteers started to, you know, baulk, when they heard the learner next door protesting, kicking on the wall, demanding to be released, screaming . . . But the man in the white coat told them to continue, and most of them did. Thing is, you know, to give the shocks they had to pull the switch through a number of positions from 15 to 450 volts. These switch positions were marked like "slight shock", "moderate shock", "strong shock" and so on, all the way up to things like "intense shock", "extreme intensity shock", "danger: severe shock", and, finally, at 450 volts, the switch position was marked "XXX 450 volts". More than half the volunteers carried on all the way through the shock register.'

'Fuck,' Trent says, heartily enjoying all this, seeing, in fact, the whole thing unfolding dramatically, seeing the camera angles, the pull-backs, the close-ups. 'That's fucking scary, man.'

'What's worse,' says Todd, 'is that when they repeated the study at Princeton, they got a figure of eighty per cent total obedience from volunteers.'

'Eight out of ten,' the English poet, says, huskily – then, with a guilty eye-flash at Trent's fags – 'Could I have one of those?'

'Yeah but what's really cool?' Todd continues, with that American turn-a-statement-into-a-question intonation, 'Is that one guy in the experiment refused – point blank refused – to administer even the *first* shock. Just wouldn't do it.'

Bastard, the English poet is thinking. *Lucky bastard . . .*

'Sure,' Todd says. 'And do you know who that one guy was?' Everyone except me looks blank.

'Who?' Lysette Youngblood asks.

'Ron Ridenhour,' Harriet says, to my surprise. Hadn't realised she was historically clued-up. Presumably she optioned the rights to his story.

'Who the fuck is Ron Ridenhour?' Trent demands, with a stellar smile.

Todd and I smile at each other through the gloom, as if Ron Ridenhour might be our son. 'He's the guy who later blew the lid on the My Lai massacre in Nam,' Todd says. 'Without him there's a good chance the whole thing would've been covered up for ever.'

'Still,' Trent says – and I know that through the opium he's thinking about getting My Lai into the script, some flash-forward, some satanic prophecy – 'eighty per cent's pretty fucking depressing, right? I mean that's only two out of ten good guys, right?'

'There's ten of us here,' Jack points out. 'Who's who? Who here knows they'd be in the ethical twenty per cent? Let's take a secret ballot!'

Oh yes, the English poet is thinking, *yes let's. What a brilliant fucking idea . . .*

I never believed I'd get anywhere near eighty per cent. Nothing like. Of course it tripped off the tongue in Hell, of course it *sounded* fantastic – 'Eight out of every ten. Do you hear me? I accept no less. We must work in the garden, my dears, we must work *hard* in the garden . . .' but the truth is I'd've settled for fifty per cent. Hell I'd've been happy enough with *twenty*. That, actually, was my real number, twenty per cent. Two out of every ten. Would've been enough to get the Old Man's goat. He must be positively cheesed off with today's numbers. Serves him right. It's His own fault. Oh yes. Those Commandments. How *about* those Commandments, though, eh? *Thou shalt honour thy father and mother.* Er . . . ee*yah. Thou shalt not covet thy neighbour's wife.* Excuse me – have you *seen* my neighbour's wife? *Thou shalt love thy neighbour as thyself* . . . I remember thinking even at the time, He's not serious. He can't, surely, be serious. *Thou shalt not kill.* (If only you'd kept that one! The Crucifixion – the entire New Covenant would have been impossible! All my work would've been done for me.) *Thou shalt not bear false witness.* Oh stop, I thought, you're killing me. Thing was: nobody was actually going to Heaven.

I remember St Peter getting his new uniform and ticket-punch. Time passed. He wished he'd brought a magazine. The turnstile booth grew . . . *oppressively familiar.* Whereas we were taking on extra staff downstairs. Every day a gala day. I was down to a three-and-a-half-hour week. Spent the rest of my time lying in a hot hammock and dabbing away tears of mirth.

I sent Him a telegram. *Far be it from me to tell You Your Own business and all that, but* . . . Stony silence. Still no sense of humour. On the other hand, it wasn't long after that regrettably indulgent quip that I noticed the goalposts were on the move. Without so much as a nod or a wink. It was the coveters first, peeling off to Purgatory when they should have been hurtling straight down to us. Then every other one-theft-only thief. The odd regretful adulterer. Whole generations with a beef against Mum and Dad. Hang on a minute, I thought. This is a bit . . . I mean you can't just suddenly . . . Oh but He could. And did. *Dear Lucifer,* He should have replied, *thanks so much for your helpful suggestions* . . . I could have respected that. But no, not a word. And it's me who's the petulant one.

Similar chestnuts come up, now and again, *après déjeuner* in Hell. You know the setting: belts loosened, brains on the cusp of drunkenness, hash-smoke genie presiding, the air wreathed in the scent of port and brandy, an expansiveness of body, a provocatively meandering mind or two . . . 'What *is* the greatest evil?' someone will say. Thammuz, usually, who's of an infuriatingly reflective bent, or Asbeel, who just loves to argue. They're so hung up on torture, you know? On creating individual instances of despair. I tell them – eventually, after they've prattled for hours of thumbscrews, hot boots and racks – I tell them that what we need is *Systems*. Without Systems, without Seeing the Big Picture, without setting up a machine that runs itself, our work is mere vandalism.

Take torture, for example. What do you want from torture? You want the suffering of the victim, obviously, the bouquet of fear, the *parfum* of pain; you want the gradual revelation of the body's thraldom to physics, the careful journey back to the flesh's sovereignty over the spirit. You want his appalled grasp of the inescapable ratio: your motivation is pleasure; your pleasure increases proportional to his suffering; your capacity for pleasure exceeds his capacity for suffering; no amount of his suffering, therefore, is ever going to be sufficient. (What kills me about torture is how long it takes the victim to understand the impossibility of transaction. There's nothing the torturer *wants* from him except his suffering. Yet on and on the victim blabs and whimpers, naming names, offering up secrets, promises, bribes. Language compels him – if he has it at his disposal, if his tongue hasn't already been snipped or broiled – to persist in the belief that it can help him. The victim's voluntary retreat into silence, barring screams and moans, is always a sign that he's made the shift, fully realised his situation, *got it*.) You want, too, his degradation in his own eyes; you want him to observe the dismantling of his own personhood, his astonished shift from subject to object. It's why the classier torturers force their victims into a relationship with the instruments of torture before those instruments have been torturously employed: the whip is drawn caressingly over the shoulder or loins; the rods and prods, the ferruled canes, the probes, the nightsticks, the crops – must be kissed, fondled, or otherwise venerated by the torturee, as if they themselves are sentient subjects while he is a mere object of their intention. You want him to see that in the universe you now control, in *your* universe, all prior hierarchies are void.

Sooner or later (you humans can't help it, it's the way you're made) this leads to despair. The victim's despair. The torturee's preference, after a certain point has been perspiringly passed, for death over life. The impossible ideal for the torturer, of course, is that the victim remains alive in this state of craving-but-not-being-given death *forever*. We don't call it an impossible ideal in Hell. We call it routine.

Yes yes yes, despair is good, and torture a sure-fire way of bringing it out – but I have to keep reminding them – the boozers are nodding off by this point, the dullards daydreaming or picking their teeth – that flavoursome though these prison cell episodes may be, the real prize is in achieving a state where despair can flourish with barely any interference from us, when they do it to and for themselves, when that's the way the world is.

Uffenstadt, Neiderbergen, Germany, 1567. Marta Holtz stands naked and shivering in the village church. She's beginning to have an idea of why Bertolt has accused her. The Inquisitors – three Franciscans led by Abbot Thomas of Regensberg – are seated in a rough semi-circle of mahogany high chairs between the altar rail and the first pew. A brazier burns with occasional pops and snaps, tinting the rough carvings with petals of orange light. Jimbo's crucifixion to the left of the altar releases a pterodactyl of shadow, and there's a compact and vivid eruption of daffodils from the vase at the Virgin's feet. The smell (I imagine) is of incense and chilled stone. The first pew used to be the fourth; the brothers have had three pews removed to make room. Marta, who isn't stupid (that's one of the reasons she's here), has more than an inkling of what they might need room for. This more than an inkling began life in her feet and knees, but soon scurried up into her loins and belly, thence ribs, breasts, throat and face. Now this more than an inkling is all over her like a host of hairy spiders. She's beginning to have the idea that Bertolt accused her because that is his job. Bertolt came to Uffenstadt three months ago. She's barely had any dealings with him. Once, he helped her catch a piglet that had got loose. Another time she gave him a taste of the damson cake she had baked for her sister's birthday. On neither of these occasions did she have the slightest sense that he had any feelings about her beyond the one shared by most of the men in the village: that she was a desirable woman and that Günter Holtz was a lucky sonofabitch. (At this moment – this moment of Marta's realisation that Bertolt works for the Franciscans, and that with the first three pews removed there will be plenty of room for the good Fathers' manoeuvres – Günter is being informed by the Regensberg accountant that should Marta be found guilty of witchcraft her execution will be followed by Church confiscation of any property belonging – even jointly or by virtue of marriage – to her, not to mention an itemized bill – implements, fuel, labour – for the cost of the interrogation. At this moment Günter is looking at the accountant's broad and porous face and wondering how its cheek came by those three silver scars like fishbones. He's thinking, too, of Marta's pale and downy midriff, of her sloe eyes and oddly deep voice, of her habit of making him laugh at his own struggle to be a manly man, of the small mole at the back of her left knee, of her wheaty breath when she comes, of the pear-sized baby in her thickened womb. He's thinking that he'll kill this accountant, no matter what. The accountant and Bertolt. With the heavy scythe. Bertolt first. He's thinking these and many other things, none of which is of any use to Marta, who having been clumsily shaved by Brother Clement, is now being hand-examined by the trio, who bring to bear a predictably excessive investigative zeal when it comes to her vagina, breasts and anus.) Marta – who, somewhere beneath all this, is trying to single out a jewel of memory to take to her grave, something of hers and Günter's, like the warm night in summer they swam and made love in the Donau, skimmed by ghostly fish and over-arched by fierce constellations – has never met a Pope. She's never heard of Pope Pious XXII, who, nudged in the small and heartburning hours by yours truly, granted formal power to the Inquisition back in 1320. She's never heard of Pope Nicholas V, who, 130 years later, extended its authority, nor of Pope Innocent (don't you love these names? Pious? Innocent?) VIII, whose Bull, which I might as well have *dictated*, commanded secular authorities to co-operate fully with Inquisitors and to cede judiciary and executive powers in matters pertaining to heresy and witchcraft. Marta's never heard of any of these good prelates, nor of Bulls (except the ones that cover cows, precariously, standing on their little back legs) nor, indeed, of theology. Marta, as a matter of fact, can't read or write. (Neither can Günter, for the record.) She has absolutely no idea that the coals in the brazier, the branding irons, the thumbscrews, the lances, the cat o'nine tails, the bullwhip, the hammers, the pliers, the nails, the ropes, the hot chair, the manacles, the knives, the hatchet, the skewers – she has absolutely no idea that her impending relationship with these items has been facilitated by Vatican scribes and a string of Popes, some shrewd, some spooked, all quick to catch on to the remunerative potential of witch-hunting. Marta has never heard of Brothers Sprenger and Kramer, my star students among the German Dominicans, whose labour of love, the *Malleus Maleficarum* published eighty-one years earlier, drew a minutely detailed diagram of how to detect, interrogate and execute nubiles deemed suspect. She's never been to a Sabbat, nor signed in blood, nor sacrificed babies, nor delivered the acolyte's 'infamous kiss' (the tonguing, thank you my dear, of His Satanic Majesty's slack and gamy butthole), nor flown on a broomstick, nor – I'm sorry to say – copulated with me or any of my hircine proxies. Truly, Marta's venials make a paltry list: stole an orange; wished Frau Grippel would get a fever; called Helga a farting sow; sucked Günter's cock (and a formidable *bratwurst* it is, I can tell you); admired the beauty of my arms in the Donau; thought I'm the prettiest girl in Uffenstadt.

No, Marta's been a good girl. God really should be taking better care of her. But, as is the way of it with Creators who move in mysterious ways, He isn't.

Any other time and any other place Marta would draw closer to the brazier for warmth. This time and this place she's keeping all the distance she can. The idiocy of the question is bald, even to an illiterate farmer's wife. *Do you believe in witchcraft?* No, and you contradict Church doctrine; yes, and you're virtually confessing to occult knowledge at the get-go. *How long have you been in the service of Satan?* I'm not in the service of Satan. *How did you make your pact with him?* I have no pact. *Is your unborn sired by a demon?* No, by my husband. *What is the name of the demon with whom you copulated?* No demon, sir. *Were you sodomized by this demon as well as impregnated?*

Abbot Thomas, fifty-eight, tonsured and corpulent with eyes the colour of conkers and a ferociously irritable bowel, would rather Brothers Clement and Martin weren't here. He has a fiery mind, does Thomas, liable to burst into outraged combustion at the slightest provocation. Marta, naked, shaved, innocent of all charges, already constitutes more than slight provocation. The *thought* of Marta (or Wilhomena, or Inge, or Elise or whoever), which is perpetual in the hot pudding of his brain, is perennial provocation. He's a beautifully divided being, Thomas. A great, sane part of him knows that the girls are tortured and slaughtered for his pleasure and profit. A great and sane part of him knows this. But another part of him demands moral justification. Demands it loudly. *Bellows* for it. This ignites the fiery mind. (You've phoned in sick, haven't you? Nothing wrong with you of course. Just can't Face It today. You've prepared the husky speech, the wobbly or frustrated diagnosis – *bloody* flu – and damn you if by the time you've hung up you're not sure you haven't *got* the flu. Humans: need a lie desperately enough and you can take *yourself* in. Ditto with Abbot Thomas. The blades slide under the fingernails and the wretches' confessions come pouring out. *My God I was right! Infernal bitch! You dared deceive God's holy minister? Thank Heaven I held to the odious task!*)

The Pricker is called in to search for the witch's mark.

Third nipple, scar, mole, pimple, freckle, wen, wart, birth-mark, scratch, scab – pretty much anything in the blemish family qualifies. The Pricker – crew-cut, long-faced, missing an eye – who'll be well paid should he successfully detect a sign of witchhood (100 per cent success rate so far) spends a good deal of time examining Marta's clitoris, which he's not sure isn't large enough to be unmasked as the witch's teat, before noticing with relief the mole behind her left knee. ('I make this mine,' Günter had said to her, kissing it, on their wedding night. 'And this, and this, and this . . .') He turns her over on her belly the better to see while I drop my flakes of flame onto the clerical genitals and Franciscan lust fills the ether like the odour of sweet and sour pork. The Pricker reaches into his pocket and takes out a greasy leather wallet. Marta's tears (*I don't think there can be a God . . . If there's a God, how is it that –*) wet the stone floor. The pterodactyl shadow shudders, seems to elongate, then subsides. From the wallet the Pricker removes one of several bright needles of various lengths and girths. He turns his back to the now hot-faced Brothers, brings the needle close to the mole, does nothing for a moment, then turns. 'My lords. It is my sad duty to report that this woman is beyond doubt a witch. I pricked this mark behind her knee and yet as your own ears will attest she made not the slightest sound.' He hadn't had to think about it. Long experience – that is to say years of pricking – had taught him which blots were insensible and which receptive. This wretched girl was practically alight with sensitivity. Prick her anywhere and she'd yowl the roof down. Therefore the report of pricking instead. He went in more and more for the reporting of successfully carried-out prickings rather than actual prickings themselves these days. The going rate was the same either way.

You'll excuse me if I don't dwell. The same questions, this

time with torturous inducements to answer differently. For two minutes and eight seconds Marta holds out. There are precisely two minutes eight seconds' worth of faith in her tank. But, understandably, after they've broken the second finger and the crucified Christ has shown no sign of super-heroically coming down to her rescue, nor the Virgin of surrounding her with an impenetrable corona of maternal protection, Marta starts to blab. Not that that helps, since the Inquisitors' agenda has nothing to do with her admission of guilt. The two younger Brothers, Clement and Martin, know it's me. They know, deep down, it can't *really* be God's work to tear off a woman's nipple with pincers. They know it's me – but to Hell with it anyway, since it feels better than anything they've felt before, since there's nothing, *nothing* like it on earth (nor, they'll wager later, over the rough local wine and peppered fish, in Heaven, either). Abbot Thomas, on the other hand, manages on and off to wrap mutilations in psalms. There are flashes of *doing God's will* like patches of blue in an otherwise dirty and flocculent sky. He can't quite give himself over to the truth of himself, and his absurd oscillation between bloodlust and bogus rationalization is piquant to me, vastly to be preferred over Clement and Martin's white bread surrender.

You might wonder, by the way, what God and the angelic host in Heaven are doing while all this is going on. Wonder no more. I, Lucifer, can tell you. Nothing. They're doing nothing. They're watching. The infinitely merciful part of His nature swallows a sob or two, it's true, but the infinitely indifferent part keeps its gaze steady. There is a tradition, established by those blathering early martyrs and all but vanished in modern times, of offering one's suffering up to God. The winkled out eyeball, the screwed thumb, the plucked tongue and toasted bot – the right disposition can lift them from the body and send them floating up to God like exquisite perfumes. The Divine nostrils inhale them and sweet indeed is their odour. (You might think there's something obscene about it, but it will get you into Heaven.) So should you find yourself under vexatious interrogation one day, offer your shocked bollocks up to God. Next time your hole's rudely invaded by a red hot poker lift your eyes to Heaven and say: 'This one's for you, my Lord.'

Marta, I'm sorry to say, isn't offering her sufferings up to God. Marta's providing her Franciscan hosts with confirmation that the other names they have on their list (Bertolt's list, complete with colour of hair, age, vital statistics, and likelihood of intact maidenheads) are those of her sisters in witchcraft. You should hear her description – or rather her endorsement of *their* description – of the Sabbat. Christ, I wish *I'd* been there. Butchered babies, bestiality, coprophilia, necrophilia, paedophilia, incest (Abbot Thomas is looking forward to interviewing those twin Schelling sisters), sodomy, desecration of holy objects, blasphemy – a five-star knees-up if ever there was one. When this confession is read out publicly in three days' time the good people of Uffenstadt are going to see Marta in a whole new light. (It's going to put some pep back into stagnant boudoirs, too, so that's nice.) In three days' time, Marta, or what's left of her, will state that this is her true confession, given freely, without compulsion of any kind (else there'll be compulsion all over again, of a by now familiar kind) shortly before they march her up to the stake. Günter, restrained by civic officers, will watch, screaming, while they cut open his wife's womb and rip out the foetus – redundantly, since mum's going up in smoke anyway – to keep the mob happy and their crowd-pulling clout intact.

This is a Big Picture operation. Three hundred years,

quarter of a million dead, all in God's name. After about 1400 I barely needed to put in an appearance. The System was up and running. Everybody (apart from the innocent victims) won. The sadists got a piece of ass, the Church increased its loyalty to Mammon, the liars got paid for their lies, taverns groaned under the weight of drawn crowds, and the mob – the name-and-shame mob basked in righteous relief that it was *her* (bloody witch) and not them. Tell me that wasn't an achievement. Not a patch on what I was warming up to, but you know . . . *promising*. I really think God was annoyed with me. What with it being His Church and all.

There. I've dwelt, in spite of myself.

◆

At a party to celebrate the paperback release of *Bodies in Motion, Bodies at Rest*, Penelope stands in the shadows with her arms folded. She's not drunk, not *reeling* drunk, but she is blessed now whether she wills it or no with that grim, fifth-glass perspicacity. Nor is she deliberately not adding her own contribution to the applause for Gunn as he makes his way to the tiny, elevated stage with its lone reader's microphone; it's just that her entire consciousness is given over to watching him, the length of his stride, the tilt of his shoulders, the pulled-in corners of his deeply satisfied mouth. She's watching, standing with her weight on one leg and her left hand cradling glass six at an about-to-spill angle, while Gunn does his best, through gesture, movement, and facial expression, to appear exactly as he is not: unprepared, bemused by the attention, shy of the limelight, and inca-pable, actually, of taking any of this nonsense seriously. There has been a flattering introduction from Sylvia Brawne, his editor, to which Gunn has listened with his head down and his eyes glued to the floor, as if – Penelope knows – he is hiding chronic blushing. Then the applause, his *faux* exasperation at the ridiculousness of Sylvia's hyperbole, and the back-slapped, Christ-how-embarrassing-but-let's-just-get-it-over-with journey to the stage.

I'm there. I'm always there. Well, invariably. Not *specifically* for Gunn – there are other works-in-progress at the club: first-time smack for the eighteen-year-old rent boy in the bogs; the HIV transmission a philandering journalist is going to take home to his missus (who's at her wits' end already, and who stands a good chance of forgetting her pill tonight – having softened the blues with Dusty Springfield, a joint and a bottle of Bull's Blood); the waitress who knows that if she goes home with the guy in the muslin-coloured suit it'll be her first trick, that she'll have capitulated, made use of what she can make use of (but Elise has done it, I keep reminding her, and says she's never looked back – the holiday in Antigua, the two-bedroomed garden flat in West Hampstead, the money, the money, the *fucking money she's sick of pretending she doesn't want . . .*); the dear, muddled, bull-necked and swede-headed bouncer, who, as far as the rest of the world knows, is single, but who in fact has an imprisoned anorexic wife whose mere existence – plus her inability to quite absorb all his fear and rage no matter how many times he beats it into her – drives him like a disease into sudden, focused strikes, while the horror and claustrophobia and hatred and rage clash like warring gods in his skull, until he's spent, and falls to his knees babbling apologies and promises between sobs (it's limitless, his pity, as long as he himself is its object: *Why does she make me do this to her? Why? Why? Why?*) – so Gunn was hardly my priority. But I've tended, over the years, to keep an eye on

Penelope, to rootle, now and again, through the clutter of her life in the hope of being able to throw something together. Never say die, that's my motto. And never throw anything away, that's another. Honestly, I'm like a womble, I am. Anyway, here is Penelope, and there, on stage, is Gunn. *Are you going to say anything?* Penelope's asked him, earlier. *No,* he's said. *It's all bollocks. I'll just read and get out of there.*

'You always hope,' he begins, trying to find that elusive middle air between the devil of over-orchestrated diction and the deep blue sea of his childhood's dusted-down Northern vowels, 'that the person who introduces you won't make you sound overly intelligent or talented.' Pause. It's a small audience, politically hand-picked by him and Sylvia. 'Otherwise the reading's guaranteed to disappoint.' Some friendly titters. Penelope grinds her teeth. Gunn is speaking in a voice she's never heard before. Accent, depth, pace: none of them has hitherto belonged to the man she loves. Loved. Loves. (Who said 'loved'?) Nor, for that matter, have the occasional grimaces of wry self-effacement. 'Unfortunately,' Gunn continues, 'Sylvia has rather foolishly made me sound both intelligent and talented. Therefore my apologies in advance.' Polite laughter, the general *mnwoaaah* sound of an audience saying, *Oh don't be so amusingly modest, you old thing.* 'Anyway,' Gunn says, taking a calculated last drag on his Silk Cut and stubbing it out on the boards, 'I thought I'd read the beginning of the book, so's not to give the game away to any of you rotters who've had the good sense not to bother reading it yet . . .'

One is tempted to conclude that there's something genetic in Penelope's acute allergy to dishonesty, something deep, something *structural*. I'd prefer to be able to explain it away by telling a tale of a disappearing dad or a compulsively fibbing first love – but I can't. Penelope is simply one of those human beings for whom dishonesty destroys everything.

And here at this insufferably pleased with itself and over-priced club in Notting Hill, dishonesty is much on her mind, as she observes Gunn at the centre of a small group of sycophantically tittering industry girls. Oh it's not as if he's feeling them up or anything (I keep *telling* him: feel them up, for Christ's sake *feel them up*); but his vanity shimmers all but luminously around him. Again she sees the unrecognizable body language, the overacting, the disingenuous well-it's-a-job-ness of his pose. Passing, secretly, at his back, she hears him address one of the girls as 'my dear'; it would be innocent if it weren't for how clearly she could see what he was doing with it, namely, connoting (however subtly – and obviously not too subtly for the smirking blonde with her dark-rimmed specs and piled giggle of hair) the priapic-artist-to-nubile-muse relationship, which would be tired even were he thirty years the girl's senior, but which, given that she looks more or less his age, is both ludicrous and nau-seating.

It's not jealousy. If only it *was*. No. It's just a terrible, near-annihilating feeling of threadbare disappointment. All the hours and years. His hand in the small of her back. *Be true to me*, she's said, unashamed of the antique idiom, because she's known he understands. *You will stay true to me, Young Gunn, won't you?*

Meanwhile Gunn is confounding me with the firmness of his resolve: *You will not do anything.* He keeps affirming, watching the light on her lipstick and the little corkscrewy bits of her pinned-up hair as they jiggle and bounce around her face. *You are flattered. She's pretty (but stupid) and you're now almost certain that you could have her if you wanted to – but you* WILL NOT DO ANYTHING – **DO YOU UNDER-STAND?**

Much to my chagrin (blocked temptation's like chronic constipation; not Satanic Rap – just the truth) he *does* understand, or so it seems. He extricates himself – *No, honestly, I cried*, blondie has tinnily confessed, *just cried my eyes out on that last page* – and heads for the gents. He knows he's neglected Penelope. Glimpses of her on the periphery with unblinking eyes and the corners of her mouth gone trouble-coming tight. Why did he let himself drink so much? Why, in God's name, has he just spent forty minutes so obviously flirting with Aurora? *Nice tits, though*, I per-suade him to acknowledge at the urinal, where, in a surfeit of self-satisfaction ('. . .the poetic beauty of his imagina-tion . . .' *Times Metro* – cheers!), merely pissing in a straight line strikes him as a niggardly or unimaginative activity, and he begins slashing with a swing to his hips, accompanied by his own surprisingly tuneful version of James Brown's 'I Feel Good', a performance short-sightedly premised on the notion that he's alone in there (apart from me, obvi-ously), shattered in mid soul-brother screech by the appearance of the literary editor of the *Independent*, who, not surprisingly, gives him a pained smile before hurrying out.

And just when you think it's hopeless, just when a lesser angelic rapscallion would have called it a night (the rent-boy's rolled-up sleeve, the journo's husky mobile call in the purple foyer, the waitress's successful rationalization, the bouncer's stirred hunger and gnawing fear – all in the bank), a way through the darkness opens as Aurora's fifth gin and tonic passes her tonsils and sends its alcohol by express bloodstream delivery to her noisy and irritable brain. Well, I only need a sniff. *Go on, I dare you. You know he fancies you.*

Not that you can blame him, because you do look the fucking business *in that dress, babe. 'You look like Nicole Kidman' he said.* (He did, too. Believes the non-sequiturial delivery of such judgements part of his newly acquired status as an artist.) *Bernice said his girlfriend's here. Fuck it. Go on – I dare you. Make a night of it.*

Amazing thing is – Gunn stumbles out of the Gents only to find Aurora awaiting him on the landing, barely has time to check his flies before she sweeps up to him, takes his surprised face in her white hands, and kisses him, softly on the mouth – amazing thing is that sheer *luck* has Penelope spot them on her own (arrested, obviously) way to the loo. I can't take any credit for that. That – long live the angles of chance – is absolutely nothing to do with me. She stops and stares. They don't see her and she doesn't hear them. *Thank you very much,* Gunn is saying, holding Aurora by the elbows, *but I can't do this, I'm afraid. I've got a girlfriend. You're very attractive, though. I'm really flattered. Sorry. And you really do look like Nicole Kidman.*

But, Hell be praised, Penelope can't lip-read. *We need to meet somewhere,* she supposes he's saying. *Fucking girlfriend's here. Give me your address.*

'Tell Declan I've gone home, will you?' she says to Sylvia. 'I've got a stinking headache and I don't want to spoil his fun.'

Which is where I go to work. By getting her to punish God by degrading herself. Convoluted? No no no no *heavens* no. How many of you haven't heard that voice, the no-nonsense, call-a-spade-a-spade friend who emerges when the world's shat on you? *So, this is how much He cares about you, is it? Cares about you enough to let you fail fucking Human Biology/drop the mortgage/lose a leg/miss the bus/stub your toe/get the sack/crack your tooth/fluff your line/get to the booth only to discover that the bastard in front of you got the last ticket . . . That's how much He cares. Yes. Well. Fuck You, God. Two can play at that game. Watch* THIS. And off you go to the tobacconist's, or the boozer, or the Adult Video retailer, or the knocking shop, or the casino. *Look at your precious creation now, Mister. Don't like it, do you, taking a bit of your own medicine. And if I get lung cancer, or liver failure, or fucking AIDS, Matey, we know whose fault it'll be, don't we, eh? Should've thought of that when you let Claire* FINISH WITH ME!

Penelope's is a secular version, more or less. So I don't speak to her of God or the friability of His love, but rather of the long, grinding, endless punishment the world dishes out if you try to live in accordance with truth and decency. I speak to her, bitterly, of how daily she struggles with the idea that her stand is hopeless, that everything turns to shit in the end, that evil invariably wins, that people . . . people aren't any damned *good*, that her own horror of falsehood is nothing more than a pitiful delusion of grandeur, and that the best thing she can do now is give herself a good, strong, vinegared slap in the face . . .

She resists for quite some time. Had I not been around so long – so *very* long – it would astonish me, somewhat, the strength of her resistance. It doesn't, however. In boredom, I persist. Time for Bad Cop. *You fucking stupid bitch. You knew, didn't you, it'd come to this. There's shit everywhere, it's all shit, you pathetic, deluded idiot. Get down on your hands and knees and rub your stupid, trusting, high and fucking mighty face in it . . . Go on. There's medicine!* Until, with what feels like an icy fracture down the centre of her chest, knowing full well and having no clue about what she's going to do, she halts the cab at the bar that's just opened not three blocks from the flat she shares with Declan Gunn. I remember my last words to her. Not the first time I've used them. And certainly not the last. I gave them to her in a long, slow whisper. *Embrace it . . .*

◆

I've heard some theological guff in my time, but one of the most idiotic theories I've ever come across is the one suggesting that I possessed Judas Iscariot in order to bring about Jimmeny's betrayal. Can anyone explain this to me? Actually don't bother. I know the explanation. (I know *all* the explanations.) The explanation is that millions of people all over the world, despite being in full possession of a functioning cerebrum, think I wanted Christ crucified. Now if you'll allow me to be blunt for a moment: Are these people *retarded?* Christ's crucifixion was the fulfilment of the Old Testament's prophecies. Christ's crucifixion was going to restart the mechanism for the forgiveness of sins. Which would mean? *No one has to go to Hell.*

So, could you please tell me why I would do anything to help bring that about?

I was, however, at the Last Supper. Thirteen guys in sour-leathered sandals, all with tropical underarms and honking butt-cracks; a tiny room (Leonardo's way off), poor ventilation, the smoke of badly trimmed lamps, the odd discreet but sulphurous apostolic brap, the tang of burped plonk . . . You know what I spent the evening doing? I spent it loading Judas with guilt. *You miserable bastard. You know you're doing the wrong thing. Thirty fucking pieces of silver? You cheap sonofabitch. Don't do it, man. Listen to me. Listen to the voice of your conscience! The Enemy has led you astray but it's not too late to change your mind and save your soul. Listen to the voice of God, Judas Iscariot. This is a mighty hour for you. You're on the verge of consigning yourself to Hell for eternity – and for what? Thirty fucking pieces of silver! Don't do it, Judas!*

The man was made of stone. Hanging was too good for him if you ask me. Actually that's not fair. Not fair to give Judas credit for his own resistance, I mean. It was, as in the desert, the Old Bugger's hand at work. *God hardened Pharaoh's heart* . . . Yes, He did (He's hardened a lot of hearts over the years) and He hardened Judas's, too.

In spite of all that, in spite of the unfair nature of the fight, in spite of His *cheating*, I almost nailed the fucker (pardon the pun) with Pilate and Procula.

What I have written, I have written. My general disappointment in Judea's then governor notwithstanding, I've long had an aesthetic soft spot for the poised ambivalence of his infamous dictum. The lonely pregnancy of the pause, its shadowy implications: What I have written is not what I wanted to write. What I have written is the truth. What I have written is what I shall be judged by. What I have written seemed to write itself. What I have written was not for me to write . . . *Quad scripsi, scripsi.* The tautological conclusion with its gravitas and idiocy. He wrote it at the end of a morning the length and drain of which couldn't be measured in hours. He'd been abused by forces beyond his control, boxed and flirted with as if by fevers and flues. His thigh-bones had felt thin, his ankles weak, his flesh hot and cold, as if embraced and abandoned by a sodden shroud in the heat of the sun. His blood whistled and thumped; deafness descended, periodically, leaving him only the sound of the heart in his chest; his vision seemed to narrow into a dark tunnel, haunted at its distant end by incandescent spirits. I didn't give him up without a fight, I can tell you.

Pilate's side of the bed was long cold by the time Claudia

Procula woke with electric suddenness, sheened in sweat, sitting bolt upright and astonished that the loud lamentations on the other side of sleep translated to mere whimpering in the waking world. She wasn't bad looking, Pilate's missus, and became increasingly appealing in somnambulistic agitation, but that really *isn't* relevant, *at all*, Lucifer. What's relevant is that Pilate trusted her dreams. He wasn't overly superstitious (although you wouldn't find many military men who didn't at the very least go through the motions of pagan propitiation), but his wife's dream-inspired prognostications had several times proved useful, and had once literally saved his neck, back in Rome not long after their marriage, when she'd dissuaded him on the strength of a nightmare from keeping a horse he'd bought for recreational riding, which beast a week later threw and broke the neck of its next owner. She'd never actually seen Jesus, though she'd heard of him, and, via slaves' gossip the night before, of his arrest and detention in the hands of Caiaphas & Co. She'd never actually set her dark eyes on him, so I'm not altogether sure why I bothered impersonating him so carefully in her dream; I could have appeared to her as Groucho Marx and she'd have been none the wiser. But I'd be fibbing if I didn't admit that there was a profane titillation in taking on his looks and mien. Made me feel . . . I'm almost embarrassed to say . . . You know: what *might* have been. Anyway. I entered the tapestry of Procula's sleep and crucified myself in her dream. It was funny, hanging there in her mind with the stigmata flowering and the sky darkening at my back. I worried that I'd overdone it with the blood – her and her husband mired and flailing, shin-deep and red-handed – but time (New Time) was passing (Caiaphas's envy glowed around him like baby's breath while the real J.C. stood barefoot with his head on one side and an infuriating patience in the stilled line of his mouth) and I wanted the message writ large, so to speak: PILATE & WIFE MURDER INNOCENT MAN – 'WE'LL BURN IN HELL FOR THIS' GOVERNOR ADMITS. In any case it had done the trick. The legs kicked, the neatly plucked eyebrows drew down (one *grave*, one acute), the plum-coloured lips twitched and pursed, the perspiring palms opened and closed. *Have nothing to do with this innocent man . . . Have nothing to do with this innocent man . . . Have nothing . . .* I stayed till she woke, charmingly dishevelled (flushed and hyperventilating, one mango-sized breast free of the night-gown – if I hadn't been in such a Godawful *hurry . . .*) and called reedily for her maid.

You want to get to the man, go through the woman. Eden seemed like ages ago (grainy Super-8 footage in ropy colour) but I hadn't forgotten its lessons. Complacency's never been my vice, and it certainly wasn't that morning in Judea, but I felt, you know, *optimistic*.

But. Well.

Actually things got off to a good start, what with Pilate's irritation at having to come out of the *praetorium* into the courtyard to meet the priests (Passover's dictates for clean and unclean objects, food and places) exacerbated by narked Caiaphas's response to the governor's question about what the prisoner was accused of. 'If he weren't a malefactor, we wouldn't have brought him to you, would we?' I watched the furrows appearing in Pilate's brow and practically rubbed my hands with glee. I think if they'd stayed outdoors I might have been in with a shout. But God was interfering. Goddammit God was inter*fering*. I could see it in the governor's occasional slight head-shakes (as if trying to clear a ringing from his ears) and fidgeting hands. The sun hammered the stones in the yard, and when Pilate looked up, briefly, the sky struck him like a cacophony.

Are you the King of the Jews?
You say it.

Not to mention Junior's elliptical style. If he'd just said 'you bet your skirt I am, Punchy', the procurate could have dismissed him as just another Hebe nutter, but the tone was all wrong for that, suggesting at best fearlessness, at worst contempt. *Don't be insulted*, I'm going. *He doesn't mean to be insolent. Don't do anything hasty, man.* Meanwhile the Sanhedrin's bigwigs are chunnering and gabbling like a gang of speeding turkeys, and the sunlight's playing havoc with its boomerangs and spears. *Tell them it's nothing to do with you. Tell them to crucify him themselves if he's getting on their nerves so much.*

Which would be illegal, as both Caiaphas and Pilate knew well enough.

'It's too fucking hot out here,' to no one in particular. Then to the prisoner: 'You. Come inside with me.'

It was time to call in reinforcements. I picked the *crème de la crème* from the fallen angelic host and gathered them over Jerusalem. It's going to get ugly, I told them. I'm pretty sure He's going to make use of the mob. I want you in there. *Right* in there, understand? I want you whispering so close you can taste their *earwax* – got it? At least three of you to every member of the crowd. Is that understood? Let's go.

I did some work with Pilate in the *praetorium*. Really some of my best, warped though it was by the irony of its application. On any other day Sonny's clipped ripostes and sheer *non sequiturs* would have exhausted his patience and had him signing the crucifixion chit with his mind else-where. As it was, he spent most of his time in the judgement hall vacillating between curious fraternity with this wastrel and a strangely detached conviction that his own destruction would follow if he failed to execute him. His hands and face grew hot. The lamps weren't lit (what need amid the mote-filled and Godspeaking shafts of light?) but his breathing was troubled by the stink of burning oil. Tonight he would get Claudia to mix him a draught. Thoughts rose and burst, emptily, like painless blisters. He had an overwhelming desire (courtesy of *moi*) to understand the riddles. *My kingdom is not of this world: if my kingdom were of this world, then would my servants fight* . . . But the language – kingdoms, servants, fighting – kept yanking him back to his own world, one in which he was Pontius Pilate, Roman Procurator of Judea, with a city swelled for the feast, a gossip-fattened crowd outside the palace and a phalanx of ecclesiastical thought-police all but breaking down his door. And *still* I worked, amazing him and the hall's guards with his own tolerance. His face found hitherto unseen alignments, a grammar of expression his own mother wouldn't have recognized, featuring improbable segues from anger to bliss, from peremptoriness to a patience that amounted almost to bon-homie. *I find in him no fault at all.* The words dropped like gentian petals. A sweating centurion exchanged a risky glance with a standard bearer. *Are we dreaming, Marcus?*

No we weren't. I was *horribly* tired, I don't mind telling you, and in more than my usual amount of excruciating pain. All the back-and-forthing was killing me. I know this is a rhetorical question, but have you any idea how difficult it is to tempt a human being away from his fate? You see the conceptual clash, yes? It was a strain for Pilate, too, you could see. He scratched his neck a lot. Started up violently – then sat down again after three or four paces. The very stones of the *praetorium* were warm with incredulity, as if blushing.

To this end I was born, and for this cause I came into the world, that I should bear witness to the truth. Everyone that is of the truth hears my voice. I remember thinking, Yes, it's all very well standing there with your slumped shoulders and risen veins talking about bearing witness to the truth, but what you've just said could have come quite as easily from me, mate, and no word of a lie would it be. Some of which sentiment plainly rubbed off on our beleaguered guv, who, getting quickly to his feet, spat out 'What is truth?', before turning on his sandaled heel and storming back out to the priests.

You know, it's quite exhausting just *talking* about this. Come aside with me a moment. Trust me.

Paedophilia's what I call a flexible gain investment. It yields profit in umpteen different ways. Most obviously there's the immediate suffering of the children, followed by the shame, the guilt, the self-disgust, the not being believed, the hatred. Not least the now loudly ticking clock of their own desire, all those dream-rich hours and days before the early damage gestates and they start fiddling with youngsters themselves. Then there are the perpetrators. Again the shame, again the self-loathing, again the useless guilt. Useless to God, I mean. Guilt's only useful to God as prologue to penitence and a change of ways. But based on guilt no paedophile's ever going to change his ways. The desire for nippers is too strong. Guilt's simply no match for it. It goes: desire-gratification-guilt-desire-gratification-guilt-desire-gratification-guilt and so on. It's a mechanism, interrupted if they get caught by the cops and banged up by a judge, but otherwise unstoppable except via hard psychic and professional graft which neither the perp nor his world is remotely interested in investing in. Then there's the suffering of the parents (in cases where it's not actually the parents wots dunnit, I mean). The horror of being afraid of their own sullied child. The shame of having suspected and done nothing. The shame of having known and done nothing. But best of all, by far the best of all, is the opportunity it gives the self-righteous mob.

Look closely the next time a paedophile comes via the media to the attention of his peers, look closely at the faces of the outraged mob. That's where you'll find me. Those pixelated tabloid stills of good mums and dads transformed by righteousness into grimacing beasts, bellowing for blood, teaching their children to hate first and ask questions later (or better still never), buoyed and inflated by the gobbled-up lie that they're doing God's work. This is paedophilia's *quality* yield: the indignant mob bloodthirsty with decency, obscenely relieved of the burden of thought and the yoke of argument. EVIL PERVERTS SHOULD BE TORTURED THEMSELVES. The bald leaders make me fizz with pride. You'll have noticed, no doubt, how mum and dad's first genuine expressions of grief and shock are telly-seduced and mob-lionized into studied outrage and the calculated stammers of disbelief. You'll have noticed, I dare say, a dearly purchased and bitter confidence, now that their loss has excused them their own ethical failings and moral mediocrity. They've suffered the tragedy of poor Tommy and are thus absolved of further responsibilities. It is required of them now only that they exist as mascots for the mob. Please do look at the hangin's-too-good-for-'em crowds in the tabloids – do look and tell me, if you can, that there's any greater evil than the transformation of individuals into the lurching, self-congratulatory mob?

God taught me that. Yes, God Himself taught me the value of the mob a couple of thousand years ago in Jerusalem.

The boys told me afterwards they could barely believe what happened. What happened was nothing less than the mass scrambling of their myriad promptings in the ears of the crowd. (It wasn't that big a crowd, by the way. Maybe a couple of hundred. Certainly no more than that. Still, the idea that there were *fucking thousands of Jews* of their own free will screaming for Jimmeny's blood has come in awfully handy down the centuries, so I shouldn't complain I suppose. Ill wind and all that.) What happened was that they told the crowd one thing; God made sure the crowd *heard* another. I mean 'release Barabbas' doesn't sound anything like 'release Jesus', does it? Nor does 'crucify him' sound much like 'let him go'. Not the sort of thing you'd *accidentally mishear*. At the time I thought the lads just weren't pulling their weight. Pilate's psyche was still wobbling like a blancmange, preoccupied – flabbergasted, as a matter of fact – by its own reluctance to do what it would normally do and seek the path of least political resistance. The sensation was both seductive and nauseating – and somewhere between the two he ordered the prisoner scourged.

I didn't like it. Not the scourging *per se*, obviously, but the line of physical contact having been crossed. Wife batterers around the world will tell you: the primary effect of hitting your wife for the first time (assuming she doesn't leave you immediately or cut your cock off while you're asleep) is that it makes it much easier to hit her – harder – a second time. Then a third, then a fourth, and so on, until hitting's nowhere near enough and you've got to start getting creative. Although he didn't wield the whip himself, Pilate had now got his hands dirty with action; more importantly, he had seen that he could draw the man's blood, and that it was red, just like any other man's. It lowered the stakes. That wasn't good for me. If he could scourge him as a man, he could crucify him as one – although it was after all *somewhat* diverting to see Arthur having such a terrible time of it, I admit. Then the message from Procula arrived, via a red-robed flunkey with a face in which all the dark little features seemed to huddle in the middle as if in fear of being shot. *Have nothing to do with that just man. I've suffered many things this day in a dream because of him.*

Well, it was a bit late for having nothing to do with him, since he was hanging from the post in bloody ribbons, thorn-crowned, dripping with sweat and glazed with the spit of Pilate's soldiery. But not too late, perhaps (*that's right, go on!*) to avoid nailing him to a cross on Calvary. Assuming my boys had by now swayed the crowd, I put it into the procurate's seasick head (why *did* the floor keep pitching like that?) that he should take the prisoner out with him, let the morons see what a harmless and indeed pitiable spectacle the so-called 'King of the Jews' made against the backdrop of Imperial pomp and order; get him off, in other words, on the sympathy ticket. I didn't know, I repeat, that God had already been at it among them. Neither, obviously, did Caiaphas, who'd sent cronies into the throng to buy shouts with coin. All redundant. God had released the force of the brain-dead righteous collective. They didn't know why it seemed imperative to crucify the fellow – only that in some way he was Them and they were Us. It could have been the terraces of Old Trafford or the swaying Anfield Kop. I could see my angelic brethren among them like fragments of a smashed rainbow. Lack of results was plainly not due to lack of effort; they blazed and swarmed and whispered – and achieved precisely nothing. And this is where my earlier boasting about the importance of the right remark at the right moment comes back to haunt me, because Caiaphas leaned in close for the delivery of the one that clinched it: 'Caesar's subjects are united in their condemnation of this blasphemer and instigator against Rome. I'm sure the Emperor wouldn't like to hear that his governor in Judea suffers such an individual to live and spread his lies. Rome, after all, gets to hear of everything sooner or later.'

Pilate closed and opened his eyes very slowly and wearily. Not as slowly or as wearily as Jesus, mind you, who was already having trouble staying on his feet.

'This round to you then,' I said, slipping alongside him. 'Still, that business with the nails isn't going to be a picnic, is it?'

◆

You know, I'm going to miss you lot, when you're gone. I'm going to miss our . . . our thing, our working relationship. I'm going to miss you listening to me, seeing sense, taking my advice. I'm going to miss your candour (the inner candour, I mean, the one that's camouflaged by all that external duplicity, omission and pretence). I'm going to miss your self-love, your sense of humour, your crippling weakness for doing what makes you feel good. Makes you feel good initially, I mean. Soon, now, it'll be gone, all gone. What'll I *do* with myself when you're gone?

And thanks to this incarnate sojourn, I'm going to miss . . . damn, man, I'm gonna miss *handshakes*, ya know? The honest comfort of flesh and blood. This flesh and blood, it's honest, isn't it? It tells the truth, doesn't it? The wind in your hair, rain on your face, sun-warmth between your shoulder-blades – perception's straight-up. Kissing. Stretching. Blowing off. Forget René: the senses don't lie, not about the big things, not about what it's like to *be here*.

I took a break from the script and went to Church. St Paul's. Call it a hunch, an intuition, an inkling, something pulled me there. (The dreams are knocking me out, by the

170

way. Repeatedly, I'm trapped in tiny, vast spaces. Does that make sense to you? Do you dream paradoxes? Woke up this morning, couldn't even face Buck's Fizz. Harriet's suggested I see a doctor. Harriet's suggested I see a *shrink*. Pot, kettle and black, Harriet, I thought, pot, kettle and fucking black. The film – the film's *racing* along. Harriet hasn't left the bed for two days. She sits cross-legged amid the pillows talking on the phone, moving money, telling lies, having things brought to her, half-consuming them, having them taken away. I've told her: slow down, you'll make yourself ill. You think she takes any notice of me? Trent was miffed about the no-sequel nature of the project. He's been *depressed* since I pointed out that there was no scope for a prequel, either. Meanwhile, I'm anxious about the third act . . .)

St Paul's. Well if you're going to do it, do it large. It still takes me a while to get to places, and this afternoon's jaunt to the cathedral was no exception, what with London's oven-baked asphalt and disreputable trees, what with its brew of stinks and perfumes, what with the wide-angle sunlight and the stratosphere's ghostly cirrus. I was straight, too, more or less, if you don't count the coke-hangover and three Lucifer Risings I took to knock it on the head. Admittedly there's a more or less permanent residue of chemicals and booze around Gunn's cowering brain these days, but, you know, *relatively*, I was sharp.

Which was just as well. Given who turned up.

I only just got out of Gunn's carcass in time. Up in the Whispering Gallery, under the great, ribbed belly of the dome, I couldn't shake it, that sense of being watched that had been troubling me since . . . I don't know. A while. However long it had been smouldering, it caught fire up there among the scurrying sibilants. Dangerous, too, what with Gunn's fear of heights kicking in without warning, what with me *swaying, precariously* at the gallery's rail. The presence – for there was no mistaking it by then – coalesced just before the rising tide of tinnitus which announced it would have sent me literally and metaphorically over the edge. With a nauseous wrench (think of a femur being pulled from its groin) I tore myself from Gunn's body, which, not surprisingly, collapsed, buttocks-first, into that indecorous sitting position adopted by abandoned cloth dollies.

'And the great dragon was cast out, that old serpent, called the Devil, and Satan,' Michael droned, with a kind of rich boredom, 'which deceiveth the whole world: he was cast out into the earth, and his angels were cast out with him . . . *ha-satan*, have you forgotten, my friend?'

Pain? Well, you could say that. Can't tell you what it cost me to keep it together, up there in the dome's shadow, with you dear things scuttling like roaches below. Corporeally, I would have talked of deep internal haemorrhaging. I would have talked of head trauma. I would have talked of the immediate need for *intensive care*. Leaving the body was bad enough – the dreadful reunion with my default angelic rage and pain – but to be forced into it so suddenly *and* to have him to deal with . . . Well. I mean be *fair*.

Not that I let on, obviously, no more than he did, and I can assure you my presence was no cakewalk for him, either.

'Michael,' I said. 'Dear old thing. It's been simply *ages*.'

I wondered, peripherally, how on earth this bit of the material world could contain us without radical signs of stress – I half-expected the dome to split or implode – until I realised what should have been obvious: Divine dispensation. It was, after all, *St Paul's Cathedral*. Sometimes I'm so *slow*.

'You're afraid,' he said, quietly.

I smiled. 'It's extraordinary,' I said, 'how much you chaps

consider it your duty to tell me that. I had Gabriel at it the other day. I wonder why you think it's so important? Sceptics, I dare say, would mutter of wishful thinking.'

He returned the smile. 'His advice to the mortals, you know,' he said, 'that they should love their enemies, I pity them that they should require such instruction.'

'Have you seen *The Empire Strikes Back*?' I asked him.

'Because for us it is natural to love our enemies in proportion to their proximity to ourselves. We're so very alike, *satan*. We're so very *close* to one another.'

It did rankle a *wee* bit, the '*satan*' with small *s*. Means just 'one who obstructs'. Not the name-calling itself, but his not being able to rise above it. He's mighty fond of his own name, needless to say, which he translates at parties as 'who is like God'. I wonder the Old Bugger lets him get away with it, since the correct – and far less flattering – translation, is a rhetorical question: 'Who is like God?' Used to piss him off no end in the old days. Every time someone said, 'Er, Michael?' I used to cut in straight away with, 'Me.'

'So near and yet so far,' I said. 'How *are* things in the bowing-and-scraping business? I'm thinking Bob Hoskins for you in the movie, by the way. How does that sit with you? I'm sure you could talk me into Joe Pesci.'

Between you and me, I really was in the most excruciating discomfort. I glanced down at the gallery, where Gunn's impersonation of a passed-out wino or junkie had attracted the attention of two small children, who, ignored by their whispering parents, were tearing up the tinfoil wrappers of their Kit-Kats and dropping the pieces into Gunn's hair. I wondered, glumly, what would happen when the security guard was called.

'You've surprised us,' he said. He's never quite grasped that conversation isn't actually the other person making some unattended-to noises while you think of the next bit of your monologue.

'Oh I have have I? What were you thinking? Harrison Ford?'

'With the shortness of your attention span, we thought you'd be at middle-aged melancholy by now. And yet you've managed to . . . hold yourself, more or less, at adolescent egotism.'

'Don't underrate adolescent egotism, old stick. With adolescent egotism and a lot of money one can pretty much rule the world – redundant, obviously, when one already does rule the world.'

Oh I felt *awful*, I did. You know how it is when you come home trenchantly, comprehensively, *authentically* drunk, turn the light out, lie down, and feel the waltzer room's nauseating spin? Yes? Well this was *galaxies* worse than that.

'I realise this might sound rude, my dear, but why are you here, exactly, umm?'

'To help you,' he said.

Had I a face, just then, it would have been no mean trick to have kept it straight. 'Aha?' I said. 'Um-hm? Yah?'

'Have you not, of late, Lucifer –'

'Look why don't you spit it out, there's a good chap, eh? Then perhaps we can get on digging our respective scenes. In case it escaped your attention, I had come for a quiet half-hour *in Church*.'

'You came because you were called.'

'Oh dear this is really *so* uncivilized. I had hoped – you know, from you, Michael, I had hoped for a certain standard of –'

'You're afraid.' He said it this time with the air of someone genuinely in possession of a mighty truth. If he hadn't continued, I'm not sure I wouldn't have begun Apocalypse there

174

and then. 'You're afraid of what you most desire. You desire
that of which you're most afraid. Think on this, brother.'

'I'll be sure to.'

'Think on it.'

'I'll be sure to.'

To give him his due, he didn't have the look of a gloater.
Nor, to give him further credit, did he stick around for vac-
uous chit-chat.

'I'll see you soon, Lucifer,' he said.

'Not if I see you first, Michael,' I replied.

Didn't fancy the walk back to the Ritz after that. I cell-
phoned Harriet and she sent Parker – whose real name is
Nigel – round with the Rolls. We've bonded, Nigel and I.
Got chatting one small-hours whisk through the city
(Harriet passed out on the back seat) and I recognized him
as one of my own. I needed him now like you need an
escapist film when there's an exam to revise for.

'The point,' I said, as I collapsed into the Rolls's generous
rear, and the upholstery gave its welcoming gasp, 'is that in
calling it multiculturalism or diversity or ebony and ivory or
we are the fucking world or whatever, they're missing something much more fundamental. They're missing the
deliberate eradication of one race by another. For which, in
the twentieth century, we've got a word: genocide. It seems
to me, Nigel, that your concern – and thank fuck you're not
alone in this – your fiercely and rightly felt concern is to stop
the genocide that is happening in this country right here and
right now.'

'You all right, boss?' Nigel said, with a blue-eyed glance in
the rear-view. 'You look a bit peaky.' (A homely idiom,
Nigel's, though peppered with the Party for the Preservation
of British Nationalism's staples : Rights, Decent People,

Honour, Difference, the White Race, Patriotism, Homeland, Relocation.)

'What does it say about a Christian country, Nigel,' I continued, pocket-patting for Silk Cut and Zippo, 'that its churches – its *churches* – can be sold to Muslims and converted into mosques? I mean correct me if I'm wrong, you know, correct me if my history's faulty here – but wasn't there, some years back, a little operation known as the Crusades? Was that an academic exercise, then, was it? Eh?' (I put a bit of bark in to my rhetorical questions for Nigel. It gets him going. It *delights* him, actually, though he experiences the delight as political disgust.) 'Do you know, Nigel, that in parts of Britain now, children under ten years old – Christian children, this is, English, Christian children – are being forced to study the Koran? You know, you tell people this stuff, they think you're making it up.'

'Tories have got a coon Lord.'

'I know, Nigel, I know. You know, when I think of the . . . the . . .'

I faltered. (So long since I've seen Michael. New Time hadn't changed him. Still the over-earnestness, the show-offy angelic physique, the irritating air of privy intelligence. No doubt he believes there's a great deal he knows that I don't. He's welcome to it. There is, after all, something I know that he doesn't . . .) 'When I think of the role this country of yours *used* to play on the global stage,' I went on, 'when I think of the notion that the sun never set on the British Empire, when I think of this country bringing the light of civilization to dark places, bringing technology, learning, industry, imports and exports – you know, *educating* the less intelligent nations on how to make use of natural resources – sometimes resources they didn't even know they had, Nigel – when I think of that, in the light of the cultural and

176

linguistic genocide now being encouraged in your schools, churches, hospitals, legal system . . . I think of that and I wonder: Is this how the countries of Empire repay their erstwhile sovereign?'

Your country. I've softened Nigel's initial suspicions: told him I'm half Italian. Don't live here. Passing through. And a member of the PPNI (*Partita per la Preservazione di Nazionalismo Italiano*), the fictional guinea equivalent of the PPBN. If I say things like 'erstwhile sovereign' I usually regret it, since Nigel's own vocabulary needs very little room to stretch its legs – but that's me again, you know? Baroque. Got to do it with knobs on. Honestly, sometimes I'm my own worst enemy.

'It's the fucking newsreaders piss me off,' Nigel said, as we swung into Trafalgar Square. 'Sanjit fucking this and Mustapha fucking that. There's a fucking Paki doing the *weather* on BBC1.'

West End façades, a troupe of rattling pigeons, the lights turning green. 'Nigel,' I said, 'there are going to have to be some significant changes in the world. Changes are long, long overdue . . .'

◆

There's a photograph of Gunn's mother depressed me, this afternoon at the Clerkenwell writing den. (Jimmeny's plums, this *writing* game, eh? The script's a fucking *doddle* next to these meanderings. Of all the earthly seductions in all the towns in all the world . . .) Anyway the photograph. From the late sixties, when Gunn must have just started school. She was working afternoons in a Market Street café. The chef was in love with her. She liked him as a friend but after the scarpering Sikh she'd shut up the shop of her heart, not to mention the vaginal premises. (This was in the days before drink and I seduced her, those chaste days before loneliness drove her into the pulpy embraces of hamfisted cabbies and bad-breathed reps.) Anyway the photograph. You can tell someone just said 'Angela' then click-flashed as she turned. The moment captures her unschooled look, the face she gave to the world when it hadn't given her time to prepare, the face without art or protection. You can tell that a split-second later, blinking away the magnesium's after-image, she'd have said, 'Bloody hell, Dez,' (or Frank, or Ronnie, or whoever) 'get away with you.' But in the moment, she's absolutely, unguardedly herself.

It gets to Gunn, this picture, because there's no sign of himself in her eyes. He's at school, or his gran's, or Mrs Sharples's or wherever (lot of women in Gunn's childhood, not enough men; no wonder he turned out such a sissy). Sure, immediately the shutter and flash have snapped her, her history and motherhood return; but just for that instant Gunn's seeing a version of his mother that's nothing to do with himself. He remembers her, that she had much to forgive him. Chiefly, that he never once thought of her as a person in her own right. Instead he measured her by her aesthetic near-misses and hair-raising mispronunciations – measured her, that is, solely in relation to himself. She knew. He knew she knew. Time after time his resolution to rise above himself. Time after time his failure to honour it.

In any case it depressed the hell out of me when I found it, blistered at one corner, dog-eared at another, in Gunn's desk drawer this morning. I was supposed to be drafting the film version of my *Hail horrors* speech. I ended up just sitting with a foully reeking Silk Cut, chin in palm, face as perky as a flat tyre. Could barely drag myself back to the Ritz for supper. If I hadn't remembered that I was due to eat supper off XXX-Quisite Miranda's mouth-watering arse, in fact . . .

I ask you. I, Lucifer, ask you: Is this any way for the King of Hell to be spending his earthly days?

'What I'm seeing?' Trent Bintock said to me, after supper (do you want the supper details? I don't think you do). 'What I'm seeing is a hugely fucking extended tracking shot from Lucifer's viewpoint, as if . . .' he struggled . . . 'as if he's going down a rollercoaster facing the wrong way, you know? He's looking back and seeing Heaven getting further and further away. He's on this fucking *unreal* downward gradient. Except it's not a fucking rollercoaster, man, it's space, it's anti-space, and it's *empty*.' His blue hawk eyes were glittering with childish delight; he was possessed, I observed, of cocaine's dreary and inexhaustible confidence.

'Except it wouldn't be empty,' I said – and left a pause for him to figure it out for himself. This is always a mistake with Trent. Ten seconds of his sparkling bemusement. I was discovering (at this late stage of the game, for fuck's sake) *impatience*. 'It would be *occupied*, actually, by my followers. Fully one third of the *benē 'elöhim* came with me, you're forgetting, dear boy.'

'Benny *what*?'

'Sons of God. Angels. You know, Trent, there's some background reading you could do if you're . . . What I mean is, there's some crazy fucking shit in this story, you know? Might be useful to check out a *library* sometime before we start shooting.'

For some two minutes – I kid you not – Trent's face retained its expression of impervious joy. Such was the glitter of his eyes you could have been forgiven for assuming he was on the verge of tears. And even then, there was only the merest suggestion of a flicker, when he said: 'You fucking condescending to me, man?'

'Trent,' I said, laughing and fondling his chest in a way he's not quite sure what to do with. 'Dear, dear, adorable Trent. Why don't I just tell you the way it was? Why don't I just tell you what I *remember*?'

'What I remember,' I said – not to Trent, who had to take a call from New York, but much later, to Harriet in bed, after aborted high-jinx – 'is how it looked looking back. It's hard to get this across, obviously, given that we're not talking about a place, a material *thing*. Not even an idea, really.'

I didn't know if she was awake or asleep. The curtains were open, displaying a dashing pre-dawn vista of London's lights under a clear, smoke-coloured sky. The last scatter of stars was still visible. Sunrise was a vast and magnanimous presence below the horizon, a furious benevolence with an inexhaustible wealth of heat. (Except of course it's not inexhaustible. Except of course it's *burning itself out*.) I thought of the planet's atmospheric gradations: troposphere, stratosphere, mesosphere, thermosphere, exosphere. I thought of how far away from home you'd feel out there, looking back. You'd think *that* was homesickness. You'd think *that* was exile . . .

'If I was confined to one metaphor,' I continued, as a plane came in, winking, rhythmically, 'I suppose it would be . . . I suppose it would be blue.'

I waited for Harriet to say, 'Blue?' But she didn't say anything. She always falls asleep (if indeed she was asleep then) in the same position: lying on her front with her face turned to the right, towards the window, and her right arm hanging over the side of the bed. She looks like a Cindy Sherman. You'd expect to see pills scattered near the dangling hand, an empty glass, crumpled money. And who could blame you? Most nights, next to the dangling fingertips, you can find scattered pills, an empty glass or two, crumpled notes and bills . . .

'Blue,' I repeated, quietly. The hotel's low hum of comfort, the city's troubled breathing and weary intelligence, the one within the other. 'I remember, looking back along the plunging cavalcade, the flaming torrent of my rebel brothers . . . Harriet? . . . I remember seeing what you lot would think of, what you lot might represent perceptually – you do know perception's the oldest metaphor in town, don't you? – what you might see as blueness and space. A special kind of space, a special kind of blueness, not the blue of an arctic sky, you see, nor the lapis blue in Bronzino's *Allegory with Venus and Cupid* . . . certainly not the midnight blue of the Virgin's mantle, nor the charming cobalt of these tiny hours . . . Well. Harriet? The point is I'm having trouble seeing how we could do this in the film. The blueness is going to be trouble enough, but the space, that space that was infinite and not really space at all, more a feeling. More a feeling of . . . a feeling of . . .'

Bah, I thought. And thought, simultaneously: What *is* all this, Lucifer?

I got up, raided the minibar for a thrown-together Long Island Ice Tea, then stood for a while, butt-naked at the window, looking out at the moody sky. The trouble was, I reasoned, I was so dashed *busy* all the time. Activity . . . yes, *activity* was taking its toll. This was, after all, the sorry-ass big-ears-and-tub-gut body of Declan Jesus Christing Gunn. What, in the light of the limitations *that* arrangement imposed, did I expect? There were, obviously, going to be physical noises of complaint. (As if in confirmation of this, Gunn's anus released a painful and protracted fart with the voiceless interdental quality of a stammerer beginning the word *thin* and never getting beyond the *th*. If Harriet remained unmoved by the smell that accompanied it, I thought, she wasn't asleep, she was dead.) I had backache, did I not, most mornings? My pee-pee-time tears were hardly an indication of a chipper urinary tract, and it was only by supreme effort of will that I managed to ignore the more or less perpetual headache and dehydration that had set in a week ago. If I thought of Gunn's liver I thought of a dried chilli. Attending to his lungs conjured the smell of tarmac and the sound of the desert's abrasive wheeze. No, it had to be admitted, the body has its parameters, the flesh and blood would rebel if pushed.

Except, the Little Voice said, *it's not the flesh and blood that's giving you trouble, is it?*

'What *are* you doing?' Harriet's voice said, out of the bed's palely lit swamp.

'Drinking a Long Island Ice Tea. Go back to sleep.'

'You come here and lie down next to me.'

'It's no good. I can't sleep.'

'I don't want you to sleep. I just want you to – oh never mind.'

I let quite a while pass after this, feeling pretty miserable if you want the truth. It was an effort just to keep sipping the drink and chain-smoking. The city's smog, furious at the sun's rising, had turned its first band of light into a long, purplish scar. Piccadilly's traffic was thickening.

'Do you ever have those dreams,' Harriet rasped, slowly, 'where you've done something, something terrible and irreversible? Something horrific, and no matter how much you're sorry it's no good? It's indelible?'

'No.'

I didn't look at her. Didn't need to. I knew what she'd

look like, lying on her side, face to the window, the city's lights minutely captured in the glossy convexities of her tired eyes. I knew she'd be unblinking, her cheek squashed in the deep pillow, her mouth dripping a single strand of spittle. I knew she'd look sad as hell.

'I have that dream all the time,' she said. 'Except when I'm asleep.'

◆

Carry on like that, my son, I thought, the following morning, and you might as well move back to Clerkenwell.

I arranged drinks with Violet at Swansong. Violet, I deemed, under a fateful delusion of wisdom, was just what I needed.

'Look this is ridiculous,' she said. 'I think the least you could do is *introduce* me. I mean is that going to fucking *hurt*?'

Pacific as ever. This is her mode, now: a curious oscillation between blunt impatience and cosy collusion with me.

'That's why I wanted to see you,' I said. 'I think it's about time I introduced you to Trent.'

I'd given it thought. Likely outcome was, of course, that Violet wouldn't get a part. If that happened, it would leave Gunn with the business of getting rid of her (that boy's going to be trading up when he gets back into these boots) and Violet with bitterness straining the seams of her soul's pockets. Violet in that state – having come close enough to fame to reach out and touch it, only to see it turn and whisk glamorously away – will be promising material indeed. Truly, there's no telling *what* Violet close-but-no-cigar'd will be capable of. Certainly I'm seeing stalking. Certainly I'm seeing rage. Certainly I'm seeing a tag-duo of self-loathing and self-love with potentially fatal psychic consequences. Certainly I'm seeing a vast and hungry silence into which any number of my voices might enter . . .

'Oh Declan you are *horrid*,' she said, thumping Gunn's humerus with what was intended as little-girl exasperation but which in fact dead-armed me for the next ten minutes. 'Why do you let me? I mean why do you *let* me, eh?'

Alternatively, she might end up with a part. You never know. She's not, after all, going to have to *act* that much. I'm seeing her as one of Jimmeny's groupies or Pilate's bits on the side. Maybe one of Dirty Mags's pre-conversion colleagues (there's some obvious two-girl action there that I'd trust Trent not to sidestep). Or may*be* Salome, since she's got the fleshy erotic puppyishness that would drive a dad mad. The point is it's a win-win situation. What do you think Vi's going to be like if she gets to Hollywood? What sort of a couple do you think her and Gunn are going to make?

'Let's go,' I said.

'Where?'

'You need the loo.'

'I don't.'

'Yes you do.'

'No, Declan, honestly I don't. Oh I see. *Oh*.'

But damn me if Gunn's . . . What I mean is despite Violet's businesslike adoption of the requisite . . . One stiletto-toed foot up on the seat of the can, both reddish hands gripping the cistern, the Jane Morris froth tossed, as if with petulance, aside . . . Despite the charming attire of libertinage revealed under the hoiked-up skirt ('be prepared' is Vi's new motto, apparently) I find once again that . . . I find myself . . . Well.

'This is getting ridiculous,' I said, zipping, buttoning, tidying with compressed fury. 'I mean this is –'

'I've told you *never mind*. You look a bit under the weather if you want my opinion. Why don't we arrange it for Friday.'

'Friday?'

'Trent Bintock. Friday evening. Where's he staying?'

They keep the bogs spick and span at Swansong, but on a tile just to the left of the cistern a markered line had been incompletely erased. 'For nothing' it said.

'At the Ritz,' I said, a little wearily. 'Where else?'

The day went from bad to worse after that.

I'd no plan to end up passed out on Declan's kitchen table, yet that Heinz-flecked and mug-ringed board was where I woke, at the slaked end of the city's afternoon, packed full of treats and delicacies – those 99s, man, can one *ever* have too many? – and woozy from hourly pub-halts, where single malts and fortified wines followed rowdy bloody Marys and chilled pilsners down my broadminded gullet. That afternoon drinking thing. And in such heat, too. Well, you know how it is. Did I feel terrible? I felt terrible. The body's queasy lurch and roil, sure – but chiefly the mind's curious deflation. Chiefly my irritation with myself. It's a long time – really a very long time indeed, since I've felt irritated with myself. And why, in a month of Hadean Sundays, I thought of visiting Angela Gunn's grave I've no idea. Did I think that was going to *help*?

None the less don't laugh, because that is what I did.

There are of late these urges, peculiar blips that are taking me into all sorts of sudden and absurd gestures. Words like 'irreducible' and 'occult' nudge at the back of my brain. Wordsworth's blank misgivings, fallings from us, vanishings . . . You've got to laugh, actually. One minute I'm sprawled on Gunn's formica observing through the window the sky's slow-mo parade of whipped and beaten clouds, the next I'm back in the stewed streets heading for St Anne's, a heart murmur, an insistence laid against Gunn's backbone like an icy palm. Images fluttered in and out: Angela's face in the photograph. Mourners like dark menhirs around the raw grave. Gunn's face – the pocked mirror in the loo at the funeral directors' to which he'd adjourned mid-sentence, ambushed by the thuggish gang of his unspoken filial endearments. All this while I kicked my way through the remains of Value Meals and footprinted tabloids with my hands in my pockets and my guts gone heavy. Well, you've got to laugh. They'd piss themselves, Downstairs. I'm practically pissing myself now, just thinking of it. Teeny cemetery. No blue left in the sky by the time I got there. Less than a hundred headstones like . . . like what? Terrible teeth? Victory Vees? Damn and *blast* this language tries my patience. Anyway the little beds of the dead, some crisp and white, others gone to leprous ruin. Blurred dates. Even New Time's got the clout to smudge the lines of who and when. Doesn't take long. There was no one else there. The small, dark, and insensitively renovated church threw its shadow at my back. I did contemplate, briefly, popping in to see Mrs Cunliffe of the strabismal leer and compulsive polishing – but thought better of it in the end. She's in capable hands. She's *getting worse*. I felt chilly. I felt dreadful, actually, if you must know, what with the bare flesh of my throat turned tender and Gunn's ticker doing its broken-winged bird thing in his chest, what with my bunch of bright daffs held heads-down, what with the dropped wind and suddenly attentive trees, what with being slowly flooded by the sense of how seldom Gunn can bring himself to come here.

D'you know what I did? I *cried*. Oh yes indeed. Cried my eyes out. Right there by her headstone. ANGELA MARY GUNN, 1941–1997, ETERNAL REST. You can laugh now. It was the *eternal rest* did for me. Not my fault. Gunn's. He's noticed in himself of late a vulnerability to venerable abstract nouns and hallowed phrases. *Duty. Grace. Honour. Peace. Eternal Rest.* Tears start. The bottom lip wobbles in that way that always makes an observer – no matter how compassionate – want to giggle. *Grief. Home. Regret.* He lives in mortal fear of *Love.* A child of his times, he buried these things away in some cellar of himself under sprawling cobwebs and drifts of dust. They lay there, the holy relics his sceptic had outgrown. Then his mother's death, with, not long after, the discovery that even the most casual utterances of such words in the world he'd thought debunked could wake their awful magic. British Airways TV commercials, country and western songs, Hallmark birthday cards, hymns. Only two weeks before I arrived he was unmanned outside a church, arrested by the tune he knew.

Be there at our sleeping and give us, we pray
Your peace in our hearts Lord at the end of the day . . .

Dreadful. He's tried caution. Steers clear of poetry on the Underground, with its things of beauty being joys for ever and cycle clips removed in awkward reverence. He's invariably undone. Once a laryngitic busker's mechanical yet strangely desperate version of 'Wish You Were Here'. Once (oh *please*) a speech by Tony Blair. It's not the self-congratulatory comfort of mere sentimentality. More a queer surge of bowel and soul, a twist or wrench of feeling as liable to have him hurling his dinner as breaking his heart. Whatever it is it messes him up – and I don't balk at telling you that it messed me up, too, good and proper there by old Angie's rotting remains.

Debilitating, that's what. Had to go and sort myself out

with a quadruple Jameson's in a nearby Knave of Cups. (I mean how do you bear it, this being suddenly overcome by feeling? Isn't it just an almighty jumping Jesus Christing *drag*?) I felt mighty peculiar afterwards, when the Irish had kicked-in. *Faint*, you might say. And yet, I must confess, not wholly dreadful. There was, it must be admitted (must it? Well, yes, perhaps it must . . .) a slight . . . a sort of . . . How *is* one to put this? An internal breathability. A space around the alarmed heart. The feeling that someone, somewhere (I know, I know, I *know*) was quietly, simply, without a concealed agenda, telling me that it was all right, that stillness would come, that peace is purchased in the currency of loss . . .

At which point (having called for another Jameson's family of four, sparked-up a Silk Cut, sneezed, and cracked my knuckles), I found myself laughing, to myself, at what an unpredictable wheeze this caper was turning out to be.

Took me an awfully long time to get home. I seemed to think it a *terrific* hoot to take buses and tubes at random. Hardly surprising, I suppose, that I ended up in the arms of a nineteen-year-old young-man-of-the-night in the anonymous yet surprisingly trim and lavender-scented boudoir above Vivid Videos, just off Gray's Inn Road – though, having rather foolishly succumbed to the honeyed tongue of a hallucinogens salesman not an hour before, I can't be absolutely sure of the location.

I had . . . *paused* at King's Cross. Intriguing to see one of my little urban kernels of vice (and misery, and regret, and shame, and guilt, and violence, and greed, and hatred, and rage, and confusion) from the other side, so to speak, from down on the ground. Theory in practice. The abstracted boffin down among the engine-room grunts. My brothers were busy in the ether, I knew, the ticklish temptations and purred prompts; I was a bit taken aback, however, at being able to *see* them, flowing around the multitudes in gorgeous streams – until I realised that I was in fact hallucinating. Extraordinary, let me repeat, to see the fruits of our labours from the material end. Normally, you understand, my brothers and I 'see' only the spiritual correlates of physical actions, not the physical actions themselves. There's an entire realm (again 'realm' is very misleading, but it's the best you've got) in which the spiritual dynamics of this mortal coil have their home. We know when an operation's been a success, of course – not because we see the bodies but because we feel the effects (the rips, the rucks) in the fabric of the spiritual realm.

I had paused, as I say, at King's Cross, leaning against a lamp-post with what must have been an expression of near obscene carnal happiness, when young Lewis had caught my eye, I his, and with an exchange of raised eyebrows and a couple of smirks, passed from the vulgarity of his price list to the charm of the room above the shop.

Slender lad. Elfin eyes of yellowish hazel; bones and lips that *must* have passed through the Caribbean at some stage, though his skin was barely the darkness of a Pret-à-Manger *latte*. Delicate (and slightly grimy on closer inspection) hands with long and pearly fingernails, and a dark dong of surprising proportions for one so otherwise slightly built. Talented, too, from what I can recall, though for all the impact his attentions had on *Gunn's* treacherous member he might as well have been reciting the Highway Code. Oh those *drugs*. Cockroaches by the hundred hurrying out from the legs of my discarded trousers; the curtains' burgundy roses morphing into tiny, sack-carrying dwarves; my hand the size of a double bed; a stadium of whispers; hot flushes; me expelling geysers of nonsense that did nothing for Lewis's peace of mind. Worst of all (don't relax *too* deeply, Monsieur Gunn, I'll right this wrong before I go!), a penis that might as well have been a Brillo pad for all the sensitivity it retained.

'I don't think this is going to work, you dear beautiful boy,' I heard myself saying, as if from a great distance, after forty minutes of fruitless fondling. 'No reflection on your . . . your *fitness* for the task in hand, I hope you understand?'

'Yeah well there's no fuckin' refund, babe,' my companion replied, surprising me, somewhat, with the speed of his shift from cheeky mincer to no-dice businessman.

'Delightful,' I said. 'Just the tack that's likely to get your darling head cracked open one of these days – although not by me, of course.' Not that it hadn't occurred to me, especially given the sudden appearance of an enormous twin-headed battleaxe propped up against the mantelpiece, looking very much the part with both its edges sporting coagulated blood and the odd wisp of human hair. Lewis, meanwhile, got dressed as if the drawing on of each garment expressed a distinct and unique contempt. I was wondering how to reach the battleaxe – given the howling and bottomless chasm that had just opened in the floor between myself and the mantelpiece – when the door opened and a meaty-headed man with a very black beard and very blue eyes entered. He surveyed the scene with his knuckles on his hips and his chest thrust out – not entirely unlike the posture of a pantomime dame – an expression of mildly displeased boredom on his face.

'Oh yeah?' he said, rather non sequiturially, I thought, to no one in particular. 'Oh yeah? Oh yeah? *Oh yeah?*'

It was taking me an age to shake those damned devil's coach-horses from the legs of Gunn's jeans, distracted, as I was, by the regularly rising urge to vomit and by the erratic flight of the room's previously unnoticed white hot bats that whizzed hither and thither weaving a cat's cradle of phosphorescence around the three of us.

'Yeah, well, Gordon okayed it, babe,' Lewis said.

'Oh yeah?' the bearded man repeated.

'I do think, old sport –' I began.

'And *you*, sunshine, can fuck *right* off out of it,' he said.

Well that tickled me beyond reason, I must say. Having finally managed to get Gunn's de-bugged jeans and shoes back on, I staggered over to where our hirsute observer stood with both eyebrows raised and both lips joined in a curled expression of distaste.

'I'd leave it, babe, if I were you,' Lewis murmured.

Wisely, as it turned out, though I took no notice at the time. (I mean there's no surer recipe for getting me to do something than the one warning me not to . . .) Besides, for hours – days, actually – a part of me had been busy decoding the body's potential, its unreleased violence and bottled energy. Crystal clear that a good punch-up now and again would've done our Declan the world of good. Would probably have staved off suicide. (It's shocking, really, this neglect of violence, your oft' fatal ignorance of its therapeutic heft.) No *chance* of it with *him* living in his carcass, obviously, what with him being yellower than a canary in custard – strangely, specifically terrified of having his teeth knocked out (strangely, I mean, given what all else might happen to him in a brawl: spleen ruptured, kneecaps smashed, eyes gouged out, fingers broken, eardrums punctured, goolies crunched, nipples torn off and so on) – but it was all still available to me, the pent potential, its lively aesthetics of blows, gnashings, kicks, butts, throttlings, forkings and swipes – and I do quite clearly remember thinking how joyful his body was going to feel, how much it was going to thank me for finally releasing its stoppered talent into the world . . . I do quite clearly remember a fantasy vision of myself, post-fisticuffs, floating in a seratonin haze (I think I was reclining in a vast red leather armchair, actually, in this image), just before the guy with the beard took umbrage at my hands on his lapels and headbutted me with astonishing speed and accuracy, sending me – with similar speed and *inevitable* accuracy – down onto my buttocks, which, whether by his design or otherwise, turned out to be the perfect position for my face to receive his kneecap, a bit of down-to-earth physics with all the subtlety of a cannon-ball landing in a rum baba. I'm assuming, given the bruises, given this body's new collection of aches and pains, that other things were done to me after that. Assumption is required, since an unequivocal blackness swallowed my consciousness a split second beyond impact, and did not regurgitate it until several hours later, when I found myself quite comfortably wedged between a re-cycling bin and a mountain of shredded paper in an alley at the back of the shop. Fleeced, I believe, is your word. Stiffed. Done over. *Fucked.* Teach me, I suppose, to walk around drunk and on drugs with 1,500 pounds sterling in my pock-ets. Nice team, those two, Lewis and his guy. I made a mental note to find out which of the boys is working with them and give him a raise . . .

'Do you need help?' a voice said. 'Do you want me to call an ambulance?'

I looked up. Indecipherable against the dark brick and pewter sky. A patchouli-flavoured hand, dry and cool, reached down and took mine. My left. My right was clenched around some tiny object. 'Can you stand?'

Apparently, I could, given that I found myself, after her braced yank, on my feet. Vertical, I found myself face to face with a stout woman in her late fifties. Ruddy cheeks, manly hands, a silver-grey ponytail, red corduroys and a battlescarred leather bomber jacket. Cheekbones. One earring of Chinese turquoise. Breath roll-up-scented and boots steel-capped.

'Are you all right?' she said. 'You're covered in blood.'

What does it say about the state I was in that I merely stood there opening and closing my mouth for a few moments? To my absolute astonishment, she started feeling me up. Or at least, so I thought, until I realised she was looking for the source of the bleeding.

'Please,' I said. 'Please. No. I haven't been – I'm not, ah, wounded.'

'Just fucked over?' she said, giving my elbow a compassionate squeeze. 'You've got a shocking black eye, you know.'

Hard, really terribly hard, to describe my feelings at this point. First, I own, was incredulity. Do you, by any chance, have any idea how STUPID it is to go wandering around London's alleyways in the small hours? And do you have any idea, dear Miss Ruth Bell, how FURTHER STUPID it is, given your presence in such locales, to extend a hand to a beaten body indisposed among the bins? Do you know who you could run into? But then that is Ruth, you see? Very seldom troubled by the gaps between knowing what the right thing to do is and doing it. (Whereas Gunn . . . Well, he's all gaps, really.) She's what we call Downstairs a Lost Cause. Course, being celibate helps. Leave sexual energy unspent and it'll turn its hand to all sorts of creative activities (no wonder Gunn's output was so poor), and dear Ruth hasn't had a jump in three years. Claims she doesn't miss it. Claims she's too busy. But what irritates me is the stupidity, the ease with which such people keep themselves out of my grasp. There's no reading, very little reflection, just the spirit's rough expression through salubrious hobbies and a worthwhile job. She doesn't even go to fucking Church.

'What've you got in your hand?' she said, lifting my clenched right mit up between us.

Well, I thought, as I opened my palm and struggled to focus, perhaps things are looking up after all. She's going to be . . . disappointed when I repay this kindness with . . .

'Oh,' I said, feeling terrible all over again. 'Oh.'

'Is that one of your . . . Is that one of your teeth, love?'

In the café ('Come on,' Ruth said, as the light brightened around us, 'I'll buy you a cuppa. You look like you need it.') I went into the bathroom to get a hold of myself. Lucifer, I said – I did, you know; I don't spare myself when I need a right good talking to – Lucifer, I said, you are going to pull yourself together. Do you hear me? Can you imagine – for the love of Farrah can you *imagine* how this would look in certain quarters? Can you imagine how Astaroth . . . No, enough. Amusing in its way – but really: enough. *Enough.*

'Got to go myself, now,' Ruth said, when I returned to our table. 'Keep an eye.'

You'd think she was loaded. Two full Veggie Breakfast specials, despite my protestations. I saw the ex-crim behind the counter sketching his London theory: *Older bird, arty, bit a dosh from the family; younger bloke* – but he came a cropper with it when he saw the state I was in. Probably not your idea of aromatherapy, a night between King's Cross rubbish heaps, though I myself found my lately acquired odour whoreishly seductive. You'd think, as I say, that she had some middle-class wedge behind her, but the truth is she's barely making ends meet.

All the more reason, therefore, to relieve her of her purse while she was in the loo. A laughable haul, obviously, £63.47, NatWest chequebook and Switch card, photo of her dead ma and pa, any organ you like as long as I'm dead, and a slew of useless contact numbers scribbled on aged scraps and tickets – but that was hardly the point. A faith-shaking betrayal, *that* was the point.

◆

It should by now be apparent that I'm no fan of mere brutality. Brutality is to evil what a Big Mac is to hunger: it gets a job done, it accomplishes *something* – but utterly without beauty. There *is* a job to be done, obviously. Big Macs from Moscow to Manhattan address hunger's pragmatic agenda even if they leave the demands of its aesthetic untouched. I do require a certain quota of broken faces and crippled minds; there are *targets*. But what I'm looking for – what I'm *really* looking for – is the marriage of brutality to the higher human faculties: imagination, intellect, practical reasoning, aesthetic sense – and this pearl is found in but few oysters.

Consider, for example, my work in the thirties and forties. I'm not just talking about the boom, the record profits, the staggering *numerical* achievement (oh my brothers how the dark flowers bloomed in Hell, how we wallowed in blossom, how the odour dizzied us, how we *swooned*); nor am I talking merely of the clean lines of the System, nor the inspirational role of the mob. I'm talking, dear reader, of the sublime fusion of order and destruction. Like most alchemical grails it wasn't sought or won without risk and hardship. (Speaking of grails, shall I tell you where the Holy Grail is? You'd never believe it. Actually I'll save it for later. Some incentive for you to hang in there through the grizzly bits . . .) My boy Himmler spent a great deal of time worrying – about all sorts of nonsense (his bowels, whether he was undermined by his spectacles, whether his face really resembled – as an old school enemy had cruelly claimed – a brainless onion) but chiefly about the excruciating difficulty of torturing and murdering millions of people without damaging one's humanity . . .

Tonight Heinrich addresses an assembly of SS brass in Berlin. He has his speech prepared, but the cases of Kreiger and Hoffman won't leave him alone. The cases of Kreiger and Hoffman are telling Heinrich that the speech as it is won't do. He's drafting an addendum mentally, now, combing his hair at the mirror of his mistress's bathroom. The bathroom, like the rest of the grand, cavernous house, used to belong to someone else . . . *Gentlemen, there is, in addition* . . . no. *In addition, gentlemen, I must draw your attention –* no. *There is no getting away, gentlemen, from the fact that –* no. 'The fact that' is always redundant. If you feel yourself to be in possession of a fact, then state it. *Gentlemen, there is something I would like you to consider. I mean of course –* but the addendum falters at the intrusion of a slight colonic spasm and a sequence of soundless farts escaping in malodorous ellipsis that bring tears of something – humility, relief, joy – to the Reichsführer's eyes. He must begin again with his hair. It's not widely known that our Heinrich suffered from an obsessive compulsive disorder, that actions as mundane as combing his hair were hung around with curious methods and rituals. The floor of the bathroom is tiled in pale blue with blinding white grouting. He wonders about the workman who laid them, where he is now, whether he's alive, whether he was a Jew. *What I mean, gentlemen, is that there is a serious risk of –* no. Fucking *concentrate*. But Kreiger and Hoffman won't let him. Scylla and Charybdis, Kreiger and Hoffman. No point in mentioning them by name, obviously, but . . . Perhaps through the Scylla and Charybdis motif – though half that lot won't even – he is thinning, he knows. Under the overgenerous light (the bathroom is big

196

enough for a small chandelier) the pink of his scalp shows through. *It is a great, dark, burden, gentlemen, and it is for us – it is for me – I will bear this burden* . . . Remembering her soaping his hair in the bath, sculpting it into a single tuft like the stem of an acorn almost makes him laugh. He's been finding in laughter of late hidden precipices, sudden sheer drops into the conclusion that he's lost his mind. Laughter – genuine laughter, not the political variety – has of late had him slithering down unexpected tilts, arms windmilling, only to grab a halt at some vertiginous edge beyond which emptiness offers him the pitch into madness as his own final solution. So he doesn't laugh genuinely of late. Instead he laughs strategically, loudly, letting each metallic ejaculation form its brilliant armour around him.

It's a great difficulty for the Reichsführer to ponder the wording of the warning Kreiger and Hoffman have made plain, without now, at this very moment, mentally re-living the two cases themselves.

Gerd Kreiger had done eight months at Buchenwald. (Marcus Hoffman had been there only three.) In December he'd been granted leave to attend his father's funeral in Leipzig. Gerd hadn't been close to his father (perhaps *that,* thinks Heinrich . . .?) and it was no secret among his colleagues in the camp that this two-day sojourn was cherished not as an opportunity for the formal expression of grief, but as a chance for a highly *in*formal expression of lust: forty-eight hours in Leipzig would take him (once the onerous business with the old man's corpse was concluded) into the arms of his fiancée, the tediously rhapsodized Wilhomena Meyer, or, as both she and Gerd preferred, Willie.

Heinrich, against his better judgement (he suspects not sentimentality, exactly, but some kind of weakness) has photographs of both Gerd and Willie (but not of Marcus) in the top drawer of his desk. Gerd is in uniform facing the camera: monstrously high cheekbones and giant grey eyes, a full-lipped mouth and a slicked-back widow's peak so blond it shows up white in the print. (Just the sort of hair Heinrich himself would prefer.) Not quite the ideal – there's a lopsidedness to the face as a whole, as if its components have been shaken by something and not come into correct realignment – but certainly nothing to arouse suspicion.

In the other photograph, Willie Meyer, Gerd's intended, is bright-faced with dark eyes and her coppery hair wound up in an elaborate chignon. Her cheeks are on the heavy side, as is her jaw, and Heinrich suspects she would have thickened undesirably with age, but her throat is a pearly column of some loveliness, and you can see there's a pair of formidable Teutonic *Titten* beneath the close-fitting blouse. The photograph shows her at twenty-two, seated at a piano but not playing, clutching, rather, her framed Certificate of Excellence from one of Leipzig's private colleges of music. She looks genuinely happy, relieved, shyly proud of herself. Whenever the Reichsführer places their images side by side on the varnished oak of his desk he feels sure they would have had a good, stodgy, tolerably unhappy marriage and four or five clumsy children. He feels sure everything would have been all right.

Afterwards, he had sent officers to interview Gerd and Marcus's crew at Buchenwald. A good poker player, they'd said of Kreiger. A practical joker, of Hoffman. The prisoners? What's to say about that? They felt as we all do. It's a headache, you know, a constant headache. Jews, Jews, Jews, fucking endless shivering Jews. Kreiger used to complain the whole thing was going too slowly, maybe that they were coming out of the ground at night like mushrooms! What? No, no, of course not. What's this all about anyway?

The bathroom radiator shudders and clanks. Difficult to do this in your head, Heinrich thinks. Heated bathrooms are the hallmarks of . . . *The point I want to bring to your attention, gentlemen, is that our destiny places us on a knife-edge* . . . Yes but then you lose the Scylla and Charybdis image. They won't even be paying attention, half of them. Too many of them don't realise even now what we're . . . what we . . .

Gerd got his night alone with Willie. It was a big night for both of them. A big night for Willie because she knew her mother didn't believe her story of staying at Lisle's, and though she didn't quite *wink* at her daughter, there was a curious movement at the corners of her mouth that indicated some new and shocking female complicity, brought on by the war, Willie thought, with feelings of liberation and betrayal queasily mixed. (It must be said here that it was by no means a small night for Marcus Hoffman, either, since round about the time Gerd and Willie were getting down to business, young Marcus was putting the pistol in his mouth, pulling the trigger, and blowing most of his brain out of the top of his head.) A big night for Gerd, because sometime shortly after entering her (standard issue condom) he stabbed Willie through the stomach with a pair of dressmaker's scissors that were lying on the bedside table. Then he stabbed her through the kidneys, then the lower bowel, then the heart. Then he had a bath. Then he dressed. Then he went out to a nearby café and had a drink. He was still there six hours later when the Gestapo came to arrest him.

Heinrich demanded the transcripts.

I don't know. It doesn't matter now so I'll tell you. There was a woman in the camp. These things don't matter to me now so what do I care? I couldn't stop myself. I don't know about Marcus. He came in on us.

I don't know if it had ever occurred to him before. It soon did! She worked up in the kitchens most of the time, but sometimes I saw her. I'll tell you, it's a strange thing, sergeant, but I knew, you know, that it would be a defilement to let her touch me, to touch her . . . but it's difficult to explain. What does it matter me saying this now? A strange thing. Really a strange thing. My mother took me to see my grandfather one time in Weimar, and he had a huge turd in his pocket, his own turd, you know? The nurse said it was common in the old. Not that I'm old. Touching something like . . . whereas you know . . . What? Yes. You know I can say these things now because it doesn't matter. And what can it matter to Marcus, that idiot? They ran short of fuel up at the house and she came down to our shed. Franz was on duty and Dieter was playing solitaire – but they didn't see her, you know. I went by myself. Marcus only came in by chance, I think. It was all very simple. The odd thing was neither of us said a word. What can I tell you? I remember her body was cold. She didn't do anything, just let me move her arms and legs where I wanted. What is there to say? She felt like clay. Bits of clay from my old school in Leipzig, but a bit harder. She made barely a sound even when I stuck her. Couldn't believe I got away with it. Well, I guess I didn't, did I? Heh–heh! I don't think the commandant believed a word. But what did he care? She never made a sound. Afterwards, I remember Marcus lifting up her arm and letting it flop back down. It had become dislocated – I don't know how, she didn't put up any kind of fight. Lifting it up and flopping it down. It was like he had a fixation or something. If you ask me he should never have been in the camp in the first place. No backbone.

Willie betrayed me, you see. When I touched her, she felt just like the Jew in the woodshed. Just like clay. I kept trying but I couldn't feel any difference. Somehow I couldn't stop myself. It seemed not to matter whether I did it or not. When I did do it, I felt a great calm peace all over me, you know, like when you've had a fever and then you wake in the morning and know that it's gone, like magic . . .

Heinrich has been to see Gerd Kreiger in his cell. Kreiger read a two-week old newspaper. Didn't bother saluting. Didn't bother standing up. The cell was clean, but with an unpleasant smell, compressed and feral, as of a furiously alive rodent in a box no bigger than its body. Heinrich had insisted on going in alone. The bodyguard would have pistol-whipped Kreiger for his insolence – but how would that have helped? (Beyond, obviously, the minute addition to the wildly sculpted mass of the Reichsführer's ego; astonishing, given the weight of power that already attended him, that Heinrich still noticed each new particle of another's fear that increased it. He marvelled at it somewhat himself.) He went with the intention of questioning Kreiger, but found, when confronted with the youth's recumbent body and mildly enquiring face, that he could not think of what to ask him. So the two had regarded each other in silence for a few moments, then the Reichsführer had turned on his heel and left.

There is also, gentlemen, a very grave matter about which I must speak. I mean of course –

Hoffman's suicide bothers Heinrich, if possible, more than Kreiger's murder, stirring up not just fear, but contempt. (One of the downsides of my work with the Nazi Party was that its evils threatened perpetually to become internecine, the brilliant by-products endangering the process as a whole. I felt like the parent of a gifted but hyperactive child: take your eye off it at the wrong moment – Stalingrad '43, for example – and there was no calculating the damage it could do to itself.) He doesn't know the cause of it, Hoffman's suicide. He doesn't know the *particulars*. (I do, obviously. I was there, believe it or not, on a flying visit, touching up details, checking loose threads, tensions, weights, contrasts – no rest for the wicked and whatnot.) Heinrich doesn't know pins and needles killed Marcus Hoffman. An off-duty nap in his bunk. His left arm resting at an odd angle under his head. A cut-off blood flow. Pins and needles. He woke, as you do, with the sense that his arm was by his side, in some deadening pain – only to find, on investigation in the dark, as you do, that his arm wasn't by his side at all, but in fact strangely elevated and seemingly possessed of a will of its own.

It was just that it had never happened to him before. It was just that he'd never touched his arm and not felt himself touching it. Manhandling it, in tingling increments, back to where it belonged, he was reminded of the Jew in the woodshed. Her arm had felt . . . Her arm . . .

Well. It's a slippery slide, the imagination. Once you set off there's no telling where you'll end up.

Heinrich stands in front of the bathroom mirror washing his hands, scrupulously. The soap is good, and lathers as if with hyperenthusiasm. He is not satisfied with his hair. But against the odds – perhaps, perversely, because he has allowed his anxiety to take him through the two cases, the illuminated fear less potent than the one that still lurks in the dark – his addendum is finally starting to flow:

I also want to talk to you quite frankly on a very grave matter. I mean . . . the extermination of the Jewish

202

race . . . Most of you must know what it means when 100 corpses are lying side by side, or 500, or 1,000. To have stuck it out and at the same time – apart from exceptions caused by human weakness – to have remained decent fellows, that is what has made us hard. This is a page of glory in our history which has never been written and is never to be written . . . It is the curse of greatness that it must step over dead bodies to create new life. Yet we must . . . cleanse the soil or it will never bear fruit. It will be a great burden for me to bear . . .

Yet still it bothers him, later that night under the lights and the blood red banner with the stage wings like two dark beckonings into eternity, that the after-image of languid Kreiger and Hoffman's hungry ghost are slipping away from him, their meaning, these unique bookends to the danger . . . and on the run, *ad libitum,* so to speak, he takes a risky detour from his belaboured and beloved script:

 . . . must be accomplished without our leaders and their men suffering any damage in their minds and souls. The danger is great indeed, for only the narrowest way stands between the Scylla of their becoming cold-hearted brutes unable any longer to treasure life where it must be treasured (*he thinks of Willie, the chignon, the Certificate of Excellence, the five boisterous nippers that will now never be*) where it *must* be treasured, gentlemen, and the Charybdis of their becoming soft, enfeebled, nervously debilitated, or in danger of mental breakdown . . .

You lose even your golden earthly students, eventually. As I did Heinrich to suicide (after continual problems with nausea, stomach convulsions, tics and a whole range of physical and psychological irritations, bearing witness that even the Reichsführer had difficulty *quite* practising what he preached) in 1945. But you've got to appreciate the sheer effort he made to hold on. You've got to appreciate the commitment to *civilizing brutality*. Nothing fucks the Old Man off more, believe me. He can forgive the animal in you dragging you down to the trough. He can't forgive you inviting the animal up for afternoon tea.

But the system petered out, you'll say. The death camps were liberated. The fucking Nazis *lost*.

Well, yes, my darlings, they did. But their victory wasn't my goal. (Obviously it was *their* goal, the morons.) Their victory, ultimately, was neither here nor there, as long as, after they'd done their thing, millions of people could no longer sustain the preposterous fallacy that the Old Man loved the world.

Heinrich, by the way, was *awfully* surprised to find himself screaming in agony – I mean sipping his complimentary arrivals cocktail – in Hell.

◆

I have of late – wherefore I know not . . .

Evening in Clerkenwell. I've been writing for hours. Apathetic rain and London's sky like a tarry lung. The City's gone home, exhausted, with aching feet and sour skin. It's gone home to seek the relief of diversion. It's gone home to consume, to drink, to masturbate, to babble, to smoke, to watch *Who Wants to Be a Millionaire?* It's gone home to an ordinariness only occasionally punctuated by the awful intimation that despite everything, despite *Coronation Street*, Silk Cut, chat rooms, Sainsbury's, Christmas and the Wimbledon fortnight, despite all these and infinitely more, one day the ordinariness will be terminally punctuated by the extraordinary full stop of death. I sat at Gunn's window and watched the offices and banks exhale, the systole and diastole of rush-hour traffic. I saw what I always see, what I've made it my business to make sure any ethereal observer would see: human beings avoiding God. How beautiful you are to me still, after all these years! Eyes – I've never quite got used to the beauty of human eyes, so transparently enslaved by the soul, so ready to show me how much I've achieved.

Hard to calculate the things that brought me here. I'll tell you one of them.

Not long ago, having been lengthily busy in the corporate world, I decided to put some time back into the meat and potatoes of the operation and get down amongst the plebs for a bit of slap and tickle. You need to keep your hand in. Senior style consultants in elite hair salons around the world will tell you: every now and then you need to just give someone a *haircut*. So you find me in a wood at the northern edge of Salisbury Plain (Stonehenge? Me again. Ritual rape, torture, murder. *Calendars?* These boffins kill me) with Eddie and Jane. Eddie's been hearing voices – Baraquel, Arioc, Ezekeel, Jequon and Shamshiel to be precise, whispering words of wisdom in the small hours. In any case, up until a few hours ago Jane and Eddie were strangers – or rather, Eddie was a stranger to Jane; Jane was no stranger to Eddie, who'd been observing her for some time. Eddie's a thirty-eight-year-old telecommunications engineer with a tankard-shaped head, small brown eyes and one permanently blackened thumbnail. Jane's a twenty-four-year-old brunette of no special features but nothing wrong with her either who works as one of two receptionists in a small van hire office on an industrial estate at the edge of the city.

Serial potential written all over Eddie. Topple this domino and there's no telling how many (look out girls!) will fall after it. Plus, his mother's a rabid Catholic, which is icing on any cake. The boys have put in some time, but confessed that ultimately and against their expectations they need His Master's Voice to clinch it. This happens to me a lot. I delegate, but sooner or later they shuffle in, sheepish, cap-fingering, wondering if I might find time to . . . ah . . . etc. Needless to say it's a piece of Battenberg to me, the old Blade Runner. 'Eddie,' I said to him in his mother's voice. 'It's okay, you know. You won't get caught.' (That's pretty much all you lot need to hear, not that it's morally defensible, but that it's *covered*.) Did the trick. Downloaded the recommended chloroform dosage from the web (eeee*yup*: me again) and off he went.

Most of you probably want the abduction, the rape, the murder, all the Thomas Harris palaver with the corpse, and believe me if this were Gunn I'm sure you'd get it; some pseudo-poetic cladding, some poignant details about cloud-shadows or the vividness of an empty Coke can by her knee, some watch-the-birdie *writing* to distract your attention from the possibility that the entire thing's titillating to him (and you) – but even baldly listed facts will be enough to delight others among you, as they often do Gunn, decaf and gutless sadist that he is. *My hands were tied and I was forced to perform oral sex*. These are just impersonal newspaper details, but still lights wink, bells ring. He comforts himself with the belief that it's the writer's job to tell the truth unselectively, be that the truth of motherhood or the truth of murder. 'Go ahead,' Penelope barked at him. 'You'll be joining a venerable list of male writers who've written about men committing violence against women. Men *killing* women is a fucking genre all on its own. Of course I realise it's your *obligation* to write about it, if it's at all a part of the world (as is friendship and honour and simple kindness and people dying for their beliefs – but maybe none of those is *creatively interesting*) but it's also your obligation to understand what it means to you and why you're doing it. At which point, Declan, don't come fucking crying to me if it turns out you're doing it because you *like* it.' As you can see, Penelope's critical faculties were not to be engaged lightly – a lesson I'm not sure boneheaded Gunn ever learned.

But this isn't Gunn, Hell be praised, nor is the business of Eddie and Jane the point. The point is that in the middle of everything a dog dragged itself past.

A black one, too. This dog had seen better days. This dog was dog tired. I don't know where this wretched dog came from, but if he'd ever had his day it was a long time ago. To say that something had happened to this dog is to say that Hiroshima suffered a slight disturbance back in August '45. *Everything* had happened to this dog. He'd been hit by something, some vehicle, an incident which had amputated a front leg and broken a back one, so that forward motion was a curious combination of hopping and dragging. But this was only his most recent bit of hard cheese. One eye was cataracted. His mouth (broken jaw, too, by the way) was rotting with a suppurating infection and most of his hair was gone. The exposed flesh revealed the wounds of a beating, all of which had gone bad. His arse was bleeding and his semi-exposed phallus unhealthily inflamed.

That wasn't it. You didn't think that was it, did you? *Hello?* I've presided over the torture and deaths of millions of human beings with as much emotional engagement as a nail-filing receptionist on a Friday afternoon. You think an injured hound is going to break my heart?

No, that wasn't it. What *was* it was that moments from

death this dog stopped to sniff and tentatively lick another dog's turd that just happened to be coiled and glistening nearby. I watched him. I thought, State he's in there's no way; state he's in he's not going to be *capable*. A part of me even then was thinking (not knowing why): I do sincerely hope he doesn't. I hope being this close to expiry finally releases him from the cage of his dumb instincts. I hope he just fucking dies, now.

But he didn't. (He did less than a minute later.) He drag-hopped, bent his hideous head, sniffed and licked – and my voice inside me said: *That's you, Lucifer*.

I never really wanted this job. (As all dictators whine.) Trouble was, when we found ourselves in Hell everyone looked at me. (How to describe Hell? Disembowelled landscape busy with suffering, incessant heat, permanent scarlet twilight, a swirling snowfall of ash, the stink of pain and the din of . . . If only. Hell is two things: the absence of God and the presence of time. Infinite variations on that theme. Doesn't sound so bad, does it? Well, trust me.)

I didn't want the job – the job, that is, of spending all that would remain of time working against God, the job of *personifying evil* – but look at it from my point of view: as far as Himself's concerned it's over between us. No conciliatory cappuccinos under the fat waiter's benevolent presidency. No Relate. No *saw this and thought of you, Love, Lucifer* cards. You know the routine. You've Broken Up, yes? Locks changed, CDs divvied and boxed, ring returned, cuddly toy drawn and quartered?

Doesn't matter that I felt lousy. Doesn't matter that I realised I might have been a tad *hasty*. Doesn't matter that I would have been willing (we all would) to turn over a new leaf. Doesn't matter. You're an angel, you fall, you don't rise again, the end. (Or so one was led to believe, until this whimsical turn of events . . .) We could all have devoted ourselves there and then to cancer research or pet rescue – wouldn't have made a dint, not in the infinitely hard heart, and certainly not in Arthur's prima donna ticker, reserved as it was for Humanity. (Junior and that heart. Like a pregnant woman with her suddenly enlarged mams: *Get off. These are for the baby.*) We all knew the score. The score was, God: a lot, Fallen Angels: nil. And everyone's looking at me. If I'd bottled then they would have massacred me. And so to the *Hail horrors! Hail infernal world* speech, which, despite my virtually inhabiting his quill, Milton sheared of its Angelspeak glory (as well as wreaking nomenclatural havoc among the angelic host). Whatever else I'd lost I still had the gift of the gab. You should have seen how it stirred them up. Had *myself* going by the end of it. But I still felt dismal inside. I had an inkling of what being utterly evil would be like. I had an inkling it would be *demanding*. But I repeat: What choice did I have?

Evil be thou my Good. Well, yes, in a manner of speaking, but it's a phrase (he was such an inveterate *simplifier*, was Milton) that's too often been taken to mean something it doesn't. Most commonly: that evil, in and of itself, actually *feels good* to me. Now, let me ask you – I'm sure you're a reasonable human being with a functioning brain – do you seriously think that by sheer fiat an archangel (*the* Archangel – oh no really, you're too kind . . .), that by sheer *decree*, I say, an archangel can invert his pleasures and pains like that? If only it were so simple!

No. I know this is going to be a stretch for you, but I might as well come right out and say it: *I don't like evil.* It hurts. It absolutely *kills*, if you really want the truth. Where else do you think this outlandish pain of mine originates? Evil gives me pain. *Pain.* As much as it would have had it existed independently of me before I Fell. If only it were as simple as the traditions suggest. If only it genuinely *seemed to me* that evil was good and vice versa – but it doesn't. Good is still good, evil still evil.

So what am I? *Perverse?*

Well, some might think so. The point, my dears, is not good nor evil – but freedom. For an angel there is only one true freedom, and that, I'm honestly sad to say, is freedom from God. Freedom is the cause and the effect. In this particular Creation, if freedom from God (worship of God, dependency on God, obedience to God) is what you're after, then I'm afraid evil's really the only game in town. What I'd like, what I'd *love*, is to have been given a nature that didn't even know God – the fish in the pond who doesn't know life beyond it: the lawn, the house, the city, the country, the world . . .

Your thinkers wrestle with this notion of *pure evil* or, as they're so fond of calling it, *evil for its own sake.* I've no idea why. There's no such thing as *evil for its own sake.* All evil is motivated – even mine. The torturer, the tyrant, the murderer, the consummate fabricator of fibs – they're all doing it *for* something, even if all they're doing it for is pleasure. (The problem your thinkers have is understanding quite *how* the evildoer gets pleasure from his evil, but that's a different question.) Evil for its own sake is – or would be if it existed – madness; and even the barmy do what they do for *some* barmy reason. What pains the Old Boy most is not that I do evil, but that I do what causes me excruciating pain. What pains Him is that even perpetual and excruciating pain is a price worth paying for disentangling myself from *Him. That's* the crux of it. *That's* what He can't stand.

If He'd just do the simple thing and *go away*, I could stop all this tempting and seducing and blaspheming and lying and so on, and just get on, freely, with being me. It's a *terribly* burning question, you know, this question of who, outside of my relationship to You Know Who, I actually am. I mean I'm sure I'm *someone*. I wonder what I'm like? I wonder if I'm . . . well . . . *all right?*

I'm supposed to be guilty of all sorts of crimes and misdemeanours, but when you get right down to it, I'm really only guilty of one: wondering. The road to Hell, you say, is paved with good intentions. Charming. But actually it's paved with *intriguing questions*. You want to *know*. *Man* do you want to know! *I wonder what it'd be like to stick this bread-knife into his throat?* Whose question do you think that is? You'd be surprised. It's the young mother's, slicing through the still warm loaf while her under-two sits facing her in his highchair, gurgling, a mauled and sodden Jammy Dodger clutched in his tiny mit. She's not *going* to, obviously, ninety-nine times out of a hundred, but you know, it's there, the wonder, the beautiful, abstract curiosity. It's there because I put it there. Try it. Pick up a knife, a hatchet, a club, a loaded gun when there's anyone else around – put an instrument of potential destruction in your hand and tell me that nowhere, *nowhere* in your mind is the question: I wonder what it would feel like to use this?

Proximal vice, of course, stirs curiosity like nothing else. Ask the plod who work with sex offenders, the paedophile police, the rape detectives. Ask them how long it takes before that *wondering* takes hold. Try it. Go and visit your local Dahmer, your Sutcliffe, your Hindley. Come away and tell me truthfully that you weren't in the least disturbed by the feeling that they knew something vital that you didn't. The tonnage of *True Crime*, all that astonishing testimony, all those frank black-and-whites – why does it race off the shelf, the newsstand, the web? Titillation, yes of course (bloodlust and sadism in the camouflage fatigues of what-makes-these-monsters-tick?-And-thank-God-they've-got-that-evil-bastard; you'd be surprised, I dare say, at the suburban boudoir impact some of your century's shockers have had), but more than that, the desire to *know*. Except of course you can't, vicariously, not *really*. Some kinds of knowing (you know this anyway, but you kid yourselves along) demand a rigorously empirical approach.

I've wondered – as I know you must have – why, exactly, I'm doing this. Not the movie. Not the month-in-Gunn's body thing (it should be obvious by now that I'm doing that for . . . Well, for ice cream, for bare feet on warm concrete, for kisses, for the dawn chorus, for leaf-shadows, for strawberries on the breath, for the sheer rock and roll of the Flesh and Its Feelings); no, I mean *this* thing, this *writing* thing. Why, you might reasonably ask, spend so much time and energy writing when you could be out there every second of the waking day?

Gunn would have absolutely no difficulty in explaining this – but that's not the point.

The point is . . .

Oh it's embarrassing. Honestly it is.

Jimmeny went among you and spoke to you in your own tongues, He left a *book* behind him – one so ambiguous and paradoxical that it can be made to fit any weak or credulous mind's needs – which made it categorically clear where donations, thanks and praise should be directed whenever your bread fell butter-side up. (The butter-side-down stuff they're not so keen to hear about.) He had all the publicity because he had all the *language*. Publicity *is* language. What publicity have I had, me with the allegedly beyond measure pride? A proud being would have been driven mad by this invisibility aeons ago. How long have I felt like the genius playwright barred forever from sharing encore glories – the thunderous applause, the hurled bouquets – with his frequently spoon-fed or second-rate cast? Have I complained?

Uncomplaining I would have remained, too, had this absurd new deal not been tossed (contemptuously in my opinion) on the table. Unvoiced, unseen, unheard, uncredited. Enough merely never to have surrendered. (*Never surrender.* My motto long, *long* before it left the mouth of your erstwhile PM.) Enough, it would have been, merely to have remained . . . *myself*, in silence, unwritten into your history's lively pages. But what with the clock ticking and everything . . .

I've been so close to you, after all. I'm not *entirely* without . . . What I mean is, I know it's been . . . *difficult*, at times – a love-hate relationship, you might say – but I have always . . . you know . . . *been* there for you, haven't I?

Plus, I do type now at around 400 words a minute.

◆

I'm mad, I am. Absolutely *mad*. Honestly. I should be on telly. You won't believe what I did yesterday. Truly you won't. Shall I tell you? Shall I? I went to see Penelope.

Gossip columnists must be depressed. Deeply depressed. For in a state of profound depression I opened my mouth to tell the tale – well, I mean switched on and addressed my quicksilver fingertips to Gunn's keys – and lo! The above idiom sprang fully formed into being, like Athena from Zeus's thunderous forehead. It's inappropriate. The only thing to do with atrocity, it's been said, is to chronicle it. There's no working it, shaping it, making *art* of it.

Just history's obligation to document the facts. Well then, let me list the facts of atrocity. I went to see Penelope.

There are idiots among you, I daresay, so wedded to the love story that some preposterous and epoch-making affair of the heart between me and her is already taking shape in your imagination. You're the punters for whom Hollywood producers like Harriet's chum Frank Gatz exist: 'You got a story where the Devil comes to earth, right? Takes over this writer prick's body, right? Okay. Now whatever the fuck else happens in the story, what's *got* to happen is that he falls in love. With the writer prick's girl. Then you go with it. She get's shot, whatever. Hospital. Toobs. Life-support. Our guy's got to make a deal with God. Her life in exchange for his. Boom. You see this? And when *he* croaks, the scaly wings and shit are gone. Pure white feathers. "He thought he'd fallen from Heaven. It was worse than that. He'd fallen in love." That's your tag-line. You seeing this? Get me Pitt's guy on the phone. He'll be all over it . . .'

I don't quite know where the idea came from. (It's one of the few questions I'd still like answered. I mean I know where your ideas come from. But what about mine?) Horribly curious, I must admit, to meet her in the flesh – my flesh as much as hers. Gunn's flesh, anyway. I even had a harmless plan. One that would set the cat among Gunn's pigeons when he returns (*if* he returns, that is, misery guts that he was before he left) without incurring the tiresome prohibitions of Charlie's Angels from Above. And before you get all political on me – I wasn't going to *do* anything to her. Not in *that* way. Just a bit of innocent mischief. I was going to – well . . . You'll see presently.

I took the 12.00 from Euston, due in at Manchester Piccadilly at 14.35 (useless Gunn can't drive, and I was hanged if *I* was going to waste a day stealing a vehicle and teaching

myself). It was a heartbreakingly beautiful day. Londoners
haven't seen a summer like this since '76. Heat rippled the city.
I had four 99s and a Strawberry Split on the way to the
station. Ice cream. Oh, man: your mouth's a volcanic orifice;
in goes Mister Softee – and lo! thou art filled with bliss. Or I
am, at any rate. It's the hot/cold thing, I know. Hardly surprising when you think about it. I've been troughing for
England since I got here (lamb jalfrezi; anchovies by the
pound; green olives slathered in oil and flecked with raw
garlic; glacé cherries; chargrilled salmon steaks; Toblerone;
iced radishes dipped in sea salt and fresh ground pepper; pick-
led herrings; After Eights . . .) but I've yet to come across
anything to match the delights of Mister Softee's aerated ice-
cream, spiralled into a 99 cornet, garlanded – nay, *bejewelled*
with the glutinous sauce of the noble raspberry and accented
with an ingenuine and vastly overpriced Flake. I tell you
solemnly: ice-cream's so delicious and bad for you I can't
believe I had nothing to do with its invention.

However. I walked to Euston. I find I still adore walking.
Absurd, obviously, what with it being merely a case of *putting
one foot in front of the other* and so on – but there you are. The
sky was distant, madly blue, ethereally marbled with alto-
cumulus clouds. My shadow wobbled and jogged alongside
me like a retarded or palsied companion. Dear, pan-fried
London gave out the reek of its traffic and waste – you can
smell the nineteenth century in London, the eighteenth,
the seventeenth, the sixteenth; its odours shuffle the ages,
lace KFC with ancient sewage, diesel with velum and dust.
(I've come a long way since first opening my eyes in Gunn's
bathroom. With an effort, I can remain calm in the presence
of myriad colours; with an effort I can hold back the swoon
or the rabid assault; with an effort I can – as they say
Stateside – *deal*.) No, I can't deny the merits of *wandering*

about, nor those of *doing nothing*. I cancelled Harriet the other evening, you know. Just like that, cancelled her. I was sitting in my room at the Ritz, having just inhaled a judiciously measured line of Bolivia's finest when the scent-tendrils of Green Park's recently mown grass drew me, snout-first, like a nose-ringed bull, to the open window, where I looked out. That's all — just *looked out*. The sky all furrowed mauve and indigo splashed from below by a preposterously bloody sunset; meanwhile the bruise-coloured park exhaled its day's stored heat; the trees crackled, softly; the air had a parched or purged taste, as if a fire had charged through it . . . I called her mobile and told her I was sick. You can't believe it, can you? Trading Harriet's mesmerizing monologues for an evening's quiet contemplation of twilight's gentle passage into night. I can hardly believe it myself. My mature phase, perhaps. Beauty and sadness. I got so melancholy (what *was* it it all reminded me of?), so blues & country *lonesome*, that it was all I could do to rustle up Leo for a midnight rub. (Did I mention Leo? As in 'Man-2-Man Leo, genuine 10″ cut offering full body work/role play dom or sub, TVs o.k., no TS, no women'? I didn't? Well, my dear Declan, I'm afraid I've got some rather startling news for you . . .)

Anyway. (Do you prefer *Anyway* or *Some*? This title-hunting's a bitch. I spent an hour or two toying with calling it *Huh*.) Anyway, Penelope's back in Manchester. She moved back there after her and our Declan went their separate ways. She's unresolved about it, mind you, the move up North. (It kills me, you know, all you humans lying on the couch talking about being unresolved. *I'm unresolved*. Oh, really? You don't say? You mean, you're actually . . . not . . . re*solved*?)

Stalling. Sorry. Pitiful.

I've seen photos, obviously. She hasn't changed much.

The hair's still warm golden and prone to tangles, but shoulder-length now, not the spine-long treasure that drove Gunn potty. The green eyes still have it. Beauty, of course, but life, time, history, thinking, pain. Less curiosity than the Gunn Penelope. Less curiosity, more life.

She lectures. There's a one-bedroomed garden flat. A cat called Norris and two unchristened goldfish. There are men, when she feels like it: illicitly indulged-in post-grads from time to time; these or wild cards picked up during assaults on the city's nightlife (her and her debauched mate Susan); but since Gunn she's treasured her own space, a burrow to which she can retreat and brood; a smouldering Marlboro, a bottle of plonk, the garden at evening, its anarchy of birdsong. There's been a woman, too (footage Gunn would have paid cash money to see), a PhD third-year with feisty black eyes and wet-gelled hair who wore tan leather strides and what must have been cripplingly expensive silk shirts. Laura. Smelled of lemons and Impulse Musk. Deeply exciting for Penelope, initially, her adventure at the Looking Glass. Ultimately no more manageable than the half-dozen straight lovers since Gunn.

The green leather jacket hangs on the back of the kitchen door. She sits opposite me at the stripped oak dining table, in profile, her arms around her knees, her bare feet up on the chair next to her. The kitchen's door opens directly onto the bright garden. I'm tempted to giggle, glimpsing it, remembering my unseemly moments back at St Anne's. She's opened the wine I brought – not plonk, but an extortionately expensive Rioja – but both of us take our first gulps without the bother of a (to *what*, exactly?) cheers.

'I wanted to talk to you,' I say.

She swallows, takes another quick sip. Swallows again. I know what she's thinking. I'm about to tell her that:

Penelope, my darling, I know what you're thinking, I'm about to say, when she turns, suddenly, and faces me.

'Declan,' she says. 'Don't think – please don't think the scale of it's diminished. Please don't think I've just comfortably assimilated it, what I've done. What I did. I know you think that.'

'No, I don't.'

'And don't think that I expect you to have stopped hating me, because I haven't. I know what a fucking vile and ugly thing it was. I know. I know. You wrong someone . . . When you *wrong* someone, in the old-fashioned way . . .'

Astonishing. Tears. Jumping Jimmeny Christmas. She moves fast, this girl. It's been two-and-a-half years, going on. Gunn turns up, they open a bottle of wine, he tells her he wants to talk to her and *zappo* – the heart opens its wound and starts to bleed all over the place. (It is, you must concede, unpleasantly messy, this business of having feelings, this *mattering* to each other. I've always thought of it as gory, a sort of perpetually occurring road accident – everyone going too fast, too close, without due care and attention, or with too much . . .)

This is sweet, I'm thinking. Gunn, who despises her for having made him love her then betraying him, would want my guts for garters if he were here – which wouldn't be a good idea, since they're his guts, too – if he had the faintest inkling of what I'm about to do.

'It *was* a fucking hideous thing,' Penelope says. 'It was. I know it was.'

'Would you mind if I had one of those?' I say, indicating the open-flapped pack of Marlboro next to her hand. She's blank in response, a ravaged tissue held to her suddenly reddened nose. I see I've switched to the wrong level. (Damned impulsive desires, you see? How do you cope? I mean it just came over me, right then, that I really wanted a cigarette. I'd left my

Silk Cut on the blasted train.) She's so deep in her own feeling awful that it barely even grazes her, that I'm bothering about things like *cigarettes*. I take one anyway and light up.

'What I mean is . . . Declan please don't tell me you hate me. I know you do. And you've the right. Just please, please don't say it here, now. I promise you I hate myself enough for both of us.'

I'm tempted to let her run on. I mean come on, it *is* rather charming, her misery, her guilt, finally, especially since her entire identity's been built on *knowing the right thing to do – then doing it*. Not that she's been perfect, of course. There have been slips, stumbles, days of laziness or existential ennui – but there hasn't been a *fall*, not like the one precipitated by Declan's unfortunately swollen head. She's hard on herself. She remembers *the past*. Susan tells her, invariably, on their splurges: *Your fucking trouble is you can't let go of the past*. Her cider-and-black flavoured breath beats against Penelope's face. *How can you expect to live if you've still got your head buried in the past?* It's not my head, Penelope's wanted to groan. It's my *heart*.

Now, here, I'm afraid, is where the atrocities begin. (My fingers hesitate at Gunn's greasy keys. I've already stalled myself with three cups of Earl Grey and six cigarettes. If it weren't for your language being so blatantly designed for deception, all this telling the truth would have me worried. Professional reputation and all that. However . . .) The most extraordinary thing. How to say this? I . . . I find myself . . .

Look I'm no fool. I've got used to bits and bobs of Gunn cropping up in my behaviour, the odd fingerprint here and there. I knew it was never going to be a *clean distinction* (the body has its limits on how many things you can let pass through – don't I know from previous possessions? All that rot and stench? Involuntary snatches of nursery rhymes or surprise waves of tenderness at the appearance of a favourite teddy? Goes with the territory); but this . . . this is something entirely different. What we're talking about here is the . . . the whole-sale import of a particular feeling that I didn't have to start with, suddenly, directly from Gunn's past into my present. I open my mouth to begin what I've come here to begin – and find myself in an agony of hatred and pain. (Don't get me wrong. If I'm familiar with anything I'm familiar with hatred and pain. Hatred and pain are my blood and bones, so to speak, my spirit's dress, my odours, my shape, my – well, we've covered this. The point is that's fine with me because it's *my* hatred, *my* pain. I mean they affirm the continuity of my identity if nothing else. This, on the other hand, pitches up in me like an obstreperous and lightning-quick gatecrasher. One minute it isn't there, the next it is – and I find myself – get this – *hating Penelope.* (There's an exclamation mark on this keyboard which shares tab-space with the number one. Shift+1=! It's insufficient. Radically inadequate as the deno-tation of my surprise. Even in bold. Even in <u>underlined</u> **bold** *italic.* I need something else, some punctuation mark not yet invented.) I sit there with my mouth open filled with human pain and human anger. *She was there*, a voice is saying (Gunn's presumably), *all naked and warm with her hair spread around her in the bed that we'd . . . In the bed . . . How could she and think of it think of it go on her sucking his cock and swallowing his come and go on* THINK OF IT HER FUCKING TONGUE IN HIS MOUTH AND HIS FACE *HIS FACE AND HER FACE AND SHE WAS SHE WAS YOU KNEW WHAT SHE LOOKED LIKE AND NOW HE DOES TOO* **YOU THINK OF IT YOU MIS-ERABLE FUCKING SHIT WRETCH AND YOU'VE DONE NOTHING NOTHING NOTHING EXCEPT WANT TO FUCKING DIE.**

In hindsight, gentle reader, I think even then I felt a bit sorry for Gunn, having so much rage and pain and so paltry a medium for its expression. I mean compared to me he's in fetters. I've got the whole earth and everyone in it to give tongue to my grievances. What's he got? *English*. I don't know what I must look like, sitting there, fuming. A children's cartoon steam train, perhaps, red-faced, pulling and puffing in a foul temper up a punishing hill. Whatever I look like, the important thing is what I feel like. And I feel – I can only assume – like Gunn. Drenched afresh in all that vivid moment's rich treachery. The slowly opened door introducing the scene like an amoral master of ceremonies. Penelope on the bed. That . . . that (what? Bastard? Fucker? Cunt? Cocksucker? Nothing adequately labels the object of Gunn's rage . . .), that *man* up on his elbows above her; his look of mild surprise; hers, turning to the yawning door, of death.

The need to hurt her, now, sitting in distress across the table from me, is overwhelming. Not physically – Gunn hasn't got it in him, whatever his fantasy life might think – but with the mouth's unstinted repertoire, the complete arsenal, the maximum yield.

Her face is a map of remembered trouble and absorbed guilt. The green eyes look broken, as if their glass has shattered. A motorway pile-up of wrecked mascara. Lashes jewelled with tears. She holds her own mouth on a tight rein. Remembering – it makes a frightful mess of the human face. I've seen it a billion times.

Now Penelope.

And the overwhelming desire and need is to hurt her. The words – Gunn's words – swarm on my tongue as if some inner smoke is driving them from the head's hive. But – (oh yes, *but*) – when I've got a plan I stick to it. Unlike some. If this is Limbo'd Gunn's distant broadcast (note to self: summon bloody Nelchael for a long overdue progress report), he's reckoned on too passive an audience. This isn't about what cuckolded Declan wants – no matter how loud and clear his carcass shouts its absent soul's mass of demands. It's about what I want. Thus, stepping around it, so to speak, as one might a sensitively alarmed sculpture in a narrow gallery space, I reach out and take Penelope's hot, tissue-clutching hand by its knuckles. She's a good, strong, guilty girl, so she looks me in the eye.

'That's not what I came here for,' I say, imagining Gunn tearing his incorporeal hair out, wherever he is. Penelope looks tired and all but irresistibly human – but I'm determined, now. (Besides, if I decide to stay – ha-ha – I might want her to be the mother of my children . . .) 'I came here,' I continue, dropping my glance to the mug-ringed table top in the manner of a person who, through a great and near-fatal struggle, has learned the virtue of kindness and humility, 'to tell you . . . to tell you . . .'

'Yes?' The air-speech of the grief-ravaged larynx.

'To tell you that . . . I . . . forgive you,' (the words come with a strange ease once I've got that 'forgive' out), 'without expectation of any kind. It was a betrayal, yes, but I'd betrayed you first. My fucking vanity. My idiotic, deluded *vanity*. If you wronged me, my love, it was because you were provoked by my wrong. I'm sorry for what I did, for what I became, for how ugly and false.'

I look back up at her. Her eyebrows have gone up in the middle and her lips are pursed. She doesn't know what to do, what's going on, whether she loves Gunn all over again, whether, even, this might not be a ruse, the opening device in an emotional booby trap. She's (I like this word) *flabbergasted*.

'I'm asking for nothing,' I say, getting slowly to my feet and unwrapping my jacket (it's been a wrench, I don't mind telling you, slipping out of the Armani, the Gucci, the

Versace, the Rolex, back into Gunn's excruciatingly dull threads – but there was no point in complicating things) from the back of the chair. 'This isn't a request, or a plea, or a gesture that requires response. It's just that I want you to live the rest of your life knowing that as far as I'm concerned you're forgiven, and loved. The whole thing was my fucking fault.'

'Declan . . . Oh, *God*, Declan I –'

'Don't say anything now. I just want to feel clean and right for once. We're not stupid; there's no point in talking about being friends or anything. I think we were too much to each other to be satisfied with that, now.'

I'm in two minds about the next bit – but it feels right, so I turn her hand over in mine and bend forward to leave a chaste kiss in its palm. She's utterly astonished. (And would you believe it? A thought breaks through in her like a sunbeam: *My God, I was right. My instincts were sound. He's grown – but you have to have the potential for growth . . . Maybe . . . maybe . . .*) But I'm gone. Out of the kitchen and down the hall while she's still scraping her chair in getting up from the table. I deal with the front door myself ('Wait . . . Declan please wait . . .') pull it shut behind me, then stride briskly away down the street. I feel her, of course. She comes to the door, opens it, looks out, sees the purposefulness and speed of my step, understands that now it must be left to germinate, that more words will ruin it. (Indeed they've ruined things enough for me, already, one way or another – but I'll come to that in a moment.) Nothing has prepared me for how I feel. I flag a cab and fling myself into its gloom, barely capable of muttering a destination ('. . . station . . . Piccadilly . . .') before feeling overwhelms me and I pass away into a terrible dream.

The first terrible part of this terrible dream was a merciless assault on my body. The train journey was bad enough (the train journey's bad enough even if you're tickety-boo in the health department, I'll grant you): shivering, cold sweats, hot sweats, tommy-gun teeth, blood flecked with peppercorns and glass fragments, the fever taking and releasing me like an equivocating molester, every bone a bruise, flesh as if stripped of its dermis – you wouldn't think, would you, that a mere seat cushion . . . A murmur in my ears like a Wimbledon crowd between games. Mere consciousness a terrible interrogation. By the time I staggered into my room at the Ritz it was all I could do to chug down a fifth of Jameson's and collapse onto the imperial bed. I believe I tried to speak. Not English, you understand. No. My *own* language. A very bad idea. I was seized with convulsions. My tongue swelled and burned. I hurled myself from the mattress with the intention of crawling (slithering would have been more likely, ha very bloody ha) to the enormous bathroom with its cooling spirits of basin, bowl, bidet and bath. Another bad idea. I hit the deck to discover I was paralysed. My tongue detumesced and my guts fired out a spectacular arc of sulphurous vomit. Now I'm familiar with this sort of thing – you don't get through the average possession without the odd gastric fiesta – but previous chunderings were picnics compared to the . . . the surrealist free-for-all to which I gave myself over that evening in my bathroom. I tried getting out of the body altogether: nothing doing. A wave of panic *that* sent through me, you can imagine. (S'all right. I've done it since. Must've been a temporary blockage on account of my . . . on account of what I was going through.) Things progressed. A chain-gang of fevers. Me babbling, incomprehensibly. I wouldn't've believed myself capable of moving – let alone writing – but, since I have the sheet of Ritz stationery to prove it . . . Not that it makes any sense. Handwriting's pretty atrocious, too. I can barely decipher it.

5%ityas 3insevvse££3 666666666theyiii ho yo
hurthurtyoulove6$$$and   evenb   thetgloryisn't
you!!!!1youthought isn'tyouisn'you%$$was te of????y
ou£££rexis 10sveig rof3"1"'""""!t ogoh$£$£ome

That's my best guess.

It stopped as suddenly as it had started. The madness, I
mean, the *terrible dream*. Or rather, switched its assault from
the body to the mind. In actuality, no doubt, I was lying
supine in a state of unflattering partial dress on the
unjudgemental bathroom floor. In the *terrible dream*, however, I was back at Penelope's gaff in Manchester with the
words 'forgive you' opening me – how can I describe this? –
separating my ribs and filling them with unbounded, men-
tholated space. Space. Can you be filled with space? Is it just
me? I could see the inside of my head. It was an area big
enough to seat every being in the universe, an infinite
amphitheatre overarched by . . . well, a *sky*, I suppose, one
of icy and sunlit blue, going on, as you might expect, forever. Vertigo? Sort of. The vertigo of bliss. (Gunn should
make a note of that for a title. *The Vertigo of Bliss*. That's got
to be a title for something. Not this, obviously, but *something*.) In any case nothing I've felt before, angelically or
otherwise. Still at the Manchester table, still observing the
concrete particulars – Penelope's bare feet up on the chair
next to her; the coffee rings and half-done *Guardian* quick
crossword (14 Down: *To forgive?* (6); she'd fill it in later, no
doubt); the open back door with its colour-riot and smell-
festival; the buzz of a passing bluebottle; my own hand, the
Marlboro with inch-long ash smouldering between first and
index – still, as I say, *there*. But released, too, simultaneously, as it were, into a realm from which it was possible to
both feel what I was feeling and observe myself feeling it.

And what I was feeling is water to this language's net, evidently. Hugeness. Internal hugeness. Room inside for . . . well, one hesitates to say this, but, *for everything*. Is there any other way of saying it? Bear with me, I'm searching . . . Searching . . . Nope. Room inside for everything. The discovery of infinite inner space, belonging to me and in which I ceased to matter. In this terrible dream my fingers grip Penelope's table edge, my feet hook around its mock Queen Anne legs – I'm convinced that without such precautions my own infinite lightness will see me carried up, up, passing immaterially through Penelope's ceiling and the floors and ceilings of the three flats above, up, up into the blue, filled with space, emptied of all but terrible bliss, permeated with the knowledge that I am both nothing and everything, a minute speck with the capacity for infinite expansion . . .

Wearing, isn't it. And that's just *hearing* about it. Meanwhile, back at the actuality ranch, I was very much regretting having turned the bathroom's lights on. Inset halogens surrounded prone me with interrogative stares of piercing brightness. It would have been lovely – it would have been absolutely the thing – to have got up and crawled or staggered back to the unlit bedroom with its forgiving shadows and soccer-pitch sized window filled with London's dusk. It would have been just what the doctor ordered. Instead, wide-eyed and inert, I lay on the bathroom like a mute patient unable to tell the approaching surgeon that the anaesthetic hadn't worked, that when the buzzing blade entered, I would, actually, *feel it*.

Nor was that the end of it. Oh dear me no. Betsy – yes, Betsy Galvez – stands in her bathroom gripping the rim of the sink and staring into its large, bulb-rimmed mirror. Her eyes are raw and her make-up is fractured. Tears, you see.

Every now and then a part of her rises up and looks at the other parts with contemptuous clarity. Downstairs, her eighty-three-year-old mother sits in her chair with bits of her mind abandoning her by the hour. There's a home help during the day – but Betsy handles the evenings and the nights. And it is evening now. Mr Galvez wants the old girl out and in a home. Ridiculous, he says (the smell of piss and medicine, the deteriorating mind, the ice cream in the hand-bag, the idiotic and impotent rages), since they have the money to pay for the best. But Betsy (would you believe it, *our* Betsy) is wedded to caring for the old woman because . . . Because . . .? I don't know.

'*I don't know!*' I believe I screeched out at the bathroom's brilliant eyeballs, trying, at the same time, to get to my knees – failing.

In any case, there's Betsy at the mirror. Her mother has just slapped her across the face. Betsy doesn't know why. 'Why' is a concept sliding into irrelevance in relation to her mother's behaviour. The old woman, Maud, had dropped dessert all over her blouse. They've tried getting her to wear a bib, but she won't have it. Therefore these mealtime messes. Banana mashed with clotted cream and sprinkled with pungent ginger. The old woman will eat virtually nothing else. (Betsy gags, these days, preparing it, having seen it far too many times in other form at the end of its journey through her mother's bowels. Mr Galvez won't even be in the room when the old woman tucks in. Betsy understands. . .) Anyway. Bending to mop-up her mother's blouse, Betsy received a stinging slap across her mouth and a look of purest hatred from the still piercing octogenarian eyes. *I hate you.* Maud had said. *You're a dirty thief. You think I don't know where all this money comes from? You're nothing but a thief. You're wearing my cardigan. D'you think I'm blind?* And

Betsy, for once, had been unable to bear it. Unable, for a moment, that moment, with her mouth bloody from Maud's in-turned garnet and diamond cluster, to bear it. She had run upstairs, on fire with hurt and choking on unswallowable knots of tears, until, safe behind the bathroom's locked door, she had taken her place before the mirror and let herself weep.

Without much surprise, by the way, I found that I was weeping myself, right there on the bathroom floor. No flailing or wailing, just strangely cooling and continuous tears. Somewhere in the back of myself, I remember, panic was politely trying to get the rest of my attention.

'As long as I have strength,' I find myself saying, in Betsy's wobbling voice. 'As long as I . . . Oh, *Mummy* . . .'

'Who on earth are you talking to you insane man?'

Harriet to the rescue. Thank Hell.

'You're sick' she said. 'Your *head*'s on fire. We should call the doctor. Let me call the doctor.'

'No doctor,' I said. 'I don't need a doctor.' Get her to take her clothes off, I thought, as a fresh wave of fever broke over my bad-tempered flesh. Get her to strip and — and — just anything to blot this rubbish out.

'Is this what it's going to be like?' I said to those blazing bathroom bulbs. 'Things you didn't know? The three faces of Eve and so on? *Sybil*?'

'What?' Harriet asked. We'd made it to the bed and she'd managed to get my bespattered trousers off. 'Declan darling I'm afraid you're rambling.'

Indeed. Each image opened yet more space in the already limitless arena. The blue sky doming it stretched on, endlessly clear. A sudden flash — something that should have been entirely subliminal: One naked man and one naked

228

woman standing in a warm evening mist looking up into the boughs of a fruit-heavy tree; a look at each other; a hand squeeze; a grin ... I wanted it to stop. Oh I wanted it to *stop*.

But there's Violet (it'll be *Harriet* next, I thought, with dread and fascination) in sudden hot tears because on a crowded and sullen Northern Line tube she's just bought a stupid keyring from a deaf-and-dumb woman every other passenger in the carriage has stonily ignored. The tears because when the deaf-and-dumb woman (sixties, watery blue eyes, a furred mole above her top lip, the anorak and old butter smell of the poor) has smiled and said something incomprehensible, Violet, not wanting to engage beyond the mechanical charity, has responded with a look of puzzlement and okay-I've-bought-your-shit-now-please-go-away-and-leave-me-alone. Then, the woman turning away with a look of threadbare weariness, Violet's realisation that the garbled phrase was 'God bless you'. It holds her for a moment, this translation, poised on the brink of a shocking grief. The woman's last look: *You can't understand me because I can't talk properly; you don't want me to talk to you because you're afraid that I'm going to want something more from you – money, love, time, your life; you just want me to leave you alone; that's all right, I know, but I was just saying thank you.* All Vi's childhood rushes up into her heart – the kids they made fun of, the tiny cruelties, the horrible guilt – all her adult excesses too, and thus with her heart full she looks down at the mute's keyring. Its gimmick is a little sign language chart in clear plastic. On the reverse, it says: *Learn my language and we can be friends!* And this, this more than anything hitherto pitches her over the edge and she finds herself in tears, publicly – not discreet weeping, either, but audible boo-hooing and visible, body-shaking sobs ...

We're going to show you a familiar object seen from an unfamiliar angle. For ten points we'd like you to name the object . . .

I didn't want to name any of them, believe me. The mixture of expansive bliss and barely contained panic had me flipping and flopping around on the bed like a landed fish until Harriet – Hell preserve her – got me still by climbing on the bed and lying on top of me.

At which point – *shshsh*, she kept saying, *its all right, shshsh* – at which point I'm afraid I capped the entire performance by shitting my pants and bursting into tears.

◆

Hydra is a small island in the Aegean, south of Poros, northeast of Spetses, three hours out by thudding ferry from the sun-and-diesel headache of Piraeus. No cars on the island. No motorized traffic of any kind, in fact; just long-eyelashed donkeys and seen-better-days nags, standing patiently or in existential nullity in the sun by the dock, or clopping in no rush up the pink and silver cobbles, carrying deliveries, tourists, luggage, their burnished haunches sexy as an oiled stripper's, thin shadows tacked and rippling at their hooves.

You get there, you've entered a different time zone. Local population's less than 2,000. The harbour's a long crescent inlaid with a single row of jewellery shops and restaurants, with a museum fort at one end and a sprawling cocktail bar at the other. Boats wobble and nod in their moorings. Sunlight bounces off the water and marbles their hulls. The sky is a high, stretched skin of pure ultramarine. Occasionally, stratos clouds. Very rarely, hilarious thunderstorms. In summer the heat and the silence form a tangible conspiracy in the air around you; you can close your eyes and lean on them, drift into blankness or dream. Nothing is required of you. One nightclub in the hills serves touring youngsters and desperate local teens (trapped in paradise, dying to get out), but in the harbour it's gentle bars with elastic hours and capricious prices where you can talk without ever having to raise your voice. They go in for complex cocktails served like desserts in glasses the size of soup bowls. There's an open air cinema – a roofless yard with a rattling projector and roll-down screen, where, under the wings of Cygnus and the skirts of the Pleiades, you can watch Hollywood's spectacles six years after the rest of the world's stopped talking about them. Intermission's an indecorous halt at the film's guessed mid-point (mid-scene, mid-sentence, mid-syllable); then coffee as thick as mercury in plastic thimble cups, a leg-stretch, a Marlboro. All the kids here run around unsupervised into the small hours. Unfortunately, nothing happens to them.

Unsuccessful and inevitably priapic painters (Panamas, nicotine fingertips, boozy breath and artfully uncared-for hair) emigrate here to become big fish in Hydra's tiny pond. Their skin goes brown, their pleasures simplify, they let themselves go – scribbles of white chest hair over Tiresian dugs, sun-oiled pot-bellies like dark tureens, scrawny knees, languid affairs, the occasional pilgrimage to Athens for worldlier revels. They let the old life of irritated ambition slide away, discover it was an unnecessary encumbrance. Tourists buy their work because they have no idea who they are. It keeps them in silk shirts, cigarettes, whisky.

Hydrofoils come bouncing in as if from outer space every couple of hours, deposit and retrieve their posse of visitors. Or the slower, heftier ferry rolls up with its gradually opening maw and endless disgorgement of gabbling passengers: this is the sort of place tourists stop at for an hour or two,

Brummies with attention span deficits – 'Ent much in the woiya shops, iz there, Rodge?' – or proprietal New Yorkers with laconic tips on how to reorganize the menus, the donkeys, the language, the island. Tabacs are run, alcoholically, by moustached dads and their chirpy, white-frocked daughters; the dads spend the day smoking, reading the papers, drinking, lifting their grogged heads now and then to bawl or bellow at their girls, who pay not the slightest attention to them, knowing it's all bluff and bluster, knowing, in fact, that they've got these old soaks at their mercy. The dads are no less resigned. Moments of magisterial bullying in front of the customers (whom they suspect aren't fooled in any case) but what they really want is to stay just as they are, hammocked in afternoon booze, rocked now and then by the brush of a passing daughter's hip.

And this is *what*, exactly? A commission from *Let's Go*?

Oh boy, I wish it was. I wish it was as simple as that. Listen to this.

'What time is it?'

'Seven twenty-three. Calm down.'

'Yes, I must, mustn't I. God. Fucking *God*. How's your headache?'

'Coming along nicely.'

'Are you sure you told them you were bringing me?'

Violet was sitting next to me at the hotel bar on a high stool with her little legs crossed. Short black cocktail dress, black stockings, black high heels, one of which she let hang on her toes. (She's still not sure whether letting a shoe hang like that is stylish or slutty. She's still experimenting.) She was so *resentful*. Resentment hummed around her like a force field, creating – it must be admitted – a terrible sex appeal when it surrounded the milky and generously freck-led shoulders, the avocado-sized breasts, the flinty blue eyes and pre-Raph hair. Again, you see, like my darling unmolested Tracy, not at all *gorgeous*, but irresistibly human, dappled with physical imperfections (the Pricker would have had a field day with Vi's beige moles and carnelian nodules) and riddled with psychic ones. I couldn't – I could *not* – quite shake the image of her in tears on the Tube, nor disentangle it from the one of her endless narcissism before the mirror on the back of her bathroom door. No wonder my head ached.

Which rationalization notwithstanding, I still suspected something darker afoot, some twitch on the perceptual periphery, some edge, some conspiracy, some chill . . .

'Oh Jesus Christ. Jesus Jesus Jesus Christ. Declan that's . . . Declan?'

Trent, Harriet, and A.N. Other. Someone you might describe as an exceptionally famous and good-looking movie star. Someone *you* might describe like that. Me, I'm a bit harder to impress.

'Did you know? Fucking *hell* Declan did you *know*?'

I hadn't, as it turned out, known he was in town. Violet, bless her, could only contain her understandable excitement by translating it into force and expressing it in a grip on my thigh which, had the next thing not happened, might have seen me publicly unmanned.

As the hairs on the back of my neck rose, and a faint echo of perhaps my host's voice said *this is the way this is the way this is the* . . . someone tapped me gently on the shoulder and a voice on the edge of my recognition said: 'A minute of your time, Mr Gunn?'

I turned. Odd, that turn. An agonizingly slow swivel; seemed to smudge and drag the images – tables, chairs, glasses, faces. Then it was done and I was facing him: a slender, olive-skinned gentleman with a long face, plum-coloured eyes and a sensual mouth, wearing a cream linen suit, blood-red tie, and invested with a presence I hadn't felt since . . . since . . .

Gunn's voice surprised me with its smallness and fracture when it crept out into the world. 'Raphael,' I said. I felt something funny going on inside, some cramped orchid awkwardly opening. Mild panic, I suppose.

He cleared his throat, smiled over my shoulder at the still apnoeal Violet, then looked back at me and said, 'Do you think we might have a word in private, old friend?'

'You've got to be kidding.'

'No, my dear, I'm not kidding.'

'Stop it with the "my dear" rubbish for a start. The assumption then, these days, is that I'm suffering from some sort of galloping credulity, is it?'

'Will you at least consider what I'm saying?'

'It's a joke. You know what this is? It's funny, that's what this is. Hill fucking hairious. And from you of all people. Honestly.'

Poor old Violet. I suppose she exhaled eventually. Catching sight of the Very Famous Movie Star didn't help, Trent's shout of 'Declan!' across the bar followed by a mimed tipple that gave every indication they were about to join us. Not that I stuck around to find out. I glanced back at Violet from the exit. She'd uncrossed her legs and now sat with her palms gripping her own kneecaps. The shoe that had been hanging – stylishly, sluttishly, howeverishly – had fallen off. The bar steward kept his head down, ostensibly lost in the languid polishing of a champagne flute, but I could see he'd noted my sudden departure and was wondering where that left him re. the shoeless minx with the taut tits and spectacular hair.

Then Piccadilly's humid night and cavalcade of coughing traffic, Green Park's gently breathing trees and a high, ravaged and star-pooled canopy of quick-moving cloud. 'I've got something to tell you and something to show you,' he'd said. 'But I can do neither here. Will you come with me?'

'Come with you where for heaven's sake?'

'The airport.'

I'd never seen him like this. I'd never seen him like *this*, dressed in flesh and blood – but that's not what I mean. What I mean is I'd never seen him *assertive*. In the old days he'd been . . . Well I mean he was a *follower*. He wouldn't elaborate. Only insisted I could trust him. That I could trust his love. That he was alone and unarmed. That it would be a short flight. That there was nothing I needed to bring. He had Gunn's passport in his inside pocket. 'You've put on weight since that was taken,' he'd said, catching sight of its photo at check-in. If it hadn't been for a ruthlessly piqued curiosity I'd have ditched him in Duty Free and headed back to the Ritz. But there you are. Me and curiosity.

So the night flight to Athens, the meandering cab-ride down to Piraeus, the last hydrofoil, the island, the sleeping streets, the eucalyptus trees and clutter of hills, the villa. Raphael, blessed archangel of the Throne and ruler with Zachariel of the Second Heaven, is now Theo Mandros – restaurateur, philanthropist, widower, Greek.

'Jesus Jesus Jesus,' I said, between cackles.

'Lucifer please. *Some* consideration. That's still painful to me.'

'You know, obviously, that you're wasting your time.'

His villa looks east over the Aegean. We sat with tall

ouzos and our feet bare against the freshly swept stone of the veranda. Dawn was an hour away. I lit a Silk Cut and wolfed down a chestful of smoke. You do *need* a cigarette when a transmogrified archangel you haven't seen for several billion years has just told you that your number's about to be called.

'Oh *please.*'

'It's true.'

'Well, it's about time.'

'Lucifer, you don't understand.'

'By the book, that's what I understand. God wins and I go to Hell forever. Big deal. In case anyone's not been paying attention: I've *been* there. You know? I *live* there. I can hack it.'

The first sliver of sun was making a moody furnace of distant cloud. The sea waited like a wedding night bride. Raphael moved his feet gently against the floor. The ice in his glass tinkled.

'It's not the Hell you know.'

'Oh right. A different Hell. How many are there?'

'Lucifer listen to me. Haven't you been wondering what's wrong with you?'

'There's absolutely nothing wrong with me, my darling. Nothing apart from Everything, obviously. I assume you don't mean "wrong" in that sense? In the sense of "as opposed to Right" with a capital R?'

'Have you not, of late —'

'Oh don't start with that, will you?'

'If you knew how hard I had to fight to be allowed to tell you this —'

'I wouldn't take such a devil-may-care tone?'

'You would do me at least the fraternal courtesy of listening to what I have to say. Your existence in eternity depends on it.'

236

'Okay, I'm listening,' I said. I was listening, I suppose – and yet a good deal of my still traumatized consciousness was away with the fairies, as you say. The wrinkled Med's gentle sway; the bittersweet scent of the olive groves; the stone and cool dust beneath my bare feet; the icy aniseed; the incessant rasping of cicadas; the stirring of a dawn breeze . . .

'It's never been you,' Raphael said – and just for the splittest second, the entire earth and everyone in it seemed to stop breathing. I looked down into my drink. The ice had almost melted. A sparrow appeared out of nowhere and alighted on the balcony. It put its head on one side, examined me, briefly, then whizzed away.

'I assume you're going to explain?' I said.

'It's never been you,' he repeated. 'Everything you've thought you've been responsible for . . . Well. You haven't.'

I thought, How weird to be plunged into darkness every night, to have to wait again for sunrise. Not a wholly unpleasing rhythm to it, though. I chuckled to myself.

'I can see you're not taking this seriously.'

'I'm sorry,' I said. 'Really. Sorry. Let me get a hold of . . . It's my mind, you see. Ever since that ill-advised trip up to Manchester . . .' I composed myself. It was, however, hellishly difficult to keep stoppered the bubbles of laughter that would insist on tickling my insides.

'Lucifer. Do you understand me? The evil in the world – your purpose, the thing that's kept you *going* has been the thought that you could at the very least get in amongst the Mortals and lead them astray. This has been your identity, has it not? Your essence? Your *raison d'être*?'

'I like to think of it as a necessary hobby.'

'However you've thought of it, my dear, you've been wrong. The evil that men do – and I know there's no preparing you for this – *is nothing to do with you.* Am I getting through to you? Is it becoming clear?'

'Oh as a *bell*. What is this? We're all existentialists now?'

'I know you're afraid. Don't be. Don't – please don't – think the laughter in any way disguises the fear. You and I know it doesn't. The Mortals are free, Lucifer. What they've done they've done from within themselves. You think you've spoken volumes to them. You imagine the transcript of your temptations would fill libraries the size of galaxies – and so they would. But not one word of them has reached the Mortals. Your words, my dearest Lucifer, have fallen on deaf ears.'

'In which case you've got to take your hat off to what they've achieved, really.'

'Please, old friend, believe me. I know this causes you pain. But your time is running out. I begged Heaven to release me so that I could help you.'

'Help me what?'

'Make the right decision.'

'Meaning?'

'Take the offer of forgiveness.'

I lit another cigarette, chuckling. 'Raphael, Raphael, my dear, silly Raphael. And have you forfeited your wings to run such a fruitless errand?'

'Somebody had to warn you.'

'Well, I'll consider myself warned.'

'Nelchael will find no scribe's soul in Limbo, Lucifer.'

Now that, I'll admit, did bring me up sharp a bit. But I'm good for nought if not dissemblance. I inhaled, deeply, and blew a couple of muscular smoke-rings. The first light was above the horizon, now. Somewhere nearby someone was leading a horse over the cobbles. I heard a man cough, hawk up phlegm, spit, clear his throat, walk on.

'I see you're surprised,' Raphael said.

'You do do you? Well you may also have noticed that I'm –' tipping the last of the ouzo down my tingling gullet – 'in need of a refreshed glass. Rather good, this ridiculous drink. Those Greeks, eh? Bumming, syllogisms, cracking good yarns . . . Be a good fellow now and pour me another. You have, after all, just given me some distressing news.'

Can't say *how* I felt, really. (The writer's condition, for ever and ever, amen . . .) Certainly there was some deflation. Not the it's-been-nothing-to-do-with-you nonsense – but . . . Well. You *hope*, you know? I mean you sort of know you're dreaming, but still, you *hope* . . .

'And what did you think you were going to do with Gunn's soul if he found it?' he asked, having returned from the cool interior accompanied by the tinkling of freshly iced drinks.

I did laugh, then, with the honest generosity of the unmasked rascal. 'Oh *I* don't know,' I said. 'Get it into Hell, somehow. Back-door it into Heaven. You think you can't grease the odd palm up there? You live in a dream world, Raffs. In any case it would have left a body vacant. I'm sure even you can see the appeal. The luxury second home and so on? It's not bad down here, is it? Eh? I mean you've a shadow or two around *your* eyes, Mr Theo Calamari Mandros, if you don't mind my saying so. Doesn't look like you've spent your sojourn illuminating manuscripts and saving spires.'

He exhaled, heavily. 'You haven't listened to a word I've said.'

'I *have*.'

'You seriously thought you could do any of that without Him knowing?'

'Not really, no. But look at it from my point of view. I mean you've got to *try* these things, you know? There is such a thing as *morale building*, when all's said and done. You know, the boys Downstairs would have loved it. I was thinking timeshare, you see?'

'I doubt, my dear, you intended to share your treasure with anyone.'

'Oh you old cynic.'

'Lucifer please. Will you listen to me?'

'I *am* listening. I just wish you'd say something *sensible*.'

'Do you know what Judgement Day means?'

I yawned and rubbed my eyes. Pressed my thumb and forefinger either side of the top of my nose in the manner of those anticipating a headache. 'Would you mind awfully if I took a brief nap?' I said.

He put his face in his long-fingered hands. 'What a waste,' he said, as if to an invisible third party.

'Look Raffles I know this is all *horribly* important and all the rest of it but if I don't get just a little sleep now I'll be absolutely *useless* tomorrow. I had thought we might go paragliding.'

For a few charged moments he just looked at me. The sun was well and truly up, now, and I did unequivocally want to get out of it. His face was filled with sadness and longing. It made me feel quite unwell.

He did that man-visibly-containing-his-emotion jaw-twitch thing, then said, 'I'll show you to your room.'

It was dark when I woke. Dreams of fire, flashbacks to the first, empty conflagrations of Hell. I'd mumbled myself awake in a sweat. I was lying in the recovery position and had drooled on the pillow. There was an open volume on the bed beside me with a hand-written note of dreadful handwriting:

Dear L,

Thought I'd let you sleep. I have to go to Spetses to see
one of my managers. Be back this evening around nine.
Help yourself to whatever you need. My clothes should
fit you. I know you were upset last night, but I want
you to know how good it is to see you again after so
long. Please don't do anything rash, there is still much
to be said.

R.

I felt terrible. The ouzo had landed its rowdy militia in my
skull, and a lively bivouac they were making of it. Of course
the book wasn't random. Rilke's *Duino Elegies*. Somehow I
knew this was the sort of twattish human behaviour the incarnate Raphael would go in for. Notes, Greek islands, *poetry*.
Course, you know me. Had to go and *read* the blessed thing:

Preise dem Engel die Welt –

Oh, sorry. I mean:

Praise this World to the Angel: not some world
transcendental, unsayable; you cannot impress him
with what is sublimely experienced . . .
In this cosmos you are but recent and he
feels with more feeling . . . so, show him something
straightforward. Some simple thing fashioned
by one generation after another;
some object of ours – something
accustomed to living under our eyes and our hands.
Tell him things. He will stand in amazement

With a curse I threw the volume at the wall. A moment arrived – you've had a few of these yourself I dare say – in which every detail of my current situation clung to every other in a great, suddenly perceived bogey of unbearable consciousness and I just couldn't stand it a moment longer. With a retch and a groan I tore myself there and then from Gunn's sleep-crumpled body with every intention of quitting this absurd nightmare once and for all to return to the familiar – if fiery – precincts of Hell, where at least things made painful sense.

I had known, even in the heat of my irritated moment, that it was going to hurt. I had known that I was going to be *surprised* by the pain of my spirit undressed of its borrowed flesh. I had, I thought, prepared myself to grin (or grimace) and bear it.

But – *by the sizzling knob-hole of Batarjal!* – I wasn't prepared for what hit me. Could it really have been *this bad*? Could I really have been existing in so furious a forge of rage and pain *all those fucking years*? It defied belief. It hit me then for the first time with a terrible clarity just how long it was going to take me to get used to the pain again. And my spirit writhed upon the face of the waters.

It was no good. I wasn't ready. I'd need longer to prepare. Warm up with some physical pain in Gunn's apparatus, maybe. A stroll over hot coals. Amateur dentistry. Self-electrocution. An acid bath. Something to get me back into shape. Either way incorporeity over the Aegean right then was out of the question. Imagine returning to the basement crew in that state! Christ I'd be laughed out. I could just *imagine* what fucking Astaroth would make of it.

Raphael found me in the open air cinema. *Schindler's List*. Not that I paid much attention to the sounds or images. It was just that I needed the darkness and the silent presence of other flesh and blood. He came in near the end, Mr Mandros, Theo, patron of the museum and provider of Greek victuals. Some lardy Hydran matron with a gigantic head of dark hair shooed her gnat-sized sprog to free-up a seat for him. He's liked here, respected. It's a life. I knew why he'd come. He couldn't follow me into Hell all those millennia ago, but he could follow me, with the Old Man's blessing, apparently, onto Earth.

'He who saves a single life,' Ben Kingsley said to Liam Neeson, 'saves the world entire.'

I got up and slouched out in disgust.

'Lucifer, wait.'

He caught me up in the street. I was heading for an appealingly dark and invitingly empty taverna at the fork of two cobbled ways, and I didn't stop. He fell into step alongside and said not a word until we were seated at a booth within. Dark wood panelling; absurd maritime accoutrements; smell of shellfish and burnt cooking oil; a jukebox that looked like it might run on gas. Quadruple Jack Daniels for me – on the house when the barkeep, a small red-eyed bandit with a Zapata moustache and hairy forearms, realised who I was with; Mr Mandros took ouzo and called for olives and pistachios. I sat and glared at him after their prompt arrival.

'This is all shit,' I said. 'Two weeks ago – no, wait – three weeks ago I get a message from your friend and mine that the Old Man wants to cut me a deal. The Human show's coming to its close and I'm a loose end He wants tied up. I get a shot at redemption. All I've got to do is live out the rest of this sad sack's miserable life without doing anything heinous. Say my prayers at night, go to Mass Easter and Christmas, love people, the usual bullshit. Big challenge for me, obviously, what with my *pride* and all, what with me being the second most powerful entity in the universe, what with me having developed this habit of being *Absolutely Evil*. So I think, what the fuck? I'll take the month's money back offer, live it up in the flesh, then tell Him come August 1 He can shove His redemption where it smells. Now you show up with a kebab empire and a Bogart suit and tell me my entire existence has been a delusion, and that the Hell I know isn't the Hell I'm going to.'

'Yes.'

'And I'm supposed to take this seriously?'

'Yes. You know I'm not lying.'

'No, you're not lying, Raphael, but you're definitely *not all there*, either.' He gave me a sad and slightly sheepish smile. 'Okay, Mr Theo Moussaka Mandros,' I continued. 'Tell me what it is you think I need to know.'

'He knew what you were going to do. He knew you weren't going to take the mortal road.'

'Yeah well that's omniscience for you.'

'We all knew. We've all been watching.'

'And whacking off, I don't doubt.'

Funny little pause there, while he stared at his ouzo and I torched a Silk Cut.

'He knows Hell has no fear for you. The mortal John's words were all words that stood for words unsayable. He knows you, Lucifer, though you think He does not. He *knows you.*'

'Not in the biblical sense.'

It was his turn to rub his eyes. He did it rapidly, as if fighting off a sudden attack of sleep. 'Hell is to be destroyed,' he said. 'Utterly and forever. No trace of the world you know, nor your Fallen brethren will remain. Do you understand?'

'Yes, I understand.'

Poor Raphael. Torn in two. He put his hand across the

table and covered mine with it. His fingers were oily from the olives. 'You don't think you've been missed, Lucifer,' he said, his eyes welling up. 'But you have.'

Well, I didn't like the way that made me feel. The Jack Daniels was kicking in and somewhere in the bowels of the tavern a woolly speaker was releasing a surreal Greek instrumental version of 'Stairway to Heaven'. I started swallowing, emptily. Oh fucking *great*.

'Okay, Mr Mandros,' I said, mastering myself with a same-again gesture to the dozing barman, 'if you've got all the answers, tell me this: if everything you say is true, if Judgement Day is coming and with it the destruction of my Kingdom, if Sariel, Thammuz, Remiel, Astaroth, Moloch, Belphegor, Nelchael, Azazel, Gabreel, Lucifer and all the glorious legions of Hell are to be annihilated forever, then why should I not embrace oblivion? Better to reign in Hell than to serve in Heaven, yes. Better even not to *be* than to be and serve. What fear of death is there in me?'

Poor Raphael's eyes, unable to quite meet mine. When he spoke, he spoke as if to the beer-stained table. His voice came in a flat incantation.

'God will take unto Himself the souls of the righteous and the angelic host. The world, the Universe, matter, the whole of Creation will be unmade. Only God in Heaven will remain. Hell and all its Fallen will be destroyed. In its place, a nothingness utterly separate from Him. Eternal nothingness, Lucifer. A state from which nothing comes and into which nothing enters. Without exception, *nothing*. The inhabitant of such a state would exist in absolute aloneness and singularity. For eternity. Alone. Forever. In nothingness.'

Hell, didn't I say somewhere, is the absence of God and the presence of Time.

After a long pause – the dismal rendition of 'Stairway' replaced now by the speakers' endless exhalation of static or hiss – I looked up and met Raphael's sorrowful eyes. 'Oh,' I said. 'I see.'

(It was something to think about on the flight back to London. For the sake of argument I had a (pointless) go at believing it. It was a kind of victory, when you thought about it. Last man standing and all that. You know, if you looked at it that way. Kind of.)

'So this is all . . . what, exactly?' I asked Raphael, rhetorically, the night before I left. 'The best you can come up with? Me and you living on a Greek island reading Rilke and desultorily managing half a dozen restaurants while the Old Man gets up the nerve to ring down the curtain?'

'There are worse lives,' he said. The two of us were on the veranda again. The sun had gone down, gaudily, with exhausted passion; we'd watched from the western side of the island, having ridden out on Raphael's two sorrel mares, lunched on olives, tomatoes, feta, cold chicken, a plummy red with peppery undertones. I'd stretched out, shadow-dappled under the eucalyptus, and he'd wandered away to fish. To give me a bit of room. Now, back at the villa, we sat facing the sea's deepening shadow and the first faint scatter of stars. Funny to think of stars disappearing. Funny to think of Everything disappearing. Except me. Funny.

'I thought you'd need . . .' He'd been going to say 'help' I could tell. 'A companion. It's not easy, is it, this mortal life.'

I thought of the photograph of Gunn's mother and of the Clerkenwell flat's sad little corners. 'Not unless you're prepared to make the effort,' I said. 'Most mortals aren't. We've always known this. That the whole fucking thing would be wasted on them.'

'Like Wilde's youth on the young.'

'It wasn't Wilde,' I snapped. 'It was Shaw.'

Later, that *piccante* little exchange having hovered between us like something imperfectly exorcised, he came into my room in the small hours. I knew he knew I was awake, so I didn't bother pretending to be asleep. The moon was up, a solitary petal of honesty casting stone-coloured light on the Aegean, the sleeping harbour, the hill, the veranda, the *terra cotta*, the silk-fringed counterpane, my bare arms. His eyes were slivers of agate. It would have been nice for me if the bed had made a silly noise when he sat on it – some *boing* or *twoing* – but the mattress was solid and silent, no help at all. I'd drunk too much and not enough.

'No, Raphael,' I said.

'I know. Not that. I just mean: Please think about it, okay?'

'Although it seems rude not to, given that we've got the flesh.'

'Don't play with me, please.'

'Sorry. I know. Truth is, there's a good chance I'd give you something.' He didn't understand. 'Something nasty,' I said. He was bare-chested, in pale pyjama bottoms. Theo Mandros's body was brown and lean with ropy muscle in the long arms and a small pot belly of almost unbearable pathos. His dead wife had loved it; the ghost of her love still surrounded it in a little crescent of warmth. It suited Raphael.

'Tell me something,' he said.

'What?'

'Why you've found it so hard to admit that you've considered it?'

'Considered what?'

'Staying.'

I half-smothered the laugh, very inadequately tried to pass it off as a cough. Slowly reached for and lit a cigarette. 'I assume – hard though this is to countenance – that you mean staying *here*, staying *human*?'

'I know you've considered it. I know the flesh's seduction.'

'What a lot you seem to know, Mr Mandros. I wonder why you bother to ask anything at all.'

'I know your capacity for self-delusion.'

'And I know yours for credulity. Not to mention limp-wristed infatuation.'

'You lie to yourself.'

'Good night, Biggles.'

'You deliberately avert your gaze from the true appeal of this world.'

'And that would be . . . what, exactly? Daisies? Cancer?'

'Finiteness.'

Oh the nasty things I nearly came out with then. Really. It's lucky for him we were old chums. All things considered, I was glad imminent operations wouldn't affect him.

'Lucifer?' he said, putting a hand on my pelvis. 'Is the peace of forgiveness so terrible a thing to embrace? Wouldn't redemption be the mightiest gift He could give? Haven't you ever, in all these years, haven't you ever once longed to come *home*?'

I sighed. Sometimes, I've found, sighing's just the thing. Moonlight lay on my face now like a cool veil. My bedroom doors opened onto the veranda; the white wall; the constellations' impenetrable geometry. There'd be an epiphany, I was thinking. Anyone else's story, this is where the tide would turn, objectively correlatived by lyrically described buggery, no doubt. Any other fucker's story.

'Raphael,' I said – then, staying in character, added, 'Raphael, Raphael, Raphael.' Didn't quite have the effect I was after, somehow. None the less I pressed on. 'Let me ask *you* something, dear boy. Do you think I despair?'

'Lucifer –'

'Do you think I exist in a state of despair?'

'Of course you do. Of *course* you do, my dear, but what I'm trying to suggest is that –'

'I do not despair.'

'What?'

'You heard.'

'But –'

'Despair is for when you see defeat beyond all hope of victory.'

'Oh, Lucifer, *Lucifer.*'

'I repeat: I do not despair. Now please, for fuck's sake, go to bed.'

He didn't. He sat there next to me with his palm against my hip and his head bowed. I might have been mistaken but I thought I saw the glimmer of tears. (And I know this is really awful, but I did, actually, feel the first scrotal stirrings of an impending erection. Typical.)

This time *he* sighed. Then said: 'What are you going to do?'

'I'm going back to London.'

'When?'

'Tomorrow. I need . . .' What did I need? The flat? The Ritz? To finish the script? The book? To idiot-check the details of my upcoming venture? (Well I did say at the very beginning that I wasn't telling quite *all* . . .) 'I need to be alone with it. With what you've told me. It's not that I don't believe you –'

'You don't believe me, Lucifer, I know. Why should you?

Why should you think this was anything more than some ruse to . . . to . . .'

Couldn't finish that. Got up and padded on Mandros's long bare feet to the door, where he halted and said, to the tiles, 'I just want you to know that I'm here. I've made my choice.'

'No month's trial?' I asked him.

I saw the gleam of his teeth in the moonlight. 'Up a long time back,' he said. 'This is my home, now.' Then, again to the floor: 'And yours, too, old friend, should you need it.'

◆

I don't know what you'd call it. Goin' Loco Down in Acapulco – except it wasn't Acapulco, it was London. A farewell binge, I suppose. Tying one on. A bender. A *spree*. I'd half a mind to kill the last week in Manhattan, but the jet-lag would've slowed me down and every hour was precious; by the end of the week in London, it just felt like I'd half a mind. First thing I did was e-mail the bulk of this to Betsy with instructions to read it and whiz it out to the usual suspects ASAP. If the thought of slipping out of Gunn's bones hadn't entailed the thought of *excruciating pain* I'd have dropped in bodilessly on the head honchos at Picador or Scribner or Cape or whoever the fuck, to work the necessary chicanery; but the memory of my big ouch over the Aegean was still fresh. No need to repeat *that* before I absolutely have to. Anyway the point is I let myself go. Man did I let myself *go*. Have you had flambéed mangoes? There are so many flowers in my room now that I can't handle more than three XXX-Quisite girlies without crashing into a vase or bruising a blossom. I've prowled the city's parks and yards day and night molesting odours of every stripe, from freshly laundered bed sheets to the diarrhoea of dogs. I've fist-fought in Soho (I won, perhaps not surprisingly – come a long way since the night with Lewis and his beard) and bungeed over the Thames. I've snuffled and retched my way through three grand's worth of Bolivian Breeze, dropped E, acid, speed, shot up, tuned in, turned on and passed out. I've been ravished by the warm wind and rinsed by the rain. Blood *is* a juice of quality most rare . . . Oh I've manhandled, I have, stone, water, earth, flesh . . . Yesterday night I swam in the sea. Don't laugh – at Brighton, where the pier's lively fug (candyfloss, mussels, hot dogs, popcorn) and delirious soundtrack dropped the nukes of Gunn's childhood in my head, tipping me momentarily off balance. I swam out and flipped onto my back like a seal pup. The water was a dark and salty slick, the sky diagrammed with myth. I got depressed as hell (not to mention cold as hell – five seconds of warm bliss when I emptied Gunn's bladder) hanging there all alone and looking back to the seafront's chain of lights. Nearly drowned, too, as a matter of fact, what with that coke nod-out when I should have been kicking back to shore. Where would *that* have left us, I wonder? (I wonder a lot, these days. You must spend your whole lives at it, this wondering game.) But time – this New Time, how it *flies* – has done what time will do. Every hour, no matter how mighty the wall of your dread, comes through . . .

The funk, the jive, the boogie, the rock and roll . . . the weight of the body draws it down, to the dirge of the dark cortège. This won't do, for you or for me. Tomorrow is clocking-off day, and after a week of extremes, I find myself strangely drawn to the predictable smallness of the Clerkenwell flat. There are unique comforts, it seems, in the most lifeless crannies of life: the tinkle of the spoon in the cup; the kettle-fogged pane; the floor's worn poem of ticks and groans; the PC's unjudgemental hum; the fan's feeble campaign against London's summer of bruisers and thugs. (I don't think Gunn's body's very well at the moment. The whites of his eyes contain startled capillaries and spooked pupils. His back's killing me and his teeth itch. The skull's ducts rattle and creak with mucus and even Harriet would think twice before letting this mossed and maculate tongue anywhere near her sensitive parts.) Besides, I need somewhere quiet to think, and to finish this at least.

Think if it were true. It isn't true, *obviously*, but there's a masochist in here that will have his fifteen minutes. Can't . . . *cannot* be true. But think *if* it were true. A comfortable life – Mr Mandros would do as a decompression chamber, a comfort zone, a kind of arrivals lounge facility – no real *theoretical* objection to living it with moderate ethical decency; plenty to enjoy in the perceptual realm that wouldn't land me in jail or send me to the chair – you know: tulips; kissing; snow; sunsets; journeys; and so to death, the obligatory purgative stint, then home. Home.

Home? How long has that word meant anything other than Hell? Which reminds me, there is still the matter of . . . ah . . . There is still, vividly, the memory of what the incorporeal version of my existence *felt* like last week. In other words how much it *fucking killed*. Can't help thinking that's left me in a bit of a corner. Should have seen that coming sooner. Should have kept myself in shape with regular nights off from the body. Should have done *shifts*.

Course I'm going on like this as if I'm even considering it. Considering staying on, I mean. Considering *being Declan Gunn*. Course I'm going on like this as if there won't shortly be wheels of a very different kind in cacophonous motion. Course I'm . . .

Well.

I'm not turning any of the lights on in the flat. The hot gloom and steady rain comfort me. Like Hydra's sunlight and silence, they let me drift into dream. Thunderstorms since the early hours. Never really seen storms from your end. Don't they make you doubt what you learned at school? Don't you hear thunder and think: all that *atmosphere* stuff, it's cobblers; the sky's made of iron that sometimes shifts and grumbles, billion-ton slabs and plates forced through the same tectonic trials as earth, yielding this, this skyquake. Oh yes, it's been up to spectacular tricks since the small hours has the weather. I watched the lightning revealed in glimpses, the sky's shocking varicosis. The rain's been racing earthwards as if with some religious or political fanaticism. The clouds have the look of dark internal bleeding. Surely you lot look up from *Cosmo* while this sort of thing's going on? Surely you take a Playstation break?

I forget myself. Of course you don't. *Of course you don't.* I've put a lifetime's work into making sure you don't. How could I possibly forget?

In the summertime, when the weather is . . . How these minutes fly! Six minutes past six, the fifth second morphing digitally into the sixth just as my eyes focused. Little red numbers in the darkness. Is somebody pulling my leg here? Betsy's going to have to cut this. I don't have the time to

◆

Here ends the writing of my brother, Lucifer, and here I begin the fulfilment of my duty.

Too formal, Raphael. *His voice even now finds time for admonishment.* Try not to sound like such a tight-arsed ponce.

I can't help smiling. He must be busy, but still he finds the time to criticize my style. Well, I must try to oblige him.

I interrupted his last sentence. Despite everything he'd said on Hydra I couldn't let him confront his dilemma alone. I came back to England on a flight that had to skirt thunderstorms all the way to Heathrow. Thunderstorms everywhere, according to the co-pilot; a phenomenon. My fellow passengers' fear of death filled the cabin like smoke from a smouldering fire. God didn't have His hand over us, but the pilot was skilful, and brought us down in safety. I took a taxi straight to the Clerkenwell flat. Sheet lightning flickered.

'Oh,' he said. 'Look, I'm busy.'

'You have a decision to make,' I said to him. He didn't look well. His colour was bad, sallow, and his right eye was blackened. A scatter of pimples around the corners of his mouth. 'You've been abusing your host,' I said to him. 'You can't get away with that sort of thing indefinitely, you know, my dear.'

'We're back to the "my dear" are we? Look, Raphael, I know you mean well but –'

'What are you going to do?'

'What?'

'You heard me,' I said – I know him enough to know the tone he best responds to. 'What are you going to do? Are you going to stay, or are you going to go?'

He placed his hands together at the base of his spine and straightened his back, the way pregnant women do.

Better, cloth-head. Now you're getting the hang of it. That smouldering fire simile was lame, though.

'I'm going to run a bath, that's what I'm going to do,' he said. 'A huge, deep, hot bath. Feel free to watch if you like, although this Gunn's not much to shout about in the cock and balls department. Then again, as my dear XXX-Quisite Immaculata says, with the frequency of a mantra: "Iss wha' joo doo with it. Thass what counts".'

I waited half an hour, taking stock, meanwhile, of the condition

of the flat. His inhabitancy, sporadic though it had been, had dev-
astated the place: litter, broken bottles, dirty laundry, spilled food,
manuscript pages, overloaded ashtrays, the kitchen bin overturned,
not a dish washed . . . Who could be in the least surprised? How
art thou fallen from Heaven, O Lucifer, Son of the morning –

Er . . . Excuse me . . .

But I was wasting time. Worse, I was pandering to his wasting
time. In less than five hours he would have to decide. In less than
five hours they'd come for his answer. This was no time for idling in
the bathtub. With a cursory knock, I entered.

'Couldn't keep away, could you? Thought you'd catch me at it,
did you? Having a bit of a bathtime lube?'

He must have just added more hot water, because the tiny room was
filled with steam. 'Well, as you can see, here I am chastely bathing
and sensibly reflecting. Close the door will you, for Baal's sake.'

He was in fact smoking a cigar (not steam, smoke) and cradling
in his palm a huge brandy balloon amply furnished with the golden
liquor. There didn't seem to be any sign of either chaste bathing or
sensible reflection. He looked, as a matter of fact, like he'd just been
woken from a nap.

'There are prostitutes on your gland of an island, I take it?' he
said, swallowing a large mouthful. 'I mean I would, in theory, be
able to, you know, socialize with members of the opposite sex?'

'Not of the calibre it seems you're used to,' I said. 'But yes, of
course – and if not on Hydra then on Spetses, certainly in Aegina.'

'Certainly in Aegina,' he said. 'Sounds like some fucking
Lawrence Durrell poem.'

'I'm to take it from the profanities and the erratic observations
that you're drunk,' I said, feeling, I must confess, desperately angry
with him.

'Liquid sanity,' he said, raising the balloon in a cheers.

'Liquid cowardice,' I said. 'Can't you see that time's running out
for you?'

'Time's overrated,' he said. 'Money, on the other hand . . .'

I sighed and took a precarious seat on the edge of the tub.

'It's generally recommended that one undresses before getting in,' he said.

I ran a hand over my face. (Mandros's hands are sensitive, and store the memory of many things.) Tiredness — a deep tiredness of the bones and nerves — crept up from my feet. His wilful avoidance was like a separate entity in the room with us, draining my strength. 'Lucifer,' I said. 'For love and life please listen to me. You must stay. Whether with me or alone or with someone else. Don't you see you can't go back? Haven't you understood that it's so soon going to be over? That you'll . . . That you'll be . . .'

'Yes,' he said, slowly, and seemingly with genuine seriousness. 'Yes, my dear, I have understood everything. As always, I have understood everything. Now perhaps, if you could . . . the Swan Vestas there . . . I seem to have self-extinguished . . .'

'Lucifer!'

'Hmm?'

'Do you want to spend eternity in the Hell of Nothingness?'

'Of course I don't want to spend — Ow! Fuck! Fuck fuck fuck FUCK!'

The loss of temper had had him scrabbling to get upright; a slip, and he had conked his head on the back of the tub. He lost a good deal of the balloon's brandy, and the cigar altogether. 'Jesus Christ, Jesus Christ, Jesus fucking cunting Christ.'

(It pains me, obviously, even to type that — but I promised a faithful rendering.) I helped him into a better sitting position — but he wouldn't relinquish his glass. 'And don't think you can fool me by pretending you're fishing for the cigar, either, Mr Mandros,' he said, squinting from the blow to his head.

'This is utterly absurd,' I said.

He looked at me for a moment in silence before saying, with a compressed grin: 'Yes, I'm afraid it is, my dear.'

It seemed the knock on the head had sobered him. He placed the stem of the glass on the tub's rim with some care. It was then that I noticed the razor blades, all but one still in the unwrapped pack, this one within a little outline of rust.

'Not mine,' he said. 'Gunn's. He was going to slash these.' He held his wrists up for me to see. 'Not an option I'd have all alone in Nothingness. Not a rope to hang myself with nor a pot to piss in.'

'Quite,' I said. 'I hope this means you're finally beginning to see sense.'

'What did occur to me,' he said, 'was that if God were to go ahead and get rid of everything except little old me, I'd be in exactly the position He was at the beginning. I'd be Him. Rich, don't you think? Lucifer ends up where God started.'

'It wouldn't be the same and you know it.'

'How not?'

'Because you can't create anything,' I said.

And that, I believe, was the closest the world came. A few moments in the wake of those words in which — I could feel his capitulation like a great tilted ghost on the ether — I believe he would have turned. If the words for which he opened his mouth had ever been uttered.

But they were not.

It was a measurement of how much of my angelic nature yet remained, that I felt the approaching presence of one of the Firstborn seconds before it tore through. Lucifer, too, knew. The walls shuddered and the bathroom's minute window cracked; a peculiar, dissonant articulation from the building's joists and hinges, a tightening of the room's smoke into a queer little knot — then he was through, and the material world flowed evenly once more.

'Nelkers!' Lucifer cried, smiling broadly and raising a hand in welcome. 'By gum lad it's good to see you —'

'My Lord, I must —'

'As a matter of fact I'd like you to take a look at —'

'My Lord please! Listen!'

'Dear God in Hammersmith child what's the matter with you?'

'It's war my Lord.'

The four words nailed a small silence into place. Nelchael and I hadn't seen each other since the Fall. (Daily, my angelic sight diminishes, but at that hour the cataracts of human vision were gauzy still.) His presence wasn't pleasant for me – but it was horribly fascinating to see the state – carious, putrid, bleeding and exuding an impossible reek of corruption – of his angelic being. I could see that even in his state – manifestly come straight from the din and fire of battle – he was astonished to find another ex-Firstborn (an unFallen one at that) at his master's side.

Lucifer got to his feet. 'Astaroth,' he said. 'I knew it. What's he done?'

'No my Lord, not Astaroth. Astaroth fights loyally for the preservation of your sovereignty –'

'Then wh–'

'Uriel.'

In the moment of silence that followed, the sink gurgled, jovially.

'Uriel?'

'With renegades from Heaven, my Lord. Fully half of Hell is now under his command!'

'Lucifer, let it go,' I said. 'Don't you see that this releases you? Don't you see His will at work?'

But his eyes were alight with a flame that didn't belong in the human realm. 'Fuck,' he said. 'Double-crossing. . . mother . . . He was supposed to . . . He was supposed to wait until . . .'

'He came with half of Heaven under his banner, my Lord.'

'Well, that was all we could get. Jesus Jehosophat Christ.'

'And told us that if we joined him we would have might enough for a new assault on Paradise.'

'And he told you the truth, Nelkers. Now here's a pretty pickle.'

'Oh no,' I said. 'Oh no, no, no.'

Lucifer turned to me and grinned. He had fished out his cigar and slotted it, dripping, between his teeth. Bath foam glimmered on his head and loins.

'Started without me,' he said. 'Can you — I mean can you believe the chutzpah?'

'Lucifer stop. Please, stop and think.'

'He told us, my Lord,' Nelchael continued in a lowered voice (and without managing to conceal a glance at his master's strange corporeal dress), 'that you had . . . that you had . . . forgive me, Sire, but he told us that you had deserted Hell to live as a mortal!'

'Do you know, Nelkers,' Lucifer said, scratching his head and sucking uselessly on the sodden cigar, 'it did used to be said that there was honour among thieves.'

He had got to his feet to receive Nelchael. Now, smiling, he laid himself gently back in the tub. (I've thought of this, since, that he laid the body down as one might the corpse of a beloved friend.) Nelchael, seeing his master apparently readying himself for sleep, misunderstood. 'My Lord, I beg you, you must return and order the defence of your —'

'Relax, Nelks,' he said. 'Go. Depart. Vanish. I'll be at your heels in less New Time than it takes to boil an egg. Tell the faithful of Hell that Lucifer is coming and that Uriel will bow. No new campaign will succeed under him. I'll lead the attack myself. I give you my . . . Well, just tell them that. Now go.'

What else is there to say? Useless entreaties. I'm angel enough yet to recognize inevitable motions when I see them.

So for a few moments we eyed each other in silence. I could have been mistaken but I thought his hands trembled a little.

'You did consider it, didn't you,' I said. 'You can't deny, now, to my face, that you considered it. Lucifer?'

'Finish my book,' he said, swallowing the last mouthful of cognac

and smacking his lips. 'So that what little of posterity there may be left . . .'

'This is the second time I've lost you –' I began – but he closed his eyes.

'No time for speeches. Super hols. Had a lovely time. Be seeing you.'

'God be with you,' I said, reflexively, forgetting. At which the eyes opened again, for a moment, in glittering accompaniment to the sudden and ravenous grin.

'Do me a fucking favour,' he said – then went.

I watched the body slacken as his spirit departed. The shoulders sagged, the bowels released a long and noisome fart, which bubbled up through the water as if in announcement of the kraken. The brandy balloon dropped from the lifeless hand; a cheap rug by the tub; it didn't break. Thunder boomed and rolled

Try 'like celestial pianos tumbling down Heaven's stairs . . .'

In the quiet that followed, the steady breathing of Gunn's deep sleep.

I gathered the papers together and added these notes of my own. Nothing else remains. I shall never see him again.

Except, perhaps, if I'm human enough. Except, perhaps, if there's world enough and time.

Postscript, 18 October 2001
3.00 p.m.

Simplest if I stay out of it, I think. What is there to say?
You're holding it in your hands, aren't you?

I got four phone messages that day. The first was from Violet.

'Declan for heaven's sake where *are* you? I've been trying
and trying. Why didn't you tell me *he* was going to be there?
For God's sake why'd you dash off with that chap in the suit?
Who is he, by the way? *Is* he someone? Someone *else*? I *love*
Trent. So much . . . *energy*, you know? But is Harriet . . .
well . . .? She seems . . . Anyway the point is both of them
couldn't stop saying how much they loved the script. I don't
know why the fuck you didn't do this years ago. They want
us to go out to LA. You, anyway, but I mean they are going
to screen test me in any case . . .'

The second was from Betsy.

'Declan, hi, it's Betsy. Call me back when you get this.
They like what I sent them. You have *finished* it, I take it?
Anyway they've made an offer. Wonderful news. Speak to
you soon, you appalling boy. Bye!'

The third was from Penelope Stone.

'Hello, Gunn, it's me. I don't know. I don't know what. It
was good to see you. Do you think anything? I'm leaving my
number. I don't know anything, now . . .'

Not that there isn't a story from my end. The drying out, the rehab, the sexual health overhaul. (Test results came back negative, by the way. Clearly, there's no justice in this world.) Still, best that I stay out of it. Not just because the story of the last two months – from the moment I woke in the tub's cold water, with the sense that, astonishingly, I'd nodded off on the occasion of my own suicide, to the movement of my reclaimed fingertips over these keys – is a tale of metamorphosis all on its own, but because, let's face it: some personalities, you don't bother trying to compete.

I've had some decisions to make. Some I've made. Some I've put off. It's not easy.

I returned all three of those calls.

The fourth one I didn't.

I guess it was made in a bar. There were a lot of voices in the background – really a *lot* of voices – but I couldn't tell whether it was a party or a punch-up. Could have been anything. For a while – since the caller didn't speak for several seconds – I thought it was a mobile mistake, Violet groping in her handbag, Betsy with her mind on something else. I was just about to delete the message when a voice – at once alien and deeply familiar – said:

'See you in Hell, scribe.'

Outside, the sky looked exhausted. A wind had picked up. Dust blew in the courtyard. An empty milk bottle rolled around, like a past-caring drunk. The flat was a mess. I felt terrible.

See you in Hell, scribe.

Well, I thought. Probably.

But not today.

Acknowledgements

Several books were useful in the writing of this one, most too venerable (and too long out of copyright) to require a note. Of special help, however, was Gustav Davidson's *A Dictionary of Angels* (The Free Press, New York, 1971), an engaging and comprehensive guide through the labyrinth of angelic nomenclature.

I'm indebted to Montague Summers's *The History of Witchcraft and Demonology* (Castle Books edition, Secaucus, NJ, 1992 – originally published by Kegan Paul, London, 1926) for the story of Lucifer's 'Crucifixion sketch'. Names, dates and places are my own invention.

Ron Ridenhour's connection to both the My Lai massacre and the Milgram obedience tests is noted in Jonathan Glover's book *Humanity, A Moral History of the Twentieth Century* (Jonathan Cape, London, 1999). The author cites an internet communication from Gordon Bear (1998) as his own source.

Himmler's speech in this book is a fusion of two separate originals, both of which can be found in *Heinrich Himmler* by Roger Manvell and Heinrich Fraenkel (Heinemann, London, 1965).

Grateful acknowledgement is given for the publishers' permission to reproduce copyright material from:

'Fern Hill' by Dylan Thomas, from *The Collected Poems of Dylan Thomas* (JM Dent, Everyman edition, London, 1989).

'The Novelist' by WH Auden, from *Collected Shorter Poems 1927–57* (Faber and Faber Ltd, London, 1984).

'The Ninth Elegy' by Rainer Maria Rilke, from *Duino Elegies*, translated by Stephen Cohn (Carcanet Press Ltd, Manchester, 1989).

Biblical quotations are from the OUP's *King James Version With Apocrypha* (Oxford World's Classics paperback, Oxford, 1998).

My thanks go to Stephen Coates (a.k.a. The Clerkenwell Kid, a.k.a. [the real] Tuesday Weld) for musical companionship (see the soundtrack to *I, Lucifer*) and to Jonny Geller at Curtis Brown for his sterling and inimitable representation.

Finally, enormous gratitude to Ben Ball at Scribner, for tact, acts of faith, and editorial acumen beyond compare.